Crime Victims, A Buck Taylor Novel

Crime Victims, A Buck Taylor Novel

Contents

DEDICATION

*Dedicated to all those families
looking for a missing loved one.*

CRIME VICTIMS

A BUCK TAYLOR NOVEL

BOOK 12

BY

CHUCK MORGAN

Chapter One

It was a crazy night on the Colorado Mesa University campus. Graduation week had been the climax of hard work, and now the student body was letting off some steam. The graduates had built a massive bonfire in the parking lot, and the dancing and singing had reached a fever pitch. The heavy metal band playing on the other side of the parking lot had the volume turned up, and the noise was incredible, but no one seemed to care. This was the end of the school year, and everyone was having fun. Over the next two days, most of the students would be packing up and moving on. Some off to travel, adventures that would take them to far-flung places; others off to summer jobs and hard-fought internships; still others heading back home for some of mom's home-cooked meals and a free washer and dryer.

He had spent the last two hours wandering amongst the students, cheering with them, and he looked like he was having a good time, but what no one knew was that he was on the prowl. He was a predator of the highest order, walking in the midst of all his prey. His eyes searched the crowds, looking for that one perfect victim. The one who would make his year complete.

He was always fascinated to read stories about serial killers who chose their victims based on hair color or sex or some other deep-seated fantasy that behavioral scientists would grab on toward when creating the profile of the killer. He never cared about crap like that. His murders would have confounded the behaviorists, except that, so far, they didn't even know he existed. He didn't have a type when it came to his victims. Male or female, it didn't matter. He could kill either one without concern. There was also no sexual component to his victims. He didn't rape them before killing them, and he didn't choose them based on some preconceived sexual fantasy. He never had sex with his victims. He didn't get sexually aroused with their deaths. That would come later, after the thrill of the hunt and the kill had subsided. That was the fastest way to get caught. You could never be sure that you didn't leave a DNA trace when you were ravaging your victim sexually.

He chose his victims based on one thing. Did he have an overwhelming desire to kill that person? He didn't stalk them for days or weeks to make sure he understood their every move. He would key on his victim, work to get them alone and then pounce. He also never worried about his DNA getting on the victims. He had never taken a home DNA test. He had no siblings who might have taken one for fun, and his parents were both dead. His DNA profile might be in his military records, but those were sealed from prying eyes. He was the perfect killing machine, having improved his craft over the years, and no one could stop him.

He had been looking forward to the bonfire all week because he knew the students would be there, and most of them would be out of control on drugs or alcohol. Their guards would be down, and they would be as friendly as they could be. Even the more reserved students he had encountered were feeling no pain. He liked them compliant, but sometimes he liked more of a challenge, and he might go for an athlete. He also knew tonight was the last night of hunting season. In two days, and for two wonderful weeks after that, he would be sitting on a beach in Mexico with his wife, looking out over the ocean from behind a margarita and sunglasses, looking for his next victim. He found that the hunting was a lot easier in Mexico. The tourists were too drunk to figure out what was happening, and the locals never considered protecting themselves since they were in a tourist environment. The local police were also notorious for not doing a great job investigating crime. He always thought that one day he might retire to Mexico and spend the rest of his life in the pursuit of his happiness.

He had reached the edge of a large group of students bumping and grinding to the music when he spotted her. The fire from the bonfire lit up her face, and from where he stood, he could tell she had a beautiful, vibrant laugh. He watched her for a few minutes and then moved away from the crowd, always keeping her in his peripheral vision.

Several students in the group offered him a beer, which he took, and he joined in the dancing for a few minutes. He was older than they were, but that didn't stop him from having a good time while keeping an eye on the young woman.

She wasn't pretty, but there was something about her besides her smile that attracted his attention. She was short, maybe five-two at the most, and a little on the heavy side, but not out of proportion. She had a nice chest and medium-length blond hair. He took a sip from the can of beer and poured the rest on the ground when no one was watching. He wondered who would miss her. She most certainly had a boyfriend or a girlfriend, probably the latter, the way she was hanging all over the young woman dancing next to her. He wondered who would call in the missing person report once she didn't show up back in Muncie, Indiana, or Pittsburgh or wherever she came from.

He never knew what it was about the victim that attracted his attention, and he never questioned his decision. He always knew as soon as he saw the person that they were it. He moved away from the dancing group and stood on the periphery, watching her but never making eye contact. Now it was just a waiting game, but he didn't have to wait long.

The opportunity came half an hour later when she handed her friend her can of beer and made a dash for the edge of the parking lot. He followed nonchalantly so as not to draw any undue attention. He found her on her knees behind a parked car at the edge of the lot. From the pile under her mouth, it looked like she had barfed up everything she had eaten that day. He walked around the other side of the car and approached from in front of her so as not to startle her. She threw up again.

"Are you all right, young lady?" he said in a soft voice.

She pushed her hair behind her ear and looked up, using the back of her hand to wipe the bits and pieces from around her mouth. She looked nervous until the parking lot light revealed his face.

Slurring her words, she said, "Oh, hi, Professor. I think I had too much to drink."

She tried to smile but vomited again and fell sideways. He stepped around the pile, helped her back to her knees and kneeled beside her. He looked at her face.

"Aren't you in one of my history classes?" he asked.

She smiled and nodded. He looked around and helped her to her feet. She snuggled against his side and tried to say something, but it came out garbled.

"Let's get you home, young lady, before you fall and hurt yourself."

He led her away from the parking lot lights and the noise from the bonfire and headed towards the dorms, making sure no one noticed them leaving. He steered her away from the dorms, towards his F-150 pickup truck parked in the next parking lot, and stood her next to the sidewall as he opened the tailgate. She looked at him and smiled, having no idea where she was but knowing she was in good hands. He helped her sit on the tailgate, looked around to make sure no one was in the area, pulled a syringe out of his back pocket and jabbed it into her shoulder. She looked up into his eyes in surprise. Confusion turned to fear, and she tried to push off the tailgate but her eyes closed and she fell over.

He rolled her into the truck bed, closed the tailgate and secured the black cover. He looked around. The sounds at the bonfire were growing louder, and he stopped to watch as the students threw more wood onto the fire, which was growing bigger by the minute. He saw four big guys throw a wooden picnic table onto the pyre, and he laughed and slid into the driver's seat. He pulled out of the parking lot, turned left onto North Twelfth Street, right onto Horizon Drive and then right onto I-70. He followed I-70 until he saw the sign for Grand Mesa Scenic Byway and exited the interstate.

Chapter Two

The bright white light woke him from an uneasy sleep, and he tried to cover his eyes, but his hands wouldn't move. Nothing would move. His entire body was rigid, like he was paralyzed. Everything was hazy, and he couldn't seem to focus. He tried to move, to call out, but nothing was working. He realized what was happening but couldn't do anything about it. His psychiatrist had told him it was night terrors from the time he spent in Afghanistan, but he knew it was something different.

He could see a shadow as it approached the bed. It was just like the last time and the time before that. The shadow looked like a person, but it was ill-defined. It had a long, thin body, stubby arms and a large cone-shaped head. He couldn't see the eyes, but he knew from television shows he had watched that they would be large and almond-shaped.

The shadow leaned over him, and a bony finger touched his neck. He wanted to scream, but he couldn't. He had no control over what was happening. All he could do was watch and listen.

He never heard the alien spaceship when it flew over the cabin and landed deep in the woods, but the experience of the visitation was always the same. He'd see the hazy, bright white light and the alien's shadow, and when he would wake up in the morning, he would be fine.

He lowered his eyes and tried to see what the alien was doing. He heard drawers and cabinets opening and closing, and he could see the shadow moving around the cabin. He had no idea what the alien was looking for, but when he woke up in the morning, he would always find something left by the alien on the small rustic table. Sometimes, it was an earring or a watch, and sometimes, it was a picture of some young guy or girl. The person in the picture never looked good, and he wondered if they were dead. Killed by the alien, or died from fright.

What was strange was that he never felt like the alien had taken him back to the mother ship or like he had been experimented on. He would lie there, immobile, while the alien rummaged through his paltry belongings. He didn't have anything worth anything, but he knew that the alien was looking for things to take that belonged to him. Not big things, but trinkets.

After one alien visit, he noticed that his purple heart ribbon was missing; another time, it was a button from his uniform. None of it made any sense. It was like the alien was trading him worthless trinkets for worthless trinkets. He wasn't an important person or special in any way. He was just a soldier living in a cabin in the woods, where he had lived for the past ten years. He didn't know why the alien didn't visit a powerful person, like the president or a high-ranking general. Someone who had the power to make a deal with the alien. He was a nothing, a nobody. Why did the alien pick him? A crazy old soldier in the woods.

He focused, and he saw the alien was standing next to the bed. Once again, the alien touched his neck with that long, bony finger. He wanted to scream and ask the alien why it was doing this, but the words forming in his brain would not come out of his mouth.

The alien held up something small and clear in its hand and used something thin to draw up what looked like liquid. The alien did something with the long tube, and he felt something wet hit his arm. Then the alien leaned down, and he felt a sharp sting in his upper arm. It was a strange sensation being paralyzed but still able to feel pain.

He watched as the alien stepped away from his bed; the bright light faded, and he drifted off into dreamless sleep.

Chapter Three

"Approaching your destination on the left."

Angie Wilde followed the directions from the navigation app on her phone, turned into the driveway and stopped behind the two cars already parked alongside the small house on Bunting Avenue. She turned off the engine and stretched back in her seat. She looked at the house. It looked much smaller than what her best friend, Gabby Cruz, had described when they agreed to rent the house two blocks from the campus.

She hoped she hadn't made a mistake. In her last year at Colorado Mesa University, she didn't want to live in the dorm any longer, but she knew she would have trouble paying for a place off campus unless she had roommates, which she wasn't looking forward to. She knew she could get along with Gabby. They had been friends since first grade, but the two new girls she had just met.

She had heard that Elizabeth Clayton, Lizzy, was a bit of a party girl and that her friend Antonia Gianelli, Toni, pretty much went along with anything Lizzy wanted to do. She figured this was going to take some getting used to.

She opened the door, slid out and stretched. The four-and-a-half-hour drive from her home in Towaoc, Colorado, southwest of Cortez in the Four Corners region of the state, had been long, but she was excited, and the scenery along the western edge of Colorado seemed to fly by. She was looking forward to the upcoming school year.

Angie Wilde was an incoming senior at Colorado Mesa University in Grand Junction, Colorado, and she couldn't wait for the school year to begin. Colorado Mesa University was a small public university with a 141-acre campus located in the heart of Grand Junction. Founded in 1925 as Grand Junction Junior College, the college had grown into a top-notch university and was ranked number twenty on the Regional Colleges West list of the best colleges. The student body consisted of about ten thousand full- and part-time students and had a faculty of about six hundred full- and part-time professionals.

So much was happening this year for Angie Wilde. Her NCAA Division II softball team would be defending their championship from last year. Angie, their star first basewoman, was prepped and ready to go, having spent the summer working out with her younger brother, Damian. She knew she had to give it her best since her scholarship depended on it. She was also excited that in the spring she would be graduating with her bachelor's degree in sociology. She had already talked to all the right people in the Ute Mountain Ute Reservation government and was looking forward to using her sociology degree to help the people on the reservation.

Angie Wilde was five foot six and slender, with long black hair and brown eyes. She was pretty and had medium-toned skin, which was the most obvious giveaway of her Native American roots. Her skin was also leathery for someone so young, developed over years of working on the family's small ranch. She was not the first in her family, like so many others of her generation, to go to college; she followed her older brother, James, who had graduated from medical school in California and was doing his residency at the small Ute Mountain Ute Health Center in Towaoc.

She opened the back hatch on her 1997 Jeep Cherokee and pulled out her suitcase and backpack. She closed the hatch and was heading towards the side door when Gabby, Lizzy and Toni came running out, screaming like a bunch of schoolgirls, which they were. They hugged and jumped up and down in the driveway, then helped Angie with her luggage and headed inside.

Gabby showed Angie to the room they would be sharing, and she stood in the doorway and wondered why she had decided to do this. The room was barely larger than her dorm room, and there was one tiny window. The kitchen she passed through was half the size of the one at home, and she wondered how they would all fit at the small corner table if they all ate at home at the same time. She shook her head and set her backpack on the small desk under the window. Gabby had already claimed half of it as her own, and it was now covered with her laptop, monitor, keyboard and a mess of small cosmetic bottles.

"I'm so glad you're here, Ang," said Gabby with a huge smile. "We are going to have so much fun."

Angie smiled. "Me too, Gabby. I couldn't wait to get here."

"Great," said Gabby. "Let's get your things put away, and then we're gonna meet Lizzy and Toni at Tiny's Bar and Grill. It is time to party."

They spent the rest of the afternoon getting their little room organized, and then, while Gabby got dressed, Angie took a shower in a bathroom that was too small to turn around in and put on some clean clothes. She felt refreshed as she sat on the edge of the bed and brushed out her damp hair.

Once Gabby finished with her makeup, they slid their money, IDs and phones into the back pockets of their jeans, checked each other over to make sure they were ready and headed out the door. The bar was a couple of blocks from the house, and they chose to walk so they wouldn't have to worry about driving home later.

Tiny's Bar and Grill was packed to the doors, and you could hear the music from a block away. Lizzy and Toni had gotten there early enough to grab a table, and after a few minutes of looking around, Angie and Gabby found them and sat down. Angie looked around the bar.

The band was live, and the music was shaking the entire building. There were several couples and groups on the dance floor gyrating to the racket. It wasn't the kind of place to hold meaningful conversations.

The waiter, a young dark-haired guy in a dirty apron and shorts, fought through the crowd and took their order. Tiny's was known for its wings, so they ordered several variations along with another pitcher of draft beer from a local brewery.

The drinks arrived before the food, and the party for the four young women was underway, except something was off. As the night wore on, Angie felt uneasy. She wasn't sure what it was, maybe all the beer she had consumed or maybe the wings that were sitting in her stomach, marinating in all that beer, but she felt like she was being watched, which would not have been unusual in a place like this.

She set her glass on the table and looked around

again. The crowd separated just enough that this time, she spotted the grubby guy in the corner by the window. His hair was long and stringy, his beard was long and unkempt and he looked like he hadn't changed clothes in a long time. She couldn't figure out why he was even there. He was much older than just about everyone in the bar, and he was definitely looking at her. She looked back at her glass when her eye met his.

Angie sat there for another half hour, checking on the grubby guy in the corner several times, but his position never changed, and his eyes were always on her. She mentioned the guy to Gabby, who told her not to be concerned, that she had seen him in the bar before. He was just some old drunk, and he never moved off the barstool or caused a scene. Several more times, she glanced through the crowd and noticed him staring. Gabby may have thought he was harmless, but Angie didn't have a good feeling about him. She was getting creeped out, and she set her glass down and stood up.

"I need to get some air," she said.

Gabby started to stand up, but the guy she was talking to filled her beer glass and handed it to her. She smiled at Angie and went back to talking to the guy. Angie made her way through the crowd and walked out the front door into the coolness of the night air. She took a couple of deep breaths and held out her hand to steady herself against the wall. She hoped the creepy guy wouldn't follow her, and she pushed through the crowd standing on the sidewalk and started walking. She should have headed for Bunting Avenue but decided to take a walk through the campus instead.

She crossed the street and walked towards the plaza, looking over her shoulder as she went to make sure the creepy guy wasn't behind her. The night was beautiful, and she felt like her head was starting to clear. She stopped in the plaza and was looking at the stars when she felt someone approaching. She turned around, ready to confront the creepy guy, but realized she knew the person who had now stepped off the sidewalk and was walking towards her. The little dog he walked yipped and pulled at the end of his leash to reach Angie.

Angie kneeled and petted the little dog. "Hiya, Archie. How's the good boy?" she said in a shrill baby voice. She rubbed his ears and stood.

"Ms. Wilde, how fortuitous to run into you here." He looked around. "Are you walking alone?"

"Hi, Professor. I needed some air." She jutted her chin in the direction of the bar.

The professor nodded. "Ah, I see. Would you mind if I walked with you a bit? It's too nice a night to waste it walking alone."

Angie smiled and continued her walk, this time alongside the professor. He was one of her favorite professors, and she felt safe with him.

"I was hoping to speak with you on Monday," he said. "I have an opportunity at the Veterans Medical Center that I would like to discuss with you. It's something I think would work well with your sociology studies. Would it be all right if I bought you a coffee, and we could discuss it further?"

Angie nodded, and they turned towards the coffee shop on the other side of the parking lot. He spotted the beautiful turquoise and silver ring on Angie's hand, and she told him it was a gift from her grandfather. He smiled and pulled on Archie's leash.

Chapter Four

The bright light and the fog woke him from a troubled sleep, and his eyes looked around in fear. He tried to sit up, but he knew that would be impossible. He couldn't believe the alien was back. It had been several months since their last encounter, and he had hoped that maybe the alien had found someone else to visit and torment.

He could hear the alien opening drawers and rifling through his meager belongings, but he wasn't sure what was left for the alien to take. He also wondered what the alien would leave him in exchange. He had grown tired of the silly games the alien played, and he hoped the alien would realize he had nothing left to exchange and move on.

This was nothing like the encounters he had watched on those alien shows while in the hospital. In those shows, the alien always took the victim to the mother ship and did horrible experiments on them. That never happened to him, and he wondered why.

The alien appeared at the end of his small bed and held up something shiny. He recognized it even through the fog. It was his KA-BAR knife. The alien waved it around in the air, making ever-growing figure eights. It stopped, looked at the sharp edge and seemed to shake its head. He wondered how the alien found the knife. It was one of the few things he had left from his time in the army, and he kept it hidden under a loose floorboard, under an old rug. He hated to lose the knife, and he hoped that the alien would at least leave him something valuable in exchange. His eyes followed the shadow around the bed, and then the alien reached out and touched his neck with that long, bony finger that he had come to hate. The alien held up a small tubelike item and then leaned towards him. He felt the sting in his arm, and then the bright light faded away.

When he woke up the next morning and crawled out of bed, he had forgotten about his late-night visitor, but he was thrilled to see his knife sticking into the small table next to the bed. Then he saw the supplies that were sitting on his small table. The pile included coffee, flour, dried beans and several cans of vegetables. This was the first time the alien had ever restocked his meager kitchen, and he was surprised and pleased.

He picked up several of the cans to put them in the cabinet over the sink, and something that sounded like metal hit the floor. He bent over and picked up the small ring. It was silver, and the turquoise stone was cut in the shape of an eagle. He admired the piece for a few seconds and placed it in the box next to the sink that contained the other trinkets the alien had left him.

He gave himself a quick wash in the basin by the door, got dressed and headed out the door. He took a deep breath of the cool mountain air and headed up the road towards the lodge where he worked. It was a beautiful day on the mesa, and he was glad he lived where he did.

Chapter Five

Vicky Talmadge finished cleaning up from breakfast, made sure all her food supplies were stored in the bear bag and hoisted it fifteen feet into the tree. She made sure the fire in the rock-encircled firepit was out, locked her old VW camper and whistled for Jasper, who came bounding out of the trees.

Vicky placed the pack on Jasper's back, checked to make sure there was enough food, snacks and water in his pack and, using both hands, rubbed his ears. Jasper, the five-year-old golden retriever, licked her hands and ran a quick lap around the campground.

Vicky lifted her pack up onto her shoulders and grabbed her hiking staff, and they headed for Z Road. This was their second day in the almost empty campground at the west end of Island Lake, just off the Grand Mesa Scenic Byway, and the weather couldn't have been more perfect. The bluebird sky and the temperature in the low fifties made for perfect hiking weather, and she planned to head up Z Road towards the Grand Mesa Visitor Center. She knew they wouldn't have many more good days since the National Weather Service was calling for snow by the end of the week, so she wanted to get as much downtime as she could. Even though it was early September, you never knew what the weather might do on the Grand Mesa. She had seen it go from the mid-sixties to a blizzard within a matter of hours, so she had loaded the car with clothes and food for any situation.

Vicky had been excited to get some downtime, and she knew the rest would be good for Jasper as well. They had been going at it hard for the last six months, working one disaster after another all over the world. They had spent the last six weeks in northern Turkey after a devastating 7.8-magnitude earthquake had leveled a small city, and they had arrived back in Colorado the weekend before. This was a much needed vacation.

Jasper was a cadaver dog and was one of the best in the world. As a team, Vicky and Jasper were called out to assist whenever a natural or man-made disaster took the lives of large numbers of people. During their most recent work in Turkey, Jasper had been responsible for finding more than five hundred bodies buried in the rubble, and although the work was rewarding, it was also hard on Jasper. Every couple of days, Vicky and Jasper would go off on their own, and Vicky would hide and let Jasper find her. It was part of their training ritual, but it also helped Jasper's mental state by letting him find a live body instead of the dead ones.

Vicky Talmadge had decided that today would be an off day and that they would spend the day hiking. They would have plenty of time to play and train during the next two weeks, provided the weather held, but even if it didn't, Jasper was equally at home looking for avalanche victims in the snow as he was looking for bodies under rubble piles.

With Jasper at her side, they headed east on Z Road, past the entrance to the boat ramp, and continued up the road. She wasn't sure how far it was to the visitor center, but she knew they were both in great shape. Since they had the road to themselves, they walked down the middle of it, stopping often to admire the view of the lake or look at something interesting on the side of the road. Every now and then, Jasper would take off and charge into the woods to chase a bird or small animal, and he'd return wagging his tail with what Vicky swore was a big smile on his face.

They took a break at what Vicky guessed was the halfway point on their journey to the visitor center, and Vicky filled the small portable dog bowl with water and gave Jasper snacks. While Vicky ate her granola bar and drank from her water bottle, Jasper ran across the road and explored along the trees. Vicky glanced over to where Jasper was and put her water bottle back in her backpack. She stood up and crossed the road.

Jasper was sitting dead still next to a small white cross that had been pounded into the hard-packed soil. The kind of cross that people put along roadsides to indicate where someone had an accident and died. Depending on where you drove, these white crosses were all along the highways and streets, and Vicky had passed several on her drive north from Durango, never paying much attention to them. She and Jasper had even passed some over the years on hiking trails, so she was surprised to see Jasper in his alert posture, since she knew they were markers and that there were no bodies buried beneath them.

She kneeled next to Jasper and ran her hand down his back. She could feel the tension, and she wondered what was going on as he looked up at her. She knew he was tired, but he had never responded this way before.

"What have you found, buddy?" she asked in a soft voice.

She looked around the area to see if maybe there was a dead animal or bird somewhere, but she couldn't find anything. She rubbed his head and told him that he did good, and that seemed to snap him out of his trance. They continued down the road, and after another quarter of a mile, he did the same thing at another cross. This one wasn't as white as the other one and looked a little weathered, but Jasper's reaction was the same.

Jasper looked up at her from his alert position, as if questioning why she wasn't calling for the crew to come dig up the body. She gave him a snack and a lot of praise, and they headed along until it happened a third time. The third cross was old and brown and tilted to one side like the snow had knocked it over, and she almost missed it, but Jasper didn't.

Vicky was concerned about Jasper's behavior and wasn't sure what to make of it. Then, another thought crept into her brain. Why were there three crosses along this stretch of straight road? These crosses indicated an accident location, but she couldn't understand how there could be that many accidents on the road.

After the same thing happened at two more crosses along the road, Vicky decided to turn around and head back to camp. She wanted to minimize the impact on Jasper, so they walked down the other side of the road from the crosses until they got back to camp. Once there, Jasper settled down and took a long nap, which was his typical reaction after finding bodies. Vicky spent a long time watching him, and then, as a chill ran up her spine, she decided she needed to do something. She didn't want to call the sheriff and look like an idiot and waste their time, but she knew someone she could call who might help her.

Ashley Baxter answered her phone on the

second ring. "Hey, Vicky, this is a surprise. How are you?"

"Hi, Ashley, I'm doing great. How about yourself?"

"Busy as always. Are you back home?" asked Bax.

"Yeah," said Vicky. "We got home Sunday, and we're up on the Grand Mesa."

They made small talk for a few minutes: Vicky asked Bax about the drag club shooting that had happened a few weeks back outside Grand Junction, and Vicky told her about their latest mission to Turkey.

"How's my buddy Jasper?" asked Bax.

Vicky hesitated for a few seconds. "He's fine, so don't worry, but he's kind of the reason for the call. Are you home?"

"No," said Bax. "I'm testifying at a trial in Custer County. I should finish up tomorrow or the next day. What's going on, Vicky?"

Colorado Bureau of Investigation Agent Ashley Baxter, at thirty-four years old, was the youngest agent in the Grand Junction Field Office. She'd joined CBI straight out of college, and, having had no experience in the field, she valued the time she got to spend with CBI Agent Buck Taylor, a seasoned investigator and her mentor, because she learned so much about running an investigation.

Bax stood about five foot six with blue eyes and blond hair that she often kept tied in a ponytail that hung through the hole in the back of her CBI cap. Some people would describe her as husky, or what used to be called having a "mountain girl" figure. She wasn't gorgeous, but she was pretty enough to turn men's heads when she entered a room, until they spotted the badge and gun clipped to her belt. She had been with the Colorado Bureau of Investigation for eleven years and had earned the respect of her teammates.

Vicky Talmadge told Bax about Jasper's odd behavior at the crosses they encountered, and she also wondered out loud about why they'd found so many crosses on a backcountry road.

"I didn't want to call the local sheriff and find out it was nothing," said Vicky. "But I also thought someone should look into it."

"You did the right thing by calling me, Vicky. When it comes to Jasper, I would always err on his side. One of my coworkers is camping somewhere up on the mesa. Let me call him and see if he can come by. His name is Buck Taylor, and he is a dog lover.
Either I'll get back to you or Buck will."

They chatted for a few more minutes and then said goodbye. Vicky sat back in her fabric camp chair and hoped she'd done the right thing.

Chapter Six

Buck Taylor threw off the top cover of his sleeping bag and stretched as best he could in the confines of his state-issued Jeep Grand Cherokee. He looked around to make sure he didn't have any company and pushed the button that opened the rear hatch. The crisp morning air rushed into the Jeep, and Buck took a few deep breaths to clear his head.

Buck liked sleeping under the stars when camping and had taught his entire family to enjoy cowboy-style, tent-free camping, no matter the weather. He had slept under the stars for the past five nights of his vacation, but last night was different. Yesterday, while walking back from the small stream where he had been fishing, he'd encountered a juvenile cinnamon-colored black bear. Careful to avoid a human–bear confrontation, he had worked his way around the bear and thought he had lost it, but later in the evening, the little bear kept working its way closer to Buck's camp, circling the campsite just within the tree line.

Buck had cleaned up around his campsite after dinner, hoisting his food bag high up on a branch, and even though he was always armed, he wanted to avoid any problems. He hated the idea that in a confrontation with people, it was always the bear that suffered, and he hated it when anyone destroyed an animal just for being an animal. So far, his little friend was nowhere to be seen, so he got dressed, slid out of the Jeep and stretched for real.

Buck Taylor was six feet tall and weighed 185 pounds—very little flab for a sixty-two-year-old man. Buck's hair was salt-and-pepper, with what seemed like a lot more salt than pepper, and he wore it longer than was the fashion of the day. Buck was always pleased when he looked in the mirror since, other than getting older, he was in as good a shape as he had been when he played defensive linebacker for the Gunnison High School Cowboys, what seemed like a long time ago. He still tried to jog five miles every day when he could, and he tried to ride his mountain bike every weekend, weather permitting. Except for a couple of sore knees coming from age, Buck was in good shape, which was important in his line of work.

Buck Taylor was an investigative agent for the Colorado Bureau of Investigation. He was assigned to the CBI field office in Grand Junction, Colorado, but he hadn't been in the office much during the past year. Somehow, he had become the favorite "go-to" guy for the governor of Colorado, Richard J. Kennedy, who was one of "those" Kennedys. The governor was in his second term in office, and Buck had been instrumental in closing several high-profile investigations during that period, which made the governor look good. As a result, when a situation came up that might get a little hairy, the governor always asked to have Buck assigned.

Buck had been married for thirty-four years before breast cancer stole the one person he cared about most in the world. He missed Lucy every day, even after all this time.

If you asked Buck, he would tell you that he fell in love with Lucinda Torres on the first day of their senior year in high school. On the other hand, Lucy always told people that Buck stalked her the entire senior year before she gave in to shut her friends up and agreed to go to the movies with him. She had always considered him just another jock, another football player who was too full of himself.

What she found on that first date was a shy, unassuming gentleman who cared more about pleasing her than bragging about his prowess on the football field. She would tell people it was love at first sight that had taken a year to develop. After that, they were inseparable.

During senior year, Buck had been approached by several college football scouts who wanted to sign him to play for their schools. Gunnison High School was a small school back in 1978, and Buck and his family were amazed at how many schools had recruited him, but for Buck, college wasn't in the cards.

Buck hated school and spent a lot of time getting himself out of trouble instead of getting an education. When he found something that interested him, he had no problem learning all he could about the subject, but regular schoolwork just bored him. After several long, heartfelt discussions, first with Lucy and then with his parents, he decided to join the army after graduation. No one was surprised.

Buck spent four years after high school in the army, and by the time his enlistment was up, he had been promoted to first sergeant. He spent three years of his enlistment in the military police and took to police work. That was when he decided to apply for a position with the Gunnison County Sheriff's Office.

Since he was already well known in the county, he had no trouble getting a job as a deputy. He proposed to Lucy the night he received the call that he had gotten the position. His life and career were set. He made the most of his time with the Gunnison County Sheriff's Office, becoming the undersheriff in charge of the Investigation Division and coming to the attention of the Colorado Bureau of Investigation.

Buck had worked with the Colorado Bureau of

Investigation on several cases inside the county and had earned the respect of the investigators he had worked with.

As twilight started to fall on Buck's career, he knew that unless he wanted to go into politics and run for sheriff, he had reached the highest position in the sheriff's office that he could obtain. He loved his job, but when the first offer came in from CBI, he sat down with Lucy and had a long heart-to-heart talk.

He'd spent seventeen years in the sheriff's office and had always figured he would retire from that job. They had three children, two in high school and one not far behind, and he was a well-respected member of the community. Did he have the right to disrupt their lives, pick up, move someplace else and start all over? The kids had friends. Lucy owned a small deli/ice cream parlor, and they had a nice life.

He could stick it out for another ten years and retire, and they could travel and see the world as they had always planned. Twice he turned down the offer from CBI, although more and more, he felt trapped behind a desk instead of doing what he loved, which was investigating crime.

The last offer came from Tom Cole, then-director of the Colorado Bureau of Investigation. Buck always remembered that day. The Denver

Broncos had just lost another game, the third one in a row, and his friends had all packed up and headed home when there was a knock at the front door.

Now, anyone who lives in a small community knows that no one ever uses the front door, and no one ever knocks. So, who could this be this late on a Sunday evening?

Buck answered the door and was surprised to see the director of the Colorado Bureau of Investigation standing on his front porch. The director smiled and said, "Before you close the door in my face, please listen to my offer."

Buck invited him in, and he and Lucy sat on the couch and listened as the director laid out his plan. He was opening a new branch office in Grand Junction, Colorado, that would house five agents and a small forensic unit. Buck could continue to live in Gunnison but would have to report to the office in Grand Junction twice a month. Otherwise, he would be free to work from his house. There would be no disruption in his life other than spending time on the road as his investigations warranted. He would work alone but would have all the branch office's resources at his disposal.

Before Buck could say a word, Lucy said, "Buck, this is what you have been waiting for, a chance to be a real investigator again. You have to take this." That was one of the things that made him love Lucy every day. She always knew what he was thinking and understood what drove him. She had nailed it this time. Buck looked at the director and replied, "Well, I guess it's settled; looks like you have a new investigator on your team."

That was twenty-three years ago, and Buck had never looked back. He had made the most of those years and was one of the most respected and feared investigators in the state, but all that work couldn't make up for the loss he suffered.

Lucy was diagnosed with metastatic breast cancer following a routine mammogram, and they set off together on their next adventure: the quest to beat the dreaded disease. After a double mastectomy and five years of chemo, they knew their time was drawing to a close when the cancer returned several times to her brain and was no longer controlled by the radiation.

Together, they decided to stop all treatment, even though they had always told the family that the decision was Lucy's alone to make. Lucy spent the last couple of months of her life taking care of her small business and spending as much time as possible with her children and grandchildren.

The end came one spring night. Lucy had been sleeping on and off for twenty or so hours a day in the end. The night she died, Buck had been lying in bed next to her, reading a report, when she snuggled into his arms and rested her head on his shoulder. Sometime during the night, Buck had fallen asleep. When he woke up, Lucy was gone, and his world was shattered.

They say that time heals all wounds, but Buck wasn't sure that was the case when you lost your closest friend. And even now, all these years later, he missed her more and more each day.

Buck always thought back to that Sunday morning when the family had gathered for a private ceremony at the little dock along the Gunnison River to scatter Lucy's ashes. Each family member got to say a few words about Lucy, and when they finished and turned to go, they were stunned to see several hundred of their neighbors and friends standing silently behind them in the park. Word had gotten out about their private service, and everyone turned out to pay tribute to Lucy. The affair turned into a huge party, with plenty of food and drinks. Lucy never wanted any kind of service, but Buck figured she would have loved this spontaneous outpouring of love.

Chapter Seven

Buck shook off the morning chill, walked over and stirred the ashes in the firepit. Once he had a flame going, he added some wood, brought down his food bag and cooked a breakfast of scrambled eggs and bacon. He washed it down with a bottle of Coke—the first of many. Buck's Coke drinking was well known around the CBI office, but it also seemed that no matter where he went around the state, someone always had a cold Coke waiting for him.

He had one more day left in his vacation and planned to fish several small lakes a few miles from camp. He enjoyed fishing on Grand Mesa because it gave him a variety of fishing opportunities.

Grand Mesa is five hundred square miles of some of the most scenic land in Colorado and is the largest flat-top mountain in the world. Geologists speculate that at one time, millions of years ago and before it eroded away, it was a mountain that would have towered over Mount Everest. Located east of Grand Junction, most of the mesa is above ten thousand feet. With more than three hundred lakes and reservoirs and miles of trout streams, it was the perfect place for Buck to take a vacation.

The weather could be unpredictable, and snow in the summer was not uncommon. So far, for Buck's vacation, the weather had been perfect.

Buck was an avid fly fisherman and fished every chance he got. His fishing gear was always in his Jeep in case an opportunity presented itself or he needed to clear his head.

Buck couldn't remember the last time he had taken a real vacation. His kids were always on him that he worked too hard, but Buck loved his job, and even though he was fast approaching retirement age, he had never even considered that he might want to retire. He figured he would be lost without his work. So, when his head got clogged up, he would take a couple of hours and hit the river.

This year, he needed that time off more than ever. He had been involved in several investigations that had put all his crime-solving abilities to the test. He and his team had spent the last month putting together the investigation and evidence files for a horrific mass shooting that had occurred at a drag nightclub just outside Grand Junction. Buck had been to some horrible crime scenes in his time in law enforcement, but this time, the number of dead and injured and the terrible violence had taken a toll on him and his team. He was ready for a vacation.

After packing his gear and ensuring the fire was dead, he slid into his Jeep and headed for his first destination, a little stream called Kiser Creek. Buck spent a few hours fishing the creek and several of the small lakes in the area, and at noon, he found a small picnic area and set about cutting up some cheddar cheese and sausage. He was finishing his lunch when his phone rang. He was surprised he had service this far back in the woods. He looked at the number and pushed the green button.

"Hey, Bax. What's up?"

"Hiya, Buck," said Bax. "How's the fishing?"

"It's been great, but I'm about ready to head back home and get back into work mode," said Buck.

"Well," said Bax. "I might have just the thing to get the old investigative juices flowing."

She filled Buck in on the conversation she'd had with Vicky Talmadge about Jasper alerting at several roadside crosses and her question of why there were so many crosses on a lonely stretch of backwoods road. Buck listened without saying a word.

Bax finished her debrief and waited for Buck to respond.

"This woman is a friend of yours?" he asked.

"She's a friend of my parents', and I've known her all my life. One of the Pulitzers my dad won was a story about Vicky and her dog Sandy, and their work at the World Trade Center in New York in the days following the nine-eleven attacks. Sandy found hundreds of bodies in the six weeks they worked there."

Buck noticed a sadness in Bax's voice and waited a few beats for Bax to continue.

"Vicky was smart enough to wear a respirator while working on the rubble pile, but Sandy couldn't do that. A year after the article was published, Sandy died from lung cancer. She was an awesome dog and was buried with full honors as a first responder."

"And Jasper is a cadaver dog?" asked Buck.

"Yeah. He's Sandy's great-grandson. I just sent you a copy of the article on Sandy and one about Jasper from an earthquake in Nepal a year ago."

Buck's phone chimed with an incoming message, but he didn't open it.

"I don't want to screw up your vacation, but when Jasper alerts the way Vicky described it, he must be onto something. She didn't want to call the sheriff in case it was nothing, but she's concerned, and I told her you would be willing to take a look first. What do you think?"

Buck finished the last of the Coke and put the bottle in the trash can next to the table.

"I'll head over to the Island Lake Campground right now. I'm not that far away, so it shouldn't take me long to get there. How will I recognize her?"

"She said she is the sole camper there, and you can't miss her," said Bax with a chuckle.

Buck wasn't sure what Bax meant, but he trusted her with his life, so he disconnected the call, packed up his gear and headed for the campground, thinking about what Bax had chuckled about. He didn't have to wonder for long. As soon as he pulled onto the campground loop, he spotted the old VW bus. It was hard to miss. It was bright pink and covered with flag stickers from all over the world. There was a big American flag hanging on the side and a large sign in the back window that had a picture of a dog's head and the words goldens are golden. He pulled in next to the old bus and turned off the Jeep.

He opened the door and started to slide out when Jasper bounded out of the bus and introduced himself by almost jumping into the seat with Buck. He licked Buck's hands and ran around in circles.

"I hope you don't mind dogs," said a voice from the van. "As you can see, he's friendly. "Vicky Talmadge laughed as she emerged from the van.

"You must be Buck," she said. "Ashley forgot to mention how good-looking you are." She walked over and held out her hand. "Vicky Talmadge." She pointed to the dog, who was now sitting next to Buck. "And you've already met Jasper."

Buck shook her hand and noticed the firm handshake and the calluses. Vicky was about five foot seven and stocky, much like Bax. She had long gray hair tied in a ponytail that hung to her waist, and her face was tanned and lined from years of exposure to the elements. Buck couldn't help but notice that she was attractive.

"Can Jasper have a treat?" he asked.

Vicky smiled. "Go ahead, but be forewarned that he'll be your friend for life."

Buck opened his hand to reveal a large Milk-Bone dog biscuit, and Jasper looked up at Vicky. She nodded, and Jasper reached for the biscuit. "Because of where we travel, I taught all my dogs to take treats or food only with my approval. With all the bad stuff we deal with, I don't want them eating something that might be contaminated."

Buck wondered if she also didn't want them eating pieces of human flesh they might find in the rubble. Vicky pointed towards the picnic table, and Buck followed her and sat opposite her. "Ashley told me you are a Coke drinker, so I apologize in advance for not having any to offer you, but I can offer you some Indonesian tea."

Buck nodded his thanks, pulled the Coke bottle from his backpack and set it on the table. "Why don't you tell me what you found," said Buck.

Vicky told Buck about their walk, and Jasper alerting at the small roadside crosses she found. She also explained that she couldn't understand why there were so many crosses along this one road. Buck listened until she took a breath and sipped from her cup of tea.

"So, you think Jasper might have alerted because there's a body under the cross?" he asked.

"I don't know what to think. Those crosses are everywhere, and you never give them a second thought, but he's trained to alert if there is a body, and he alerted five times this morning. I don't want to think about what's going on in my head right now."

Buck put his Coke bottle back in the holder of his backpack. "Well, let's take a look and see if we can calm your concerns."

Vicky stood, walked over to the van, pulled out a yellow safety vest and put it on. Jasper looked up and trotted to the van, where Vicky put a yellow vest on him too. Buck watched the process.

"This time, we'll approach the crosses as work and see how he reacts."

Buck led them to his Jeep; Jasper jumped in the back, and Vicky slid onto the passenger seat. Buck pulled out of the campsite, and Vicky pointed him towards the first cross. He slowed down as they approached the cross and pulled to a stop across the street from it. They all climbed out of the Jeep, and Jasper sat at attention next to Vicky's leg. She pointed to the other side of the road. "Find," she said, and Jasper trotted across the road and started sniffing the dirt. They followed behind him.

Jasper approached the first cross, circled it with his nose to the ground and sat next to it. Vicky called him back to where she and Buck stood and gave him a small treat from her pocket.

Buck walked over to the cross and looked around. The ground was covered with leaves and pine needles, so, using his foot, he brushed some of them away from around the cross. He noticed the ground looked like it had been disturbed. It didn't appear as hard or cracked as the surrounding ground. The drought conditions this year had been bad, and there had been little rain in the past couple of months, so the ground all around was hard and cracked from the sun.

Buck had pulled an old army camping shovel out of the back of his Jeep when they arrived, and he kneeled next to the cross and scraped the top layer of dirt. He wouldn't say it was easy digging, but he had seen a lot worse, which surprised him.

It took him a little while to dig down a foot, at which point he stopped and put down the shovel. The smell had worsened the deeper he dug, and after all these years, he knew what the smell was. He reached into the hole with his hands and pushed aside the soil, exposing a black plastic bag. He needed to be sure before he called out the troops that it was human remains and not an animal someone had buried, so he stopped digging and pulled his pocketknife from his belt. He slit the exposed plastic bag and separated the two sides. He looked down at the pale hand with the four red nails and one black nail and stood up. He walked back to Vicky and Jasper.

"There's a body, isn't there?" asked Vicky.

Buck nodded. "Looks like Jasper was right. You said he alerted at five crosses; do you know how many are on the road?"

"No. We headed back after he alerted the fifth time."

"Let's find out," said Buck.

They headed back to the Jeep and climbed in, and Buck drove along the shoulder of the road. By the time they reached the Grand Mesa Scenic

Byway, they'd counted eleven crosses. They drove back to the last cross and Buck asked Vicky to have Jasper do his thing; she sent him on his way. It took longer, but after several minutes, he sat next to an old, broken cross lying on the ground. Vicky put her hand over her mouth, unable to speak. Buck pulled out his phone. It looked like his vacation was over.

Chapter Eight

Kevin Jackson answered his cell phone. "Hey, Buck. I thought you were on vacation. What's up?"

Kevin Jackson, the director of the Colorado Bureau of Investigation, had been the youngest person to run the bureau when he was appointed by Governor Richard J. Kennedy. He'd had a stellar career with the Colorado Springs Police Department before being tapped for the top post at CBI. He was more bureaucrat than cop, having spent most of his career on the administrative side at CSPD, but he was well respected in the law enforcement community, and Buck was impressed with him.

"I think my vacation has come to an early end, sir," said Buck. Director Jackson could sense the seriousness in Buck's voice, and he was quiet for a moment, wondering what this phone call would bring.

"What's going on, Buck?"

"We discovered a fresh body buried under a roadside cross this afternoon," said Buck.

"Okay, Buck. You have my attention. Fill me in, and who is 'we'?"

"'We' is a friend of Bax. Her name is Victoria Talmadge, and she called Bax this morning because she was concerned. Her dog alerted next to a cross as they walked along the road at Island Lake on Grand Mesa. I forwarded you an article Jack Baxter wrote about Vicky and one of her dogs and the work they did at the World Trade Center in New York City after the attack on nine-eleven. Victoria Talmadge runs a cadaver dog, and she and Jasper, that's the dog, had just returned from spending several weeks in Turkey working on the rubble piles after an earthquake leveled a city. She and the dog are up here camping and taking a much-needed break, and they've been doing a lot of hiking in the area.

"Today, they followed the road on the south side of Island Lake and passed a small white cross on the shoulder at the edge of the trees. The kind of cross you find all over the place to mark the location where someone was killed or injured, usually in an accident. As they passed the cross, the dog alerted. Ms. Talmadge thought it was just overwork, so she gave him a treat, and they continued their walk. Long story short, they passed five crosses along the road, and the dog alerted at each one. She also wondered why there were so many roadside crosses on this stretch of backcountry road. She called Bax to see what she thought, and Bax called me.

"This afternoon, we followed the same road, and I witnessed the dog alerting just like she told Bax. I dug through some loose dirt next to the cross, and about a foot down, I encountered a black plastic bag. To make sure it wasn't a buried animal, I cut a slit in the bag. What I could see was a decomposing hand with red nail polish."

Director Jackson had been reading the article on his phone while listening to Buck. "She sounds like a pretty amazing woman, Buck."

He waited for the other shoe to drop, but Buck was silent. He decided to ask the question he didn't want to ask.

"Buck, how many crosses did you find along the road?"

"Eleven, sir. I didn't have the dog check all of them, but he alerted at the last one we found. I assume he would have alerted at the rest of them as well."

"Fuck, Buck. We're looking at a body dump site. You think we're looking at a serial killer?"

"I don't like to speculate, sir, but that would be my initial read. I'm going to need the troops. Can you call Franklin and Paul and get them on the way? Bax is still tied up in Custer County but should be finished tomorrow. We will also need an anthropologist. I'll call Max and see who she has available. Do you want to call Delta County Sheriff Buckman, and I'll call Sima?"

"I'll get the ball rolling. Send me your coordinates, and I'll call Hal Buckman. Secure the scene until I can get some deputies up there. I'll see if the troopers have anyone they can send to help block the road. Shit, Buck. Hell of a way to finish your vacation."

"Yes, sir," said Buck. He disconnected the call and looked at Vicky Talmadge. She petted Jasper, who was no longer wearing his yellow vest and was lying beside her, snoring softly.

"Looks like I was right to worry," she said, looking down at her hands.

Buck nodded, took a sip from his now-warm bottle of Coke and pulled up the contact list on his phone. He picked a number and dialed. Max answered the way she always did.

"Buck Taylor. How's my favorite cop?" asked Max Clinton. "What the hell have you gotten yourself involved with this time?"

Dr. Maxine Clinton was the director of the State Crime Lab and one of Buck's oldest and dearest friends. She was a matronly woman in her late sixties, about five foot five, with short gray hair. She thought she carried around an extra fifteen pounds she didn't need, but she was still a handsome woman. Married for forty years, Max had four children, eleven grandchildren and six great-grandchildren. She lived in a 150-year-old farmhouse in Pueblo, where she liked to tend her garden, sit on her porch and drink iced tea. She was also a bourbon girl and could drink most people under the table. She was loud and outspoken, but she knew her job.

Max had received her PhD in biology from the University of Colorado and worked as a biology professor for twenty years before joining CBI. She was the head of the State Crime Lab, which she enjoyed. She was a tough taskmaster with a belief system that didn't allow for defeat. Her goal was to give the crime investigator, no matter which department or municipality they worked for, all the information they would need to solve any crime. She held that as a sacred obligation to the victims. She was dedicated to her job and her staff, and the team at the lab worshipped her.

Buck would have been included in that group. Many times, during a challenging investigation, it was Max and her team that lit the spark that led to a breakthrough. Max was one of Buck's favorite people, and she felt the same way about him.

"Doing good, Max," said Buck. "I'm gonna

need your help." He gave her the same debrief that he'd given Director Jackson.

"Sounds like you're going to need an anthropologist," said Max. "I'll make some calls and see who's available. And I'll let the lab know to get ready for whatever you send us. You sure manage to get yourself into some strange situations, Buck."

The people Buck worked with always joked that there wasn't anyone in Colorado that Buck didn't know. But the truth was, Max was way ahead of him in that department. She had contacts worldwide and never failed to get him the answers he needed.

During one recent case, Buck was looking for information on infrasound weapons and their effect on the body. Within a couple of hours, Buck was on the phone with a colleague of Max's who was an expert in those types of weapons.

Buck laughed. "Yeah. That's why I don't like to go on vacation."

Max laughed and ended the call the way she always did. "You're a good man, Buck Taylor; God will watch over you."

Buck wasn't much of a religious man. He hadn't been to church in forty years. He had been raised Catholic but left the church right after confirmation. He always had too many questions about the teachings and too many people telling him that he had to have faith. That wasn't the answer he was looking for. He had a lot of friends, Max among them, who had always offered up a prayer when Lucy was dying. He never once rejected any of those offers, often smiling and thanking them for their kind thoughts.

Buck had realized long ago that it wasn't God and faith he had a problem with; it was organized religion. In his many years in law enforcement, he had seen too many times the aftereffects of someone's religious beliefs. It amazed him that so many people of faith could cause so much hatred and crime. But then, nonbelievers created just as much havoc.

Buck always believed there was a higher power, but he didn't believe that whatever that power was, it cared about one individual over another. His football coach always offered up a prayer before each game, asking for help in defeating the other team. He always suspected the other team's coach was doing the same thing. So, how did God decide which team should win?

He knew a lot of people who said a lot of prayers for Lucy over the five years she was sick, but in the end, she still died. And she was the last person who should have gotten cancer. But Buck didn't carry any hatred. Whom could he get mad at? Whom could he blame?

Buck believed that there are spirits or a force all around us, and he always thanked them for allowing him to enjoy the hike, catch fish, or see the sunrise and the sunset. It wasn't religion. It was something deeper. Something Buck didn't understand. He just accepted it. But no matter what, he always appreciated it when Max told him God was watching over him. After all, what could it hurt?

Buck slid into his Jeep, pulled out of the campsite and headed for the first cross. He parked next to the cross, slid out and opened the back hatch. He pulled out a roll of yellow crime scene tape, walked over to a big tree a couple of yards from the cross and tied it around the tree. He then tied it to his rear bumper, then to his front bumper and then to another tree. He stood looking at the small cross and wondered where this case was going to take them.

He slid back into his Jeep, pulled out his phone and dialed. Dr. Sima Kalishe was a forensic pathologist. She worked under contract with the Mesa County coroner, based in Grand Junction, Colorado, and several other counties in the area, including Montrose and Delta Counties.

Colorado was one of about a dozen states that still used the coroner system instead of the medical examiner system. The coroner for each jurisdiction was an elected official, and that person did not have to have any experience or even be a medical professional. Anyone could run for coroner.

The system was evolving so that the coroner was required to complete a formal training program in death investigations, but it was a slow legislative process. Unlike in the medical examiner system, and since the coroner did not have to be a doctor, coroners would contract with a licensed forensic pathologist to handle any investigations that required an autopsy.

These forensic pathologists were trained doctors who split their time among several jurisdictions to keep costs down. Many forensic pathologists were current or former medical examiners, and several were retired, working part time to keep their hands in the game. Sima Kalishe, in Buck's opinion, was one of the best.

Buck gave Dr. Kalishe the same debrief, and she told him she would gather up her team and head up. He sat back, closed his eyes and waited for the teams to arrive.

Chapter Nine

Buck slid out of his Jeep as three Delta County Sheriff's Department vehicles stopped in front of him. Sheriff Hal Buckman slid out of the black Ford F-150, stretched and walked up to Buck with his hand extended.

"Buck. Been a long time," said Sheriff Buckman.

"Hal," said Buck, shaking his hand. "Good to see you. Sorry about the circumstances."

Hal Buckman was six feet tall and trim. His brown hair was cut short, and he had a thin mustache. Buck had never seen the sheriff in his uniform, and today was no different. Hal Buckman wore jeans, boots and a flannel shirt with his badge pinned above the left pocket. He also carried a pearl-handled revolver in the holster on his left side. With his scowl and slight Southern accent, he liked to let people think he was a simple, old-school sheriff, but Buck knew different. Hal Buckman had received his juris doctorate from the University of Denver almost twenty years ago. He had also graduated with honors from the FBI National Academy for Law Enforcement and was one of the smartest men Buck knew. He had been with the

Delta Sheriff's Department for seventeen years, the last eight as sheriff. His wife of seventeen years, Lauren, made the best cherry pies Buck had ever tasted.

The sheriff looked over his shoulder. "Deputies Sterling and Cruz, and you already know Detective Apodaca. Guys. Meet Buck Taylor, CBI."

Buck shook hands all around. Deputy Alisha Sterling was tall, stocky and had short brown hair. She had three stripes on the cuff of her uniform shirt, indicating she had been around awhile.

Deputy Armando Cruz was taller than Buck and the sheriff and thin. His wavy black hair was trimmed, and he was clean-shaven. His uniform had some of the sharpest creases Buck had ever seen, and he looked like he might have just left the military.

Detective Vince Apodaca was short, stocky and had a bit of a beer gut hanging over his belt under his suit jacket. Buck and Vince had worked on several cases together, and Buck knew he was a seasoned, no-nonsense investigator.

"So, Buck," said Sheriff Buckman. "Director Jackson didn't give us a lot to go on. Want to fill us in?"

He stepped over to the edge of the hole Buck had

dug, stopping at the crime scene tape. He looked at Buck. "No denying the smell."

Buck nodded. "Yeah. I didn't notice it when I first got here, but once I slit the plastic, it was ripe."

"Director Jackson told us that a dog discovered the body," said Detective Apodaca.

"Yeah. A dog named Jasper," said Buck. "He's a cadaver dog. He and his owner, Victoria Talmadge, are camping just down the road. They walked along the road this morning; they were going to the visitor center, but they never got there. The dog started alerting at several roadside crosses."

"How many crosses are we talking about?" asked the sheriff.

"He alerted at five crosses, and then he alerted again at the one farthest down the road. We didn't check the rest. There're eleven crosses along this road."

"Holy shit," said Deputy Sterling. She looked embarrassed by her outburst and apologized for her language.

"No apology needed," said Buck. "I thought the same thing. I've got the forensic team on the way and have called the State Crime Lab to send up an anthropologist. What I need from you folks is to set up a roadblock at the turnoff from the byway and another one at the junction for the campground. No one in or out. You okay with that, Hal?"

Sheriff Buckman turned to his two deputies. "You heard the man. Alisha, take the turnoff by the visitor's center; Armando, set up down by the campground." He turned back to Buck. "I'm gonna call the office and have them send up the mobile command center. We're gonna need someplace to work. I'd like Vince to work with your team, if that's okay?"

Buck laughed. "It's your county, Sheriff. We're just visitors here."

Sheriff Buckman laughed. He knew from experience that when Buck Taylor was working a crime scene, there was no doubt who was in charge. He turned to Detective Apodaca. "Vince. Whatever Buck and his team need."

"No worries," said Detective Apodaca.

Sheriff Buckman walked away from the group, keying the mic on his shirt. Buck could hear him tell Dispatch to have one of the deputies bring up the trailer. While the sheriff was talking, the two deputies headed for their SUVs. Buck stepped up to Detective Apodaca.

"Vince, how's the new grandkid?"

Detective Apodaca pulled his wallet from his

jacket pocket, opened it and handed it to Buck. The pictures were of a chubby baby boy with a full head of black hair. Buck smiled and handed him back his wallet.

"He looks just like you," said Buck.

Vince placed his hands on his belly. "Yeah, right down to the beer belly." They both laughed.

"You ready to get dirty?" asked Buck.

Detective Apodaca nodded. "Got some coveralls in the back. What's the plan?"

"I want to expose this body as much as we can. We are in for a long night with this many crime scenes, and I'd like to get a head start. We'll pile the dirt on some plastic so my guys can go through it when they get here."

Detective Apodaca headed for his SUV, pulled a pair of white Tyvek coveralls out of the back and removed his jacket. Buck walked back to his Jeep and did the same thing. Sheriff Buckman walked up and stood next to the open hatch.

"You're thinking serial killer, right?" said the sheriff.

Buck looked up while he was putting on his Tyvek booties. "Yeah, that's my first impression."

The sheriff nodded. "The body you exposed smells pretty fresh. That means he or she is still operating."

"Yeah," said Buck. "And if all the crosses we found represent a body, he or she has been operating for a long time."

"Did you hear that Jackson turned in his papers?" said Sheriff Buckman.

"Yep," said Buck. "Had a feeling that was going to happen. The drag club shooting took a lot out of him."

Jackson Foley was the sheriff of Mesa County, an area that included the city of Grand Junction, which had been the scene of a horrific mass shooting at a drag club that led to the deaths of more than seventy people and the injuries of dozens more. It also led to the death of Colorado Republican Congressman Royal Sanders, a staunch opponent of drag clubs. The case went viral when it was determined that the shooter had been a follower of several far-right podcasts. After a riot incited by one of those podcasters injured several of the family members of the victims, Sheriff Foley took a lot of political heat.

"He's a good man," said Sheriff Buckman. "The law enforcement community is going to miss him."

Buck nodded, stood up and picked up his folding

camp shovel. "Let's see what we can find." They headed to the grave site, and Buck and Detective Apodaca started digging.

Sheriff Buckman directed the deputy pulling the mobile crime scene trailer on where to park, and he helped him set up the trailer and the generator and then haul out several portable work lights. The sun was setting, and it wouldn't be long before they needed the lights.

The sheriff stepped away for a minute, called his wife and told her they were going to be in for a long night. He also asked her to run by one of the fast-food restaurants in Delta and bring up enough food and drinks for a dozen people. She told him she would pick up a case of Coke for Buck, and he laughed.

Chapter Ten

Bax found a seat in the last row of the courtroom, stepping past three other people to get to it. She planned to head to Grand Mesa right after she finished testifying but had decided to listen to the closing arguments. She knew the case against Custer County Commissioner James Warton was cut-and-dried, but she was curious how his attorney was going to try to explain away the charges against him.

Bax had spent several weeks investigating the corruption charges against James Warton. Warton had been a county commissioner for almost thirty years, and everyone who knew him thought he was a great guy. His troubles began when his wife, Donna, developed breast cancer several years back and passed away just over a year ago.

Money had always been tight for the Warton family, and his county salary of $64,000 a year and his medical insurance didn't cover all his wife's bills, so James Warton started looking at other opportunities. There weren't a lot of opportunities in the small county that sat between Pueblo, Colorado, to the east and the Sangre de Cristo mountain range to the west, and James needed to be careful because everyone knew everyone in the small town of Westcliffe, the county seat.

The opportunity presented itself when an out-of-state developer wanted to build a collection of expensive town houses on the way to the Crestone Needle, a 14,000-foot peak a few miles out of town. The development would require water rights, but the developer also had plans to expand and refurbish the Silver West Airport, south of Westcliffe. It would have been a boon for the small county of 4,700 people.

James Warton worked a deal with the developer, and in exchange for his help getting county approval for the project and helping to secure the water rights, he received a nice payday. That was until things went bad, and due to pressure from the citizens, the deal fell apart, and a pissed-off developer brought James Warton's involvement to the attention of the sheriff.

Sheriff Albert Mitchell had known James Warton for his entire life, and he didn't feel comfortable investigating the crimes against him, so he called the director of the Colorado Bureau of Investigation for help. Bax was assigned to the case, and she dove into James Warton's life. When her investigation was finished, she brought the evidence to the sheriff and the district attorney of the 11th Judicial District, which covered Custer, Chaffee, Fremont and Park counties. What she found stunned the locals who knew James Warton, and he was arrested and charged with corruption, bribery, malfeasance and a host of other lesser charges. It seemed that James Warton had not just started taking bribes due to his wife's medical problems; he had been at it a long time.

Bax uncovered two out-of-state bank accounts and a condo in Cabo San Lucas that Warton had paid cash for. She got testimony from several local businesses that had been too ashamed to say anything until Bax approached them. Each local business was providing James Warton with kickbacks for services he provided to the county, and it had been going on for years. James Warton had set himself up for a nice life after he retired. Now he would never get the chance.

Bax had testified for two days and felt good when she was finished. The defense counsel had attacked her investigation, but she had learned from the best. In all his years in law enforcement, Buck Taylor had never lost a case in court because of something missing or incorrect in his files. He was a stickler for details, and his files were always perfect. He had instilled that same ethos in Bax when she came to work for CBI, and it had paid off. In the eleven years Bax had worked with Buck, she'd never lost a case because of her investigation files, and this case was no different.

Sheriff Albert Mitchell slid onto the bench next

to Bax and removed his hat. Sheriff Mitchell had been sheriff of Custer County longer than anyone could remember. He was a stocky man with broad shoulders and a tough demeanor. His handlebar mustache and gray Stetson made him look like an Old West sheriff. Today, he wore jeans, western boots, and a snap-front shirt, his badge clipped just above the pocket and his black Glock 41 pistol riding high on his hip in a worn brown leather holster.

They listened to the short closing arguments as each lawyer tried to make their final points to the jury of eight, consisting of five women and three men. Judge Tommy Ray Tillis had given each lawyer twenty minutes for closing arguments, and he was a stickler for time. He had stated at the start of the trial that he would adhere to a strict timeline and each side had better be ready.

Judge Tillis was a frail-looking older man with short gray hair, but he roared like a tiger when someone stepped out of line in his courtroom. He had been the county judge for twenty-five years and had been reelected every four years since he always ran unopposed. He was considered to be a fair judge, but he would also take anyone in his court to task if they crossed a specific line. No one knew where that line was, so everyone behaved themselves.

The defense attorney finished his oration and sat

next to his client. The judge spent the next fifteen minutes giving the jury their final instructions, and then he adjourned the case and sent the jury off to deliberate.

Bax and the sheriff, along with the rest of the courtroom, rose as the judge left the bench, and she asked the sheriff if he had time for lunch. He nodded, and they left the courthouse, walked up Sixth Street to Main Street and grabbed a table in the Crestone Café. The waitress dropped off a couple of menus, took their drink order and promised to be right back.

"Pretty much a slam dunk," said the sheriff. The waitress set two coffee cups on the table and filled them. She left the pot and smiled at the sheriff. They each ordered the cheeseburger platter with steak fries, and the waitress walked away.

Bax smiled. "Seemed that way to me," she said. "It must be hard watching someone you grew up with going through this."

The sheriff sipped his coffee. "Jimmy and I grew up next door to each other and were friends since we could walk. It's a shame what happened to him." He took another sip.

"Until you uncovered all those other issues," said the sheriff, "everyone respected the man. It was hard to sit through your evidence presentation and not feel betrayed. He let a lot of people down and I'm glad Donna isn't around to see his downfall."

The food arrived, and they made small talk while they ate. The waitress was taking the plates away when the sheriff's cell phone dinged with an incoming text. He pulled his phone from his pocket and read the text.

"Jury's back," he said. "Less than an hour. Must be some kind of record. The judge wants everyone back in twenty minutes. We'd better get going."

Bax was surprised at how fast the jury had reached a verdict, but after the time she'd spent being cross-examined, she knew the case was solid. They left money on the table and walked back to the courthouse. The courtroom was crowded—word had gotten out about the quickness of the verdict—and Bax and the sheriff stood along the back wall next to the double door. Bax looked at James Warton and his lawyer and they both looked dejected. They knew what was coming. The question remaining was how hard the judge would come down on Warton.

"All rise," said the bailiff over the noise in the courtroom, and everyone fell silent. Judge Tillis, in his long black robe, stepped up onto the bench and asked the bailiff to bring in the jury. Once the jury was seated, the rest of the room took their seats and silence filled the space.

"Madam Foreperson, has the jury reached a verdict?" asked Judge Tillis.

"We have, Your Honor," said the foreperson.

The jury foreperson handed a piece of paper to the bailiff, who handed it to the judge and then stood by. The judge took a few seconds to read the verdict and handed it back to the bailiff, who returned it to the foreperson.

"Will the defendant please rise," said the judge, and James Warton and his attorney, a short bald-headed man in a rumpled suit, rose and faced the judge. The prosecutor, a stern-looking woman with her dark hair pulled back in a tight bun, stood and smoothed out her skirt. She placed her hands at the front of her skirt, crossed them and stood looking at the jury.

"Madam Foreperson, in the case of Custer County versus James Warton, how do you find?"

"We find the defendant guilty on all charges."

A slight murmur rose from the gallery, and the judge smacked his gavel on the bench. Silence took over the room without the judge needing to say anything. The judge looked at James Warton, who was using one arm to support himself against the defense table. The judge thanked the jury for their service and asked them to wait a minute while he passed the sentence they had recommended.

"James Warton, having been found guilty by a jury of your peers . . ." The judge stopped and took off his glasses. "Jimmy, I can't for the life of me understand what you thought you were doing. We have been friends longer than I can remember, and I still find it hard to believe that you could do this to the people I always thought you cared about."

James Warton had tears in his eyes, and he lowered his head and looked at the table. The judge put his glasses back on and picked up the paper.

"Having been found guilty by a jury of your peers, I sentence you to twelve years in the state prison. You will not be eligible for parole until you have served at least eight years. You will remain in the sheriff's custody until such time as you are handed over to representatives of the state prison system and transported to Cañon City. This case is adjourned. Bailiff, please take the defendant back to the holding cell until the sheriff can take him back to the jail."

Bax and the sheriff looked at each other. The judge had given James Warton the maximum sentence, and they both believed that he would have given him a lot more if he could have. Just then, the conversation in the courtroom was stopped by screaming coming from multiple directions, and Bax and the sheriff turned to look at the front of the courtroom, both placing their hands on their pistols.

The bailiff, Ralph Groves, had approached James Warton and asked him to place his hands behind his back. Ralph Groves had been a Custer County deputy sheriff for thirty years before retiring due to two bad knees. Judge Tillis hired him to be the court bailiff since it was easy work, and Groves hadn't seemed ready to retire when he was all but forced to.

Groves had gotten one side of his cuffs hooked around James Warton's wrist when Warton spun around, stepped behind Groves and pulled out the bailiff's pistol. He shoved Groves, causing him to stumble over the chairs at the defense table, and shoved his lawyer out of the way. The lawyer fell over the short wall separating the gallery from the defense table. James Warton raised the pistol and pivoted to face the judge. He held the pistol in both hands and aimed towards the bench as the people in the gallery dove out of the way.

The explosion echoed off the old cinder block walls, and James Warton flew backwards and slammed into the low wall, flipping over it into the first row of seats. A bright crimson spot blossomed across his white shirt.

Bax and Sheriff Mitchell managed to push

through the crowd of stunned onlookers and reached the body with their pistols drawn. Bax kneeled and checked his pulse. She looked up at the sheriff, who nodded. James Warton was dead. They looked towards the bench as Judge Tillis placed the single-action .357 Magnum Colt revolver back in the shoulder holster he wore under his robe, a wisp of smoke swirling above the desk.

Bax pulled a pair of nitrile gloves from her back pocket and picked up the pistol. She looked at it and then held it so the sheriff could see what she was looking at. The judge walked over, and she held it up for him. The safety was still on. The judge shook his head and walked towards the door leading to his chambers.

"Suicide by cop," said the sheriff. Bax nodded.

The sheriff cleared the courtroom, and Bax called Director Jackson to request a forensic team from the State Crime Lab in Pueblo. She found her backpack where she had dropped it at the back of the courtroom, pulled out an evidence bag and placed the pistol in it. She handed it to the sheriff and then pulled out her phone and took pictures of the body. She opened her laptop, opened a new investigation file and typed out her statement and that of the sheriff and the bailiff. She was interviewing the judge when the forensic team arrived, and she turned the crime scene over to them and the county coroner, who had just arrived after closing up the convenience store he ran.

Bax sat in the jury box and downloaded the pictures into the investigation file. She sent a copy of the file to the sheriff and a copy to the district attorney. She closed her file and looked at the mess in front of her. She shook her head, loaded her laptop into her backpack, thanked the sheriff for his hospitality and offered her condolences. She walked out of the courthouse and headed across the street to the sheriff's office, where her Jeep was parked. She slid into the seat, started the engine and pulled out of the lot. She wondered what would be waiting for her as she headed towards Grand Mesa.

Chapter Eleven

Paul Webber parked his gray Jeep Grand Cherokee next to the mobile command center, which had arrived moments before. He turned off the engine, opened the door and slid out. He pulled his backpack from the passenger seat and walked towards Buck's Jeep.

Paul Webber was over six foot four with a muscular physique. He had joined CBI seven years earlier after spending ten years with the Dallas, Texas, police department. His last post had been as a homicide detective. Paul may have seemed like a giant, but those who knew him knew he was a pussycat. He was one of the most soft-spoken men Buck had ever met.

He paused momentarily to watch a deputy and one of the county's maintenance men disconnect the mobile command center from the hitch on the back of the county public works truck and fire up the generator. The lights inside the command center flickered and then stayed on.

Paul walked up to Buck and Sheriff Buckman. They shook hands all around, and Paul walked over to the small hole that Buck had dug. He stood behind the yellow crime scene tape and leaned over it enough to see the slit in the black plastic and the red nail polish on the victim's hand. He looked up as Buck walked up.

"Forensics is on the way," said Buck. "Should be here any minute. Did you hear about what happened in Custer County?"

"No," said Paul. "Bax had that case buttoned up tight. Was there an issue?"

"You could say that," said Buck. "The defendant, James Warton, grabbed the bailiff's gun after sentencing. The judge shot him. According to Bax, the safety was still on when Warton pointed the gun at the judge."

"Fuck," said Paul. "Suicide by cop? Anyone else hurt?"

"More like suicide by judge. The bailiff has a knot on his head from where he got pushed and hit his head on the table, and the defendant's lawyer broke his wrist falling over the gallery wall. The defendant was killed."

"Judge didn't mess around, huh?" said Paul.

"Everyone in the county knew the judge carried a revolver. I guess Warton didn't want to spend time in prison. Such a waste."

"So, what do we think about this?" asked Paul, jutting his chin towards the hole in the ground.

"This is just the beginning," said Buck. "Vicky Talmadge is a friend of Bax's. Her dog, Jasper, is a cadaver dog, and this morning, they were on a walk when the dog alerted next to that cross. Vicky was concerned, so she called Bax to figure out what to do. The dog had alerted next to several other crosses along the road. When I got here, we took the same walk. I skipped the crosses after the fifth one and drove to the end of the road to the last cross. The dog alerted again. There are eleven crosses along this road."

Paul looked at Buck. "Fuck, Buck. You think this is a dumping ground for a serial killer?"

Buck nodded. "We'll know more once we can open the hole, but yeah, I think we are dealing with a serial killer, and this body"—Buck pointed at the hole—"hasn't been here long."

"Hell of a way to wrap up your vacation," said Paul. "What do you want me to do?"

"Work with George and Mel and put together a list of missing persons. Start with women and go back four months. Let's keep it local for now until we know more. Delta County and the surrounding counties."

Buck, Paul and the sheriff stepped aside as the

county maintenance man set up four work lights around the hole and fired them up. The light lit up the whole area. Paul nodded to Buck and headed for the command center.

The sheriff looked down the road as two black SUVs and a white Ford Transit van pulled to a stop next to the command center. Buck turned and looked at the first SUV. The door opened, and Franklin Williams slid out of the driver's seat and walked towards Buck and the sheriff.

Franklin Williams was the lead forensic tech based out of the CBI office in Grand Junction. He was a distinguished-looking black man who stood about four inches taller than Buck but weighed about the same. He had short gray hair and a gray goatee. He had been with CBI for more than thirty years. He shook hands with Buck and the sheriff.

"Aren't you supposed to be on vacation?" asked Franklin.

"Yeah," said Buck. "That's the last time I take a vacation."

Franklin laughed as six forensic techs gathered at the back of the van and started gearing up.

"So, we think there could be as many as eleven bodies along this road?" asked Franklin.

Buck repeated the same story he'd told Paul, and

Franklin pulled a small flashlight from his belt and focused it on the hole.

"You dug the hole?" he asked.

"Yeah, I needed to be sure what we had before I put out the call," said Buck. "I put the dirt next to the hole and slit the plastic to make sure we had a human body and not someone's pet or trash. I stopped as soon as I saw the hand. The crosses are spaced about every two hundred feet and start a couple hundred yards from the visitor center. I think this might be the most recent victim. How do you want to handle this?"

Franklin stood still for a few minutes and looked at the scene. "I called in some favors and have three more teams coming from Grand Junction and the surrounding counties. I think we work them in order so we don't cause any confusion. We'll start with this hole and the first five crosses from here. As each team finishes, we'll hopscotch to the next cross and start again. We'll handle the digging. We are going to have enough people in this area, and I don't want to bring in any outsiders. Have you called Sima?"

"Yeah," said Buck. "She'll be here by the time we expose the first body. What else do you need?"

"We've got more work lights, so I think we are good for now. Gonna be a long couple of days."

Franklin laughed. "You sure do keep things interesting, Buck."

He nodded to the sheriff, walked back to the van, gathered his team around and explained the plan. The two teams grabbed their gear. Franklin and one team headed back towards Buck, and the other team headed down the road towards the second cross.

During the next three hours, more forensic teams arrived and received their assignments from Franklin. There was little conversation as the teams went to work.

Chapter Twelve

Buck stepped into the command center, grabbed a cold Coke from the small refrigerator in the corner and sat next to Paul, who was tapping away on his laptop. Paul stopped typing and handed Buck a stack of papers.

"So far, twenty-seven missing women, and that's going back two months," said Paul.

Buck leafed through the papers, looking at the face of each woman. There was nothing to indicate any of these women had met with foul play. Some of them could be runaways, some might have escaped an abusive relationship, and some just might have said, "Fuck it," and walked away from whatever they were dealing with. Many of the women in the pile were young, some just in their teens, and a couple were in their fifties and sixties. They had their work cut out for them.

Paul slid his phone closer to Buck. "Guys, Buck just walked in."

"Hey, Buck," said Mel. "Hell of a way to end your vacation."

"Hiya, Buck," said George. "Looks like we're

not going to get much sleep in the next couple of days."

George Peterman and Melanie Hart were the CBI cybersecurity team based out of Grand Junction, Colorado, and they couldn't be more different.

Melanie Hart was about five foot two, with shoulder-length black hair; she wore black jeans and dark gray hoodies and had several piercings. Anyone meeting her for the first time would think she was a high school kid, but she had received her doctorate in computer science from MIT about a dozen years ago. She'd joined CBI right out of college.

George Peterman could have passed for her father. George was about the same height as Buck, a shade under six foot, but where Buck still weighed what he'd weighed when he played football in high school, George had added a few pounds over the years. George had joined CBI after retiring from the navy, where he'd spent his entire career working in cybersecurity. As far as Buck was concerned, George and Melanie were two of the best computer people he knew. Paul Webber was good. Ashley Baxter was better, but these two were world-class.

"Any way we can narrow the search parameters?" asked George. "I can't believe the number of people that are listed as missing persons."

"I wish we could," said Buck. "We might be able to adjust the parameters, but until we open the first body bag, we have no idea if our victims are young, old, blond, brunette, Black, Caucasian, Hispanic, Indigenous, or what. Give us a few hours, and we'll have a better idea."

"No problem," said Mel. "By the way, we've already gotten a call from a Grand Junction detective. She had a flag set up on the missing person files she's been working on, and when we pulled up the info, it triggered a text alert. She'd like you to call her once you have more to go on and see if one of them might be hers. I just texted you her name and number."

Buck picked up the pile. "Which MP is hers?"

Buck heard Mel clicking keys in the background. "Angie Wilde," said Mel. "She was a student at Colorado Mesa. Disappeared the weekend before school started."

Buck flipped through the papers until he found the one for Angie Wilde. He sat back and read the details. She was reported missing on Saturday morning after not returning to her rental home from a night out at Tiny's Bar and Grill. Buck looked at the picture, and something caught his attention. He leaned into Paul.

"Can you enlarge this photo?" Buck pointed to a picture of Angie Wilde standing with three young women outside a house. Paul pulled up the MP flyer on his laptop and enlarged the picture.

"What are you looking for?" he asked.

Buck pointed to the young woman second from the right, noted as Angie Wilde. "Zoom in on her hand."

Paul clicked his mouse and zoomed in on Angie Wilde's hand, and a cold chill ran up Buck's spine. When Buck was younger, his mother had always said that spine-tingling feeling happened when someone walked on someone's grave. She may have been right.

Buck sat back in the chair and Paul looked at him.

"What?" asked Paul.

"The hand I exposed had four red nails and one black one. Look at the picture."

"Fuck," said Paul.

"Shit," said George. "We'll start a deeper discreet background check on her and see what other details we can add. You'd better call the Grand Junction detective and give her a heads-up before she gets a bunch of text notifications."

"Okay," said Buck. "Let me know what you find."

He slid the chair away from Paul just as Sheriff Buckman stepped into the trailer. He looked at Buck and then at Paul.

"What have you got, Buck?" he asked.

Buck handed him the MP flyer on Angie Wilde. "Could be our first victim. Same nail polish in the picture as the victim I uncovered."

Sheriff Buckman took off his Stetson and ran his hand through his hair. "What are the odds of two women having the same nail colors on the same fingers?"

Detective Apodaca stepped into the trailer and looked at the flyer over the sheriff's shoulder.

"Could be pretty good if it is some kind of school thing, but even so, how many missing women would have that same setup?" said the detective.

Buck pulled out his phone, found Mel's text and dialed the number for Detective Jennifer Blackthorn, who answered on the second ring.

"Missing persons, Detective Blackthorn, how may I help you?"

"Hi, Detective, Buck Taylor, CBI. Do you have a few minutes to chat?"

"Is it Angie?" asked Detective Blackthorn. "I got a text that you guys were looking at her file."

"Right now, we're not sure," said Buck. He told her about how they'd discovered the grave, and about Buck exposing a hand and that the nails were painted the same as in her MP flyer.

"Detective, is the four red and one black nail some kind of school thing, a club or a sports thing?"

"No," said Detective Blackthorn. "According to her best friend, Gabby Cruz, who reported her missing, it was something she did all the time. For whatever reason, she never painted all her nails the same color. Maybe some kind of rebellion thing. Gabby told me she had been doing it since grade school. Do you think it's her?"

"I don't want to get your hopes up, Detective. We're a long way from exposing the body."

"Would you mind if I came up there? I promise not to get in the way."

"That's fine, Detective. Hopefully, we will have

her out of the ground by the time you get here. We'll talk more when you arrive."

Buck disconnected the call and looked at the dour expressions on the faces of everyone in the command center. Detective Apodaca broke the mood.

"I came in to tell you that the pathologist is here. I showed her the first hole, and she and her team were gearing up."

Buck clipped his phone to his belt and stepped out of the command center. It looked like they may have gotten their first break.

Chapter Thirteen

Joker was troubled. He didn't like what he had heard today but wasn't sure what to do about it. He didn't have the best record, and most people tuned him out when they found out that he had spent time in a military prison for assaulting an officer. It also hurt that he'd received a dishonorable discharge when he was paroled from Leavenworth. Did you ever try to get a job with those things hanging over your head?

He finished his glass of beer and signaled Mitch, the bartender, to bring him another. Alcohol was his way of coping with the day-to-day shit he had to deal with, but this was different, and he was thinking that he should be drinking something harder than beer, but his pockets were almost empty.

How could they do that to his best friend? Mike Kirby was a good cellmate, and they had been tight since they got out of prison. He was envious that Mike, who was also dishonorably discharged, had been able to get a decent job that came with a decent place to stay, but they were friends, and he was happy for his friend. Besides, picking fruit and loading trucks wasn't a bad gig, but the growing season was drawing to a close, and then he would need to look for work again.

Maybe he should forget what he'd found out earlier today. He figured it was going to bring him nothing but trouble, but he felt it was his duty to tell someone. His source had told him that the CIA had closed down the MK-Ultra project years ago, but what if they hadn't? His buddy had never lied to him before; why would he do it now?

Joker was confused and drank half his glass of beer in one gulp. The CIA was supposed to have stopped the program in 1973, after twenty years of using various drugs to manipulate people to talk while under interrogation. Once the public became aware of the project, the outrage was massive. The idea that the U.S. government was using illegal drugs on unsuspecting citizens was appalling, and Congress put an end to the program. During the program, many drugs, including LSD, were tested on various subjects, most times without their knowledge, to see if they could achieve different results. Now he found out through his source that someone he trusted was using the same experiments on his best friend and had been doing it for years. His source didn't know if the doctor was working with the CIA or if this was some rogue operation, but Joker felt he couldn't let it go. The question, of course, was: Was it true? He had heard a lot of things while in the army that made him shake his head, but what if the CIA hadn't stopped the program? What if they had taken it underground?

Joker had called Mike Kirby earlier, when he first found out the information, and left him a voice mail to call as soon as possible. He wanted to let Mike know what he'd learned before meeting for their weekly group session. He was worried that if he brought it up during the session, things would get confrontational, leading to ugly. He also wanted to tell someone else who might be able to stop it. He knew that part would be hard. He could call Army CID and let them know, but he never had a good experience dealing with those folks. He could call the local cops, but they would look at him like some conspiracy nut, as would the FBI. He didn't know what to do.

If the doctor was doing this to Mike Kirby, then it had been going on for more than twenty years, even before Mike was locked up for killing those five Afghan women. Now, thinking about it, he wondered if Mike had committed those murders or if he had been manipulated into thinking he had. He pulled out his phone and checked his messages. Nothing from Mike. Frustrated, he put his phone away, finished the beer and signaled for another.

The more he drank, the more paranoid he got, and he wondered if he had been given this information to help his friend, or if someone was after him. He looked around the bar. Most of these people he had seen in the bar before, so he wasn't worried about them, but maybe he should be. After all, he didn't know most of them other than to say hello. He lowered his head closer to the bar top and, resting his head on his arms, perused the bar, looking at the faces. He spotted several people who could be agency spies. His paranoia had drifted into the crazy range, and he was starting to freak himself out.

Joker reached for his beer, fumbled it and tipped over the glass, spilling what was left in it all over the bar. He laughed, and everyone in the bar stopped what they were doing and looked at him, even though it wasn't unusual. Joker did something stupid every time he drank, and that was most nights.

The bartender walked over, put the empty glass into the plastic tub under the bar top and wiped the top with a bar rag.

"Time to leave, Joker."

Joker looked at the bartender through bloodshot eyes. "You cuttin' me off, Mitch?"

"Yeah. Happy to get you a coffee or call you a cab, but you're done drinking here tonight."

Joker pushed back the barstool, and it fell and crashed to the ground. He stepped back, kicked the chair out of the way, missed and fell against the bar. He staggered to his feet.

"Fuck you, Mitch."

Mitch didn't say a word as Joker staggered towards the door, bumping into tables and spilling drinks as he went. He turned at the door, gave Mitch the middle finger and pushed out into the night. The cool night air hit him in the face, and he took a deep breath. Reaching into his pocket for his keys, he pulled them out and dropped them in the shrubs next to the door. He looked bewildered and reached around, trying to find them. Having no luck, he stood and kicked at the shrub. "What stupid fuck puts bushes next to the door to a bar? Fuck it. I'll walk home."

He kicked the shrub again, shook his head and walked around the parked cars, staggering as he went, and headed across the parking lot towards the street. He didn't need his car, anyway, since he lived a mile and a half from the bar. He'd done it before, and he would do it again. He'd find his keys tomorrow when his head was clear.

Joker headed up the street towards home, and as he passed a small mom-and-pop Mexican grocery store, he felt the urge to pee. He walked behind the building and was peeing against the brick wall when he felt a presence behind him. His body shook, and the urine ran down his leg. He was afraid.

"You should be more careful, Joker. Look what you did to your pants," said the voice behind him.

He knew who it was without turning around, and his knees grew weak as he zipped up his pants and reached out for the wall.

"You've been a bad boy, Joker. The information your friend gave you was confidential, and he had no right to share it with you or anyone else. I'm afraid he won't be sharing it with anyone else again. He left me no choice. I don't understand why you had to get involved. You knew that nothing good was going to come of it."

He grabbed Joker by the shoulder, swung him around and slammed him into the brick wall. Joker's head hit the wall with a thud, and he closed his eyes.

"I didn't tell anyone," he said, slurring the words. "I promise I won't say anything to anyone. I swear."

"Well, that's a problem, Joker. Because I know you left Mike Kirby a message to call you and that you wanted to tell him something important. We can't have you passing along unfounded information, can we? So, I need to know who else you told."

Joker started to cry. "No one. I swear to god, I didn't tell anyone."

He smiled at Joker. "You see, Joker. That's a problem, because I can't trust an ex-con like you. So, the question now is, what do I do with you?"

Joker's eyes grew wide with fear as the man's face moved closer to his. "We have a problem, Joker, and we have to make it right."

Joker felt the needle enter his arm just below the sleeve of his dirty T-shirt. He tried to pull away, but he was pinned to the wall. He felt the liquid flow into his arm. It was warm, and he felt sort of at peace until a screaming pain arose from his chest, and with his free arm he grabbed his shirt and pushed against the pain. He had never felt something so terrible in his life, and he wondered if this was what a heart attack felt like. He tried to scream, but no words came out, and he felt himself sliding down the wall, landing in the puddle of urine. His eyes fluttered as his brain tried to make sense of what he was feeling, and then the lights went out.

The man removed a junkie's kit from his back pocket and placed it on the ground next to the body. He placed the rubber band around Joker's lower arm and tied it tight, then he took the syringe, wiped it clean, rolled it in Joker's lifeless hand and inserted it into his vein through the same hole as the first injection. He stepped back and admired his handiwork.

He hated killing people in such an impersonal manner. He liked the feeling of his victims dying as he choked the life out of them, but sometimes, he had to use another method to protect himself. He stood and looked at what used to be Joker—just another junkie, dead in an alley. The drug problem in America took such a toll. He turned and walked away.

Chapter Fourteen

Dr. Sima Kalishe, dressed from head to toe in white Tyvek, was putting on her N95 mask when Buck walked up; she turned and shook his hand. Dr. Kalishe stood about five foot two. She had medium-dark skin and jet-black hair tied up in a bun, but her most striking feature was her incredible blue eyes.

"Is this how you spend your vacations?" she asked with a smile.

Buck laughed. "I just can't seem to escape dead bodies." He looked into the hole. "We may have an identity on this one. Young student from Colorado Mesa. There's a Grand Junction detective on the way up."

While Buck and Sima spoke, one of her assistants took pictures of the black plastic body bag from every direction, moving the work lights as he needed to get the clearest pictures.

"Okay," said Dr. Kalishe. "Let's see what we have."

She put on her mask and kneeled beside the hole and the exposed black plastic body bag. Using a powerful flashlight, she checked every inch of the exposed black bag and then switched to a black light. Seeing nothing worth noting on the bag, she had her two assistants reach into the hole and lift out the bag, which she placed on top of an open body bag. She had her assistants roll the old body bag from side to side while she checked the rest of the bag. Satisfied that she hadn't missed anything on the bag, she took a small pair of scissors from the black medical bag sitting on the ground next to her and cut the bag, following Buck's cut from each direction. The smell coming from the bag was horrendous. Sima looked at Buck.

"She stewed in her own juices, but I can tell you she hasn't been in the ground long—a couple of weeks, maybe, but no more than two or three months."

Buck noticed a presence standing next to him, and he looked over to see a medium-height middle-aged woman. She had grayish-blond hair tied back in a French braid and wore a dark gray business suit with a white shirt. A Grand Junction detective shield hung from a silver chain around her neck. She reached out her hand.

"Agent Taylor, Jenny Blackthorn. I appreciate you letting me watch."

"Detective," said Buck. He turned his attention

back to the body. "Sima, let's see what she looks like."

Dr. Kalishe and her assistant pulled open the original black body bag while her other assistant recorded the proceedings. She stepped aside, and there was an audible gasp from Detective Blackthorn. The body was in the early stages of decomposition. The skin was translucent. Lucky for everyone, the critters and insects hadn't been able to get at the body, so everything was still intact, just bloated. Dr. Kalishe took out her flashlight and worked her way down the body from top to bottom. She turned to Buck.

"Early guess would be manual strangulation." She pointed to two clear imprints on the front of the neck. "We'll know more once I get her on the table. Also looks like a small pinprick on her right shoulder. Small spot of red on her T-shirt. We'll test it to see if it's blood. Otherwise, I don't see any other obvious external injuries."

She moved down the side of the body and held up the translucent hand so Buck and Detective Blackthorn could see the fingernails. Her assistant took several pictures. She asked Detective Blackthorn to step across the crime scene tape and take a closer look at the young woman in the black bag.

Detective Blackthorn steeled herself and stepped

under the yellow tape. Buck handed her a small tube of Vaseline. She put a small dab under her nostrils to cut some of the smell and kneeled next to the body. She pulled a flashlight from her jacket pocket and shined it on the face. To be sure, she pulled out her phone and opened a file containing the driver's license picture of Angie Wilde. She wiped a tear from her cheek with the back of her hand, stood and walked back to Buck.

"It's her," she said. "It's Angie Wilde."

She stepped away from Buck as Sheriff Buckman walked up. "Is it her?"

"Looks like it," said Buck. "Detective Blackthorn identified her from her driver's license picture. We'll still need Sima to confirm the identity, but right now, it gives us a place to start."

The sheriff looked at his watch. "I'm heading home to see if I can grab a few hours of sleep. Sack out in the command center if you need to. Vince will keep an eye on things until I get back in a few hours. I'll send up some breakfast."

Buck nodded and spotted Franklin walking down the shoulder. He stepped up next to Buck. At some point he had walked off to check on the other teams. He looked as tired as everyone else.

"We've uncovered three of the bodies so Sima can keep moving. I've got ambulances coming up from Delta to take the bodies to Grand Junction as we get them ready to move. I told my guys to grab some shut-eye for a couple of hours. We'll begin again at first light. The team working on body number five were the last to arrive, and they said they'd keep going and then move on to the next grave. I'll give them some downtime when the other teams are ready to go back to work."

Buck looked over and saw Franklin's team setting up a couple of dome tents next to the command center. He thought about sleep, but he still had a lot to do. A Delta County ambulance pulled to a stop next to the first body. Sima signed the release and turned the body over to the ambulance crew, who zipped up the new body bag, loaded it on the gurney and placed it in the ambulance. They headed out the opposite way they had come, and Buck looked at Sima.

"Franklin has the next two bodies ready for you."

"No problem, Buck. Let's go see what we have."

They headed down the road to the next grave site, and Buck stopped for a minute to talk to Detective Blackthorn.

"I just put in a call to homicide," she said. "Jessie Maldonado and Mark Ridgeway will meet the body at the morgue. I'm going to head back to Grand Junction."

"We're about to expose the next body. Why don't you stick around a while longer and see if you can help us ID another victim," said Buck.

She nodded and walked with Buck to the next site. Sima and her team were going through the same process as they had with the first body. The smell was noticeable but not as bad as at the first body. Sima nodded to her assistants, and they lifted the black plastic bag out of the hole and placed it on top of a new body bag. She cut open the old bag and did her cursory examination, then called over Buck and Detective Blackthorn.

The second body was in a much more severe state of decomposition, but a lot of the skin was still in place. Detective Blackthorn leaned closer and looked at the sagging face. She looked along the body and then stepped back to Buck and Sima.

"I think this might be Susan Raynes. Hair color, tattoos and build look right. She disappeared at the end of the last semester of the school year. She was last seen drinking heavily at the end-of-year bonfire. Her roommates didn't report her missing until three days later. They thought she might have either hooked up with someone or left the school and headed home. They called us when her family called them to see if they had seen her."

Buck called Paul and asked him to see if they had an MP flyer on Susan Raynes, and a few minutes later, Buck's phone chimed with an incoming message. He pulled up her driver's license picture and held it next to the body. Sima nodded. "Looks like it might be her. We'll confirm her identity and let you know," she said.

The second ambulance arrived, and Sima watched the EMTs move the body into the ambulance and pull away from the site. The procession moved to the third site, and Sima and her team followed the same procedure. The third body was in much worse condition. The plastic bag had ripped in several places, and water and insects had gotten to the body. They were able to get the old bag out of the hole and onto the new body bag without causing too much more damage to either the body or the black bag. Most of the flesh had decomposed, and Sima estimated that the body had been in the ground for at least a year. Using scissors, she cut open the old black bag and stood back in surprise. The body, what was left of it, was male. There were remnants of a beard on what remained of the face. Sima waved over Buck and Detective Apodaca.

"Shit," said Buck as he glanced at Detective Apodaca. "This changes everything."

"Damn, you've had Paul looking at missing

women," said Apodaca. "This is going to expand our search exponentially. We have to start over."

Buck nodded. "Yeah," he said, pulling his phone from his belt. He dialed Paul.

Chapter Fifteen

"Something's going on at the lake."

"What's going on at the lake, Mike?" asked Dr. Brian Davidson.

Former army sergeant Michael Kirby was troubled when he walked into the VA Health Center in Grand Junction. He hadn't been sleeping well since the last visit from the alien, and as he drove down the dirt road leading from his cabin, he'd noticed several cop cars and what seemed like a lot of activity farther up the road. He had slowed down and was going to ask the deputy standing in front of the yellow crime scene tape what was happening, but he grew fearful. The deputy waved him on and told him to keep moving. He turned onto the highway and headed towards Grand Junction.

Mike had been attending this weekly group session at the health center for the past ten years. It was one of the conditions of his parole, and he made sure he was on time every week, even if it meant leaving his cabin before dawn to make the hour-long drive to the center. He had no desire to go back to Leavenworth, and he was proud of the fact that even during the winter and all the snow that fell on the mesa, he had not missed one session.

This morning, he had been one of seven men and two women in the session, and for an hour, they talked about how they were coping with civilian life and not being incarcerated. Today, he was quiet. Two things were bothering him. One was that Joker wasn't in the session. He had first met Joker at the Leavenworth military prison when they shared a cell. Joker had been incarcerated for hitting an officer. He and Joker got along well and were paroled a few weeks apart. Joker had told him that he came from a place called Grand Junction in Colorado, and over the years, he described how beautiful the area was, with lots of forests, lakes and rivers. It was the kind of place where a man could settle down and find his emotional and spiritual center. The kind of place where a man could get away from his past.

Mike Kirby didn't have any family—well, that wasn't entirely true, since he had an alcoholic father, who was the reason he'd joined the army, or was forced to join the army. After he had fought back one night when his father came home drunk and decided to beat him up again, Mike had been arrested for stabbing the old drunk. Everyone knew it was self-defense, but they also knew that Mike's father had become a pitiful human being, and people felt sorry for him. Mike was given a choice by the judge: army or jail. Mike chose the army and flourished, finishing Green Beret training at the top of his class.

Through two tours in Afghanistan, Mike Kirby excelled and was an exemplary soldier. That all changed when he was reassigned to a new unit, part of a PSYOP program the CIA was running with the help of a group of special forces soldiers and some local insurgents.

Mike and the other soldiers in the unit were there as protection for the psychiatrist and his team as they engaged in various forms of psychological warfare. The torture of the high-ranking Taliban leaders that they captured was enough to make anyone squeamish, but he felt they were on the right side of history. Until that night, so long ago.

He led a small group to a village about four klicks from their base. Intel had told them that a local village leader was hiding weapons for the Taliban. That night, his team snuck into the village, raided the man's house and captured him and his three teenage daughters. The things the PSYOP team did to those young girls while their father watched in horror drove the old man crazy. By the time they were done, the three girls were dead and mutilated, and the father was lying dead in a corner. He never admitted to the crimes he was accused of.

A week later, the Taliban attacked the small base in retaliation for the deaths. The base was overrun, and everyone would have been lost had it not been for the quick reaction force that got to the base in time to save Mike and several others. Mike sustained several injuries and a bullet grazed his temple. He was found unconscious amidst a pile of Taliban bodies.

Mike recovered from his wounds, but when he woke up in the hospital a couple of weeks later, something was different. He had this feeling of rage that he couldn't seem to control, and he took out that rage on several of the female nurses. After three months, he was released and returned to his unit. He had been doing better and was under the care of the psychiatrist from the PSYOP unit. With the help of some counseling and the medicine the doctor provided, he felt in control again, and he was excited about getting back into the field.

That feeling of euphoria didn't last long. He had been having nightmares that seemed so real that he thought he was losing his mind. That was also the first time the alien had come to visit, something he didn't understand. When he discussed this with the psychiatrist, the doctor adjusted his meds, and for a while all seemed fine. Then, one night, four MPs burst into his barracks and dragged him out of bed. He was charged with the murders of five Afghan women over a period of twelve months and suspected of numerous other murders. His DNA had been found at the scenes of the five murders, and Army CID had been keeping an eye on him. He was convicted and sentenced to ten years in Leavenworth. He could have received more time, but the war was not going well, and the government wanted to avoid the embarrassment, so he was quietly tried and convicted. The psychiatrist requested a transfer to Leavenworth and took over his care until he was released.

Since Mike had no place to go and since Colorado sounded great, he followed his friend Joker to Grand Junction, but he found it hard to live around ordinary people. He found a job at a lodge doing maintenance and settled into an old cabin on the property, but far enough away from people to avoid confrontations. A month after arriving in Grand Junction, he started group therapy and was thrilled to see that his old friend, Dr. Brian Davidson, was working at the VA Health Center and was in charge of his group. That was ten years ago.

"Where's Joker?" asked Mike.

"I don't know," said Dr. Davidson. "I called his cell phone, but it went straight to voice mail. What's going on at the lake?"

Mike looked at him. "Joker told me he would be here, said he had something important to discuss with me."

Dr. Davidson lowered his voice. "Mike, what's going on at the lake? Have you seen the alien again?"

Mike looked at him again. "I hope Joker is okay. He wanted to talk to me about something."

"Mike, focus. What about the lake?"

Mike seemed to snap out of wherever his mind had gone, and he told the doctor what he had seen. "What if I did something wrong, and they are coming to get me?"

"Did you do something wrong, Mike?" asked the doctor.

"I don't think so. I mean, I don't know, but what if I did?"

Dr. Davidson looked at the man who seemed to be unraveling in front of him. He told Mike to follow him to his office and had him take a seat. Unlike the psychiatrist's offices you see on TV, Dr. Davidson's office didn't have a couch. As a matter of fact, it was quite bare. There were no personal items in the office, no pictures or mementos, no framed medical certificates, nothing that would reveal anything about the doctor and his personal life.

The doctor unlocked his side desk drawer and removed a small bottle. He closed the drawer, locked it, walked around the desk and sat next to Mike. He handed him the bottle.

"Mike, I want to adjust your meds. You seem

a little out of sorts today. Take two of these pills after you get off work tonight, and then take one each night after work, but make sure you continue to take the other meds I gave you. We'll talk next week and see if these help, and if they do, I'll give you a prescription for more."

Mike took the bottle and placed it in his pants pocket. He stood and thanked the doctor, and they shook hands. He was still concerned about Joker, but he let that go. He was focused on what he had seen this morning at the lake. He left the VA Health Center, slid into his old beat-up pickup truck and headed back to Grand Mesa. It was time to start work, and he didn't want to be late.

Dr. Davidson watched from his office window as Mike Kirby left the property. He shook his head and frowned. Now *he* wondered what was going on at the lake.

Chapter Sixteen

Bax pulled up to the deputy standing in front of the yellow crime scene tape that blocked off the road from all traffic. The sun was coming over the trees and dawn was still a few minutes away. The deputy was involved in a discussion with a man and woman in a side-by-side ATV. She put her Jeep in park, slid out and approached the deputy.

"Hi, folks, Ashley Baxter, Colorado Bureau of Investigation. Can I be of assistance?"

The deputy nodded. "These folks own the lodge just up the road a piece and would like to speak to Sheriff Buckman. I explained that he was not on the site, and they asked to speak to whoever is in charge," said the deputy.

"May I ask your names, folks?" asked Bax.

The man, wearing a shearling-lined Carhartt vest, jeans and an old battered Stetson, reached out his hand.

"Ray and Nancy Rasmussen," he said. "We own the Island Lake Lodge and Campground and wanted to find out what was going on. Some of our guests spotted all the activity last night and are concerned."

Bax shook their hands and pulled out her phone. She dialed a number and waited.

"Hey, Bax. What's up?" asked Buck with a sleepy voice.

"Hey, Buck. Hope I didn't wake you." She explained the situation and asked if she could bring the Rasmussens to the command center. Buck told her to come on up, and she put her phone back into her pocket. She signed the clipboard the deputy was holding and noted the names of her guests. The deputy unhooked the tape from the small barrier on the side of the road and stepped out of the way to let them pass. Bax pulled through, followed by the ATV.

She spotted the mobile command center up ahead and pulled in behind Buck's Jeep. She spotted the forensic teams and several deputies and troopers standing behind a Ford pickup truck where a middle-aged woman in jeans and a flannel shirt was handing out what looked like breakfast burritos and coffee. Bax waited for the Rasmussens to slide out of the ATV and led them into the trailer. She introduced them to Buck, who stood in front of a covered whiteboard.

"What can I do for you, folks?" asked Buck.

"We own the lodge on the other side of the lake, and some of our guests noted all the police activity, and they are concerned. We were hoping you could tell us something that might help calm their concerns," said Ray Rasmussen.

"Well, Mr. Rasmussen. What I can tell you is that we found human remains along the road and we're working to determine how they got there. As of right now, we don't know if this is foul play, and we don't know how long the remains have been here, so I would let your guests know that at this time, we do not think there is a threat to their safety."

Mrs. Rasmussen had been looking out the window of the trailer while Buck was giving his explanation. She turned and faced Buck.

"Seems like a lot of activity for one set of bones," she said.

Buck smiled. "You're very observant, Mrs. Rasmussen. This would be a lot of activity for one set of remains. I wish I could go into more detail for you, but at this time, we can't comment on the investigation. I promise to keep you updated, and with any luck, we should be out of here in a day or two."

Mrs. Rasmussen looked like she wanted to continue the conversation, but her husband thanked

Buck and Bax and ushered her out the door. Buck watched as they approached Sheriff Buckman, who was sliding out of his SUV. They had an animated conversation, and then the Rasmussens climbed into the ATV and headed back towards the lodge. The sheriff pulled open the door and stepped inside.

"She was not happy with your explanation," said the sheriff. "Nancy can be a little stubborn when she doesn't get her way."

"How long have they owned the lodge?" asked Bax.

The sheriff thought for a moment. "I'd guess they've been here about forty years or so. Started with just a small building, maybe five or six rooms, and expanded to fifty rooms, a dozen cabins, a restaurant, bar, stables and then, five years back, they bought the old campground and added that to the lodge. They turned it into a year-round resort, and they are always busy. Ray was new to the area when they first opened. Came out here after serving in Korea. Nancy's family is from Grand Junction. Regular salt of the earth folks. But Nancy can be a little grating at times."

Buck looked at Bax. "We should go talk to them at the lodge. We'll need a list of employees, and we should interview the staff and anyone who was around, say, four to six weeks ago."

The sheriff laughed. "If Nancy wants to hold a grudge, it may take you a while to get anything from them. Let me send Deputy Sterling with you. She's related to them in some way. She can help smooth things over a bit."

Bax nodded, and the sheriff keyed the mic on his radio and asked Deputy Sterling to swing by the command center. She acknowledged, and he turned to the whiteboard that Paul was uncovering.

"Looks like we have two possible identities already. That's quick."

"Yeah," said Buck. "Having Detective Blackthorn here for a few hours yesterday got us a jump on things. She headed back to Grand Junction earlier this morning, and I figure the homicide team from Grand Junction should show up any minute. We're going to have a lot of fingers in the pie before this is over. We can take the lead on this if you prefer. It's up to you."

"That works for me, Buck. I'd like to have Vince Apodaca work with you guys. It will give him some good experience. Not that I want to see this repeated in my county anytime soon."

They all laughed. "No problem," said Buck.

Deputy Sterling stepped into the trailer. "You wanted to see me, sir?" she asked.

"Yeah, Alisha. I'd like you to head to the lodge with Agent Baxter and help her get what she needs."

Deputy Sterling smiled. "You're worried we might not get what we need from Aunt Nancy, sir. She didn't look happy when they drove past the roadblock."

Sheriff Buckman laughed. "Yeah, something like that."

Bax shook hands with Deputy Sterling, grabbed her backpack from the floor next to the door and they headed for Bax's Jeep.

"So, what's next, Buck?" asked Sheriff Buckman.

Buck ran his hand through his hair. "First thing I'm gonna do is get one of those burritos your wife bought up. They smell awesome. That was nice of her to do that. Then let's huddle up and figure out where we are."

"I'll call Franklin and Sima and ask them to join us," said Paul. He pulled out his phone and dialed as Buck and the sheriff stepped outside into the cool morning air.

"You get any sleep last night?" asked the sheriff.

"Yeah, I was able to grab a few hours on the

floor in the corner. A little stiff this morning. Getting too old to pull these all-nighters anymore."

They laughed as Buck accepted a burrito from Mrs. Buckman and thanked her for bringing the breakfast up, then stopped to chat with one of the forensic techs from the State Crime Lab. Sheriff Buckman poured himself a king-sized coffee from the big urn in the back of his wife's SUV and kissed her on the cheek, and he and Buck headed back to the command center. It was a beautiful fall mountain morning, with just a hint of the upcoming winter in the air and not a cloud in the sky as the sun came over the treetops, but they knew it was going to be another long day.

Chapter Seventeen

Mike Kirby parked his truck in the parking lot and slid out. Today, he was working with Gus Kramer, and they were installing a water line to a new cabin. Mike liked working with Gus. He was older than Mike but strong and could go all day. The thing he liked most was that Gus rarely spoke when they were working. He hoped today wouldn't be any different, because his mind was on what he had seen on the other side of the lake. His mind was also on Joker. It wasn't like Joker to miss a session, and he was worried that something might have happened to him. Mike walked to the edge of the lake and looked across, holding his hand up to shade his eyes from the early morning sun.

"Hey, Mike. You with me?" asked Gus. Mike turned his head and looked at Gus. "You okay, Mike? I've been calling you for like five minutes. What's going on?"

Mike lowered his hand. He seemed confused, but he shook it off. "Sorry, Gus. I didn't hear you."

Gus walked to the edge of the lake. "What do you think is going on over there? Cops have been there all night. A couple of ambulances came by early this morning. I wonder what they found. Did you hear anything last night?"

Mike looked startled and took a step backward. "Wha-what do you mean? I didn't do anything?"

"Wow, Mike. Nobody's accusin' ya. I asked if you heard anything last night after you got off work. Man, you sure are jumpy. You sure you're okay?"

"Sorry, Gus. I haven't been sleepin' so good. Got my nerves all a'jangle. We better get to work. Mr. Rasmussen wants that water line finished today."

They headed towards the maintenance building to grab the supplies they would need for the work ahead and didn't talk much while they loaded up the ATV. They climbed into the ATV and headed for the shell of the new guest cabin. As they drove past the main lodge building, Mike noticed the gray Jeep pulling into the parking lot. He slowed down and watched two women, one dressed as a deputy, slide out of the Jeep and head inside the lodge. He added gas and the ATV jumped forward, dumping a roll of plastic pipe off the back.

"Jesus Christ, Mike. How about you get your head in the game and stop watching the pretty ladies."

Mike stopped the ATV, jumped out, grabbed the

roll of pipe and threw it into the back of the ATV. He climbed into the driver's seat, apologized to Gus and headed up the hill to the building site. He wondered why the cops were at the lodge. He was sure he hadn't done anything wrong, but they must be here for a reason.

The general contractor's crew was already on-site, ready to install the sheathing on the roof trusses and seal the building from the weather. Mike parked the ATV next to the hole that had been dug for the water connection. He and Gus unloaded the ATV, fired up the trenching machine and dug the trench from the valve box to the new cabin. It was hard work, and they focused on getting it done by the end of the day.

* * *

Bax and Deputy Sterling pulled open the wood double door and entered the warm, cozy lobby. The rich, honey-colored logs and the fire in the massive rock fireplace gave the room an orange glow.

"What do you want?"

Nancy Rasmussen stepped through a door behind the front counter and approached Bax.

"Mrs. Rasmussen, I'd like to talk to your employees and see if anyone saw any unusual lights on the other side of the lake over the past couple of months?"

"Your boss was rude to us. Why should I give you the time of day?"

"Aunt Nancy," said Deputy Sterling. "This is an ongoing investigation that has just gotten started. We can't divulge information we don't have, and if you felt Agent Taylor was rude, then I apologize on his behalf. It's important we talk to the staff. Would that be okay?"

"It's okay, Alisha," said a deep voice from behind them. They turned and saw Ray Rasmussen coming through the door. "Talk to whomever you need and tell them I said to please cooperate."

Nancy turned with a huff, stepped back through the door behind the counter and let it slam. Ray smiled a weak smile.

"Don't worry about Nancy. She'll be fine." He paused for a moment. "Most of our employees are seasonal. You might have better luck talking to Mike Kirby."

"And Mike Kirby is?" asked Bax.

"Mike is one of our two maintenance men. He, along with Gus Kramer, keep this place humming. Mike is the only one besides us who lives on the property. He lives in a cabin we own west of the campground. Been living here a long time. You'll find them both up the hill where we're building a couple of new cabins." He stepped behind the counter and put his hand on the doorknob. He turned to face Bax. "Mike's uncomfortable around people. He's had some rough times in his life." He pushed through the door and disappeared.

Bax and Deputy Sterling went back through the main doors and turned towards the sound of hammering. They followed the narrow road past several cabins and a hotel building and spotted several cabins under various stages of construction. After asking several of the workers, they found Mike Kirby and Gus Kramer laying flexible pipe in a deep trench. Mike and Gus stopped what they were doing and watched the two women approach.

"Mike Kirby?" asked Bax.

"Uh oh, Mike. It's the law. Whad'ya do now?" Gus meant it to be funny and slapped Mike on the back, but Mike's reaction indicated he didn't like the questions.

"Didn't do nuthin'," he said, looking harshly at Gus.

"Whoa. Easy, pal, I was kiddin'," said Gus.

Bax and Deputy Sterling stood at the edge of the trench, and they noticed that most of the construction workers had stopped and were watching.

"Mr. Kirby," said Bax softly, hoping to take the

edge off what had happened. "We were hoping you might be able to help us." In a louder voice so all the other workers could hear, she said, "You're not in any trouble. Mr. Rasmussen said you might be able to help us out."

Mike looked at Bax and then at Deputy Sterling. "You're Mr. Rasmussen's niece." He said it more as a statement of fact than a question.

"That's right," said Deputy Sterling. "My uncle told us you've lived here for a long time, and he thought you might be able to answer our questions."

"Questions 'bout what?" he asked. "I didn't do anything wrong."

While Deputy Sterling attempted to coax Mike out of the trench, Gus climbed out and stood next to Bax.

"Mike's a good sort, but he's had some troubles in his life. I don't know all the details, but he told me he was hurt in Afghanistan while he was in the army. I know he takes some pills, but I'm not sure what kind. Be gentle with him. It doesn't take much to get him upset."

Bax nodded, and Gus stepped over to give Mike a hand getting out of the trench.

"Deputy. Why don't you take Mike down by the lake while I talk to Mr. Kramer?" said Bax.

"This about all the activity on the other side of the lake?" asked Gus.

Bax nodded. "You've worked here a long time, Mr. Kramer?"

"It's Gus, and yeah, about thirty years or so."

"Bet you've seen a lot over that time?"

"Sure have," said Gus. "People get into the woods and they lose all inhibition. Could tell you some stories make you blush, but I'm guessin' that's not what you're interested in."

"No, sir. Have you noticed any strange lights or odd things going on on the other side of the lake?"

"Nothing strange. I'm not around here at night. Wife and I live in Delta. That side of the lake is always busy, especially in the summer and fall. Lots of people camp along the road so they don't have to pay Mr. Rasmussen to use the campground. Course, the campground is full all summer, so the boss doesn't care."

"You haven't asked me what's going on over there," said Bax. "Not interested?"

Gus smiled. "Interested? Sure, but if you wanted

to tell me, you would have. Learned a long time ago to stay out of other folks' business."

Bax smiled, shook his hand and thanked him for his time. She turned and walked towards the lake, where Mike Kirby was waving his hands around.

"What's going on?" she asked as she approached, and Mike stepped back.

"Mike is insisting he didn't do anything wrong, and he's getting upset," said Deputy Sterling. "He keeps saying he's not going back, but he won't tell me where. He also told me that things always disappear when the alien comes."

Bax looked at Deputy Sterling. She nodded, but as she stepped up to him, he backed up again. She held up her hands to calm him down and lowered her voice to just above a whisper.

"It's okay, Mike. No one is going to send you back."

He stopped looking around and seemed to focus on her voice, which she kept very low.

"Mike, no one is going to hurt you. We would like to know more about the alien. Can you help us out?"

Mike was focused on her mouth and tilted his head like a puppy listening to its master.

"He don't come around much, every couple months," he said. "Scares me so bad I can't move. He comes at night and leaves little things in my cabin."

"What kinds of things, Mike?"

"Just junk." Mike was shaking, but he kept his eye focused on Bax. "Don't want to talk no more. Got to finish the pipe by the end of the day."

Bax thanked him and told him that he could go back to work, and she watched as he went back to where Gus was standing. Gus patted him on the back, said something to him and led him to the trench; he looked back at Bax and waved.

"How did you do that?" asked Deputy Sterling. "Everything I asked him just got him more and more aggravated."

Bax laughed. "Something Buck taught me a long time ago to de-escalate a situation. When someone is screaming at you or agitated, lower your voice and keep lowering it until they focus on what you are saying. It's some weird twist of human nature that if someone is talking and we can't hear them, we get quieter, so we can. That man is troubled, but I'd like to know more about this alien who comes to visit him."

"What do you want to do?" asked Deputy Sterling.

"Let's stop back at the lodge and see if we can get a list of employees with their contact info, and then we can head back to the command center. I want to run this by Buck and Paul."

They headed back to the lodge, got the list of employees from a pissed-off Mrs. Rasmussen, who told them that they had better not harass any of her employees or guests, climbed into Bax's Jeep and drove out of the parking lot. Something was nagging at Bax, but she wasn't sure what it was.

Chapter Eighteen

Buck grabbed a bottle of Coke from the small refrigerator in the corner and sat at the end of the table. Everyone took a seat, and Buck looked at all the tired faces.

"Okay, folks. It's been a long night, and I know you're all tired, but we still have a lot of work to do. Let's go over what we know so far."

Before he could begin, the door opened, and Bax walked in and grabbed an empty seat. She was followed in by an older, heavyset woman wearing cargo pants and a flannel shirt. She took the seat next to Bax.

Buck looked at the woman and then at Bax. Bax poured herself a cup of coffee and looked around the table.

"Morning, everyone." She pointed towards the newcomer. "This is Dr. Andrea Kellerman. She comes from the state anthropologist's office. She and her team will be working on the next sets of remains."

"Doctor, welcome to our little team. We

appreciate you taking the time to join us," said Buck.

Dr. Kellerman nodded. "From the information I was given, it sounds like it could be a challenge. Can't wait to get started."

"With that in mind," said Buck, "Franklin, why don't you give us a status report."

Franklin pulled his laptop closer and consulted his notes. "So far, we have removed three sets of remains from the graves. We have tentatively identified two of the bodies, which were still in good condition. I will leave that portion up to Sima. We uncovered the next two sets as far as we could go. We were waiting for Dr. Kellerman to arrive so she could take over. I have three teams working on the next three. Once we've gone as far as we feel comfortable, we'll move to the final three."

"Thanks, Franklin," said Buck. "Sima, you're up."

"Thanks, Buck. As Franklin mentioned, with the help of Detective Blackthorn from the Grand Junction Police Department, we have tentative IDs on two of the victims. The most recent is a young woman named Angie Wilde. According to Detective Blackthorn, Ms. Wilde was a student at Colorado Mesa and disappeared sometime during move-in weekend. GJPD homicide has been notified, and they are witnessing the first autopsy, which started about an hour ago. The second victim has been tentatively identified as Susan Raynes. Ms. Raynes was also a student at Colorado Mesa and disappeared the night of the end-of-year bonfire. The third victim is in bad condition and will take more work to identify. That victim is a male, age unknown. The autopsies on our first three victims should be completed by the end of the day today."

Buck looked across the table at Detective Apodaca. "Vince, what do we know?" asked Buck.

"We know very little. I have the missing person files on both young women and am reviewing those. Since we don't know where they were murdered, Sheriff Buckman suggested we let GJPD start the homicide investigation and once we have more details, we can figure out jurisdiction. I am working with Paul on the other missing person files, but we had to backtrack once it was determined that victim three was a male. The sheriff had to go back to Delta to talk to the county commissioners, but he'll be back soon. He mentioned when he called me that the parking lot at the visitor center is filling up with news vans."

That last piece of information did not make Buck happy, and he wondered how they'd found out about the gruesome discoveries. He put that thought aside for now.

"Paul," said Buck. "Anything to add?"

"Not right now. I've got George and Mel compiling missing person reports from the surrounding eight counties, but it's gonna take some time."

Buck took the MP reports for Angie Wilde and Susan Raynes and taped them to the whiteboard. He stepped back.

"It's early in this investigation, so we don't have a lot to go on," he said. "So, let's keep digging."

He turned to Bax. "Bax, any luck with the employees at the lodge on the other side of the lake?"

She shook her head. "Got something I want to follow up on, but nothing so far."

Buck took a sip from his bottle of Coke. "Okay, folks. Let's get back to it, and I know it was a long night for some of you, so if you need to crash for a couple hours, feel free."

The meeting broke up, and everyone headed out the door. Bax waited until they were all gone except for Buck and Paul. Buck was looking at the whiteboard photos of the two young women, and he turned towards Bax.

"What's on your mind, Bax?"

"I'm not sure," she said. "I spoke with the two maintenance men from the lodge. They told me there is always a lot of activity on this side of the lake. I guess folks don't want to pay to camp in the campground, so they camp along the road for free. We know the two most recent bodies had to be buried during the past three months based on their estimated disappearance dates. That puts them in the middle of the busiest camping season up here. How'd the killer do it?"

She paused momentarily to give them time to think about an answer. When none came, she continued. "There's something odd about one of the maintenance men. He lives in a cabin down the road from the campground and has for years. He got agitated when we tried to talk to him. I gather he has some issues from when he was in the military. We should take a closer look at him, but the thing that struck me was he talked about being visited by an alien who comes at night and leaves things in his cabin. Not sure what that was all about."

Buck looked from Bax to Paul.

"That's kind of creepy," said Paul. "He didn't go into any more detail?"

"No," said Bax. "I tried to get more out of him, but he shut down and wanted to go back to work."

Bax pulled the list of employees out of her

pocket and handed it to Buck. She pointed to Michael Kirby's name. "This guy right here," she said.

Buck looked over the list and handed it to Paul. "Would you call Mel and George and ask them to do a deep dive on this Mr. Kirby, and, while they're at it, have them do some quick backgrounds on everyone else on this list, including the Rasmussens?"

Paul nodded and pulled out his phone. Buck turned back to Bax. "Head back to Grand Junction, sit in on the autopsies and work with the homicide detectives, most likely Maldonado and Ridgeway, and see if we can pinpoint where these young women were murdered."

"No problem," said Bax. "Call me if you need something."

Bax grabbed her backpack and headed out the door. Paul put away his phone. "George and Mel are on the list. What do you make of this alien visitation thing?"

Buck thought for a moment. "Not sure, but for now, everything is relevant until we find out it's not. Keep working on the missing person lists. I'm gonna check on the team."

Buck grabbed his backpack, finished his Coke and headed out the door. As he walked up the road to the next grave site, he pulled out his phone and dialed the director to give him a quick debrief.

Chapter Nineteen

Bax turned off North Seventh Street and pulled into the parking lot for St. Mary's Medical Center. St. Mary's was the largest hospital between Denver and Salt Lake City and was a Level II trauma center. It was also where Sima sent the bodies that required autopsies for any number of reasons. It had the most morgue space, which she was going to need, thanks to the number of bodies they would be working with.

Bax grabbed her backpack, slid out of her Jeep and headed into the hospital, taking the elevator to the basement. The morgue was at the end of the hall, and Bax pushed through the double doors into a small office area. She signed in with the morgue attendant, deposited her belongings in a half-sized locker along one wall and put on a Tyvek suit and a pair of Tyvek booties. Her hair was already in a ponytail, so she pushed the tail into a quick bun and shoved it into a Tyvek cap. She put on the N95 mask the clerk handed her, and he pushed a button under the desk, which allowed her to enter the autopsy suite.

Dr. Eric Faraday was middle-aged with a bald head and a trimmed goatee. He looked up from the table. "Ah, Agent Baxter. They didn't tell me you would be joining us, or I would have waited. I was just finishing up with victim number one."

Detective Mark Ridgeway turned towards the door and waved her over. Detective Ridgeway was average height and wore a three-piece suit when investigating a crime. Today, he was dressed all in white, just like Bax and Dr. Faraday. Standing next to them was Detective First Class Jessie Maldonado, dressed from head to toe in Tyvek.

Jessie was a large woman with a booming voice. She could have played on the offensive line for the Denver Broncos. What most people couldn't see under her saggy suit was a hard body. Jessie was not fat. She was a weight lifter and had won numerous regional competitions. When not tucked under a Tyvek cap, her long black hair hung past her shoulders, and she wore tortoiseshell glasses. Jessie was a first-rate detective, and Bax had worked with her on several cases, including the mass shooting at the drag club out in the county.

Bax stepped up to the stainless steel table and looked at the body of the young woman occupying it. Dr. Faraday was putting the final stitches into the *Y* incision in her chest.

"Hey, Bax," said Detective Maldonado. They didn't shake hands but tapped each other elbow to elbow. Dr. Faraday was a stickler for keeping the autopsy suite as clean as possible, which meant no touching.

"What do you think, Doc?" asked Bax.

Dr. Faraday finished closing the *Y* incision and told the tech assisting him to bring over a gurney. "What I think, Agent Baxter, is that this young woman was too young to die. It's a shame when they die this young. My youngest daughter is the same age. It makes me sad, but to answer your question, this young woman was strangled. Whoever did it was strong enough to do it by hand."

He stepped over to the counter and turned on the computer monitor, revealing a picture of the young woman's neck. He pointed to the U-shaped hyoid.

"As you are aware," he said, "the hyoid bone takes thirty-five to forty-five pounds of pressure to fracture, and it fractures in a small percentage of strangulations. As you can see in the X-ray, this bone is shattered. Someone squeezed the life out of this young lady. Hard enough that it left deep imprints on her neck, and before you ask, the person who did this wore gloves, so no prints."

He stepped back to the body, pulled down a magnifying glass mounted above the table and turned on the light. "She was also drugged before she was murdered."

He pointed to an almost microscopic pinprick in her shoulder. "We took a sample, but my guess would be whoever strangled her first immobilized her with something like succinylcholine. We may never know what the killer used. There have been reports that sux has been found in bodies up to a year after death, but in most cases, the enzymes in the body start to break it down right away." He covered the body with a sheet.

"Doc," asked Detective Ridgeway. "Was she sexually assaulted?"

"With the level of decomp, it's not easy to say, but since there is no evidence of anal or vaginal tearing, I would say that she was not sexually assaulted."

Bax moved closer to the table. "Any defensive wounds?"

"None that I could find," said Dr. Faraday. "And here's something to note in your reports. It looks like the killer scraped away any evidence that might have been under her nails."

"Doc," said Bax. "From what you're saying, it sounds like she was killed right after she was abducted."

"That's correct, Agent Baxter. I'm no psychologist, but my take is that your killer kills for one reason. He enjoys it."

Bax looked at Jessie Maldonado. "Is the ID positive?"

"Yep. The body is Angie Wilde. Since we don't know where she was killed, we thought we'd take the lead until we can determine jurisdiction."

"That's not a problem. I'll be along for the ride if you don't mind. I'll give Buck a call and see if he wants us to do the notification."

Bax was about to step away when Dr. Faraday stopped her. He held up a clear evidence bag, and Bax took it. She looked in the bag at the small metal object. It was a brass button that said u.s. army on it. She looked at Dr. Faraday.

"We found that in the bottom of the plastic bag," said the doctor. "Not sure what it means, but I was going to send it to the State Crime Lab along with the victim's clothes, hair, skin and fluid samples and the body bag the body was buried in."

Bax pulled her phone out of the inside of the Tyvek suit and took a couple of pictures of the pin. She handed it back to the tech, who placed all the evidence in a large evidence bag, sealed it and signed the flap. Bax told him she would call a secure courier to pick everything up. She put her phone away as the tech wheeled in a second gurney containing the second black plastic bag inside a newer black body bag. The two techs lifted the body bag onto the second examination table, and while one tech removed the newer body bag, the second tech removed the seal from a sterile five-gallon bucket and placed it under a drain hole in the table.

Dr. Faraday, wearing a new Tyvek jumpsuit, hat and booties and a new mask and gloves, pulled down the magnifying glass over the table, fired up the light and examined the body bag from top to bottom. After he completed the top and sides, the techs rolled the body bag so the doctor could perform the same exam on the bottom. Not seeing anything of note on the bag, they rolled the bag onto its back, and, using a scalpel, Dr. Faraday slit the bag from top to bottom. The smell was horrendous, and a large amount of liquid flooded the table as they removed the body bag and placed it in an evidence bag on the counter. The liquid flowed down the drain and into the plastic bucket.

As they were removing the body bag, something metallic clanged onto the table. Dr. Faraday halted the process and checked through the goo with his gloved hand. He lifted something, pulled out the spray nozzle and hosed off the object, which he handed to Bax. She held it up, and Ridgeway and Maldonado moved in for a closer look.

"That's a Silver Star service ribbon," said Ridgeway. "My brother received one for gallantry in Iraq. What the hell is it doing in there?"

"Good question," said Bax. She walked over, laid it on the counter, pulled out her phone, took pictures of the front and back and placed it in an evidence bag. She stepped back to the table as Dr. Faraday removed the victim's clothes, which fell apart as he did so. The clothes went into an evidence bag. Dr. Faraday examined the exterior of the body, making note of several tattoos and piercings. The tech photographed the items as the doctor pointed them out.

Dr. Faraday stepped back, and the first tech turned on the sprayer and washed the body, not putting too much pressure on the already rotting skin. Once finished, the tech took a series of photos of the body. The other tech wheeled a portable X-ray machine to the exam table and took head-to-toe pictures that popped up on a second computer monitor.

The second body, also of a young woman, was much further along in decomp, and the smell made Detective Ridgeway gag. Bax moved closer and looked at the body as Dr. Faraday used the magnifier and covered the entire body. He stopped at the victim's shoulder and pointed to a tiny spot.

"Same pinprick as the last victim," he said.

He pushed the magnifier out of the way, stepped over to the monitor and flipped through several of the X-rays. He stopped at the picture of the throat.

He looked at the picture and then looked at the detectives.

"Same kind of damage to the hyoid bone."

Bax and the detectives watched for the next two hours as Dr. Faraday proceeded with the rest of the autopsy. When he was finished, he bagged all the samples, signed the evidence bags and the tech sealed the five-gallon bucket. The doctor stepped back from the table.

"Death by strangulation," said the doctor. "My opinion is that both murders were committed by the same person."

Bax looked towards Detective Maldonado. "Can we confirm her ID?"

Detective Maldonado had been holding the missing person report. She laid it on the counter. "From the tattoos and piercings, I would say this is Susan Raynes. We'll confirm with DNA before we call her parents. I would rather they didn't see her like this."

Bax looked at the detectives. "Let's take a break before we go into the next autopsy. I'll call the courier and get these samples moving."

They all agreed, thanked the doctor and the techs, removed the Tyvek clothes and stepped out of the autopsy suite. Bax pulled out her phone and dialed the courier, and they headed for the cafeteria, where they had a lot to discuss.

Chapter Twenty

Buck walked up the road and stopped at the hole for victim number four. Dr. Kellerman had two people working at this location, and they looked up as Buck stepped up next to the hole.

"Find anything useful?" asked Buck, not expecting anything. The young man dressed in Tyvek coveralls and wearing a mask and nitrile gloves set down his trowel and handed Buck an evidence bag.

"We found this on top of the rib cage. Not sure what it is."

Buck accepted the bag and looked at the small metal band with pieces of fabric still attached to it. He reached into his pocket, pulled out his reading glasses and put them on. He looked at the item in the bag.

"I'm no expert, but I think that's an Afghan campaign ribbon," he said. "And you said it was lying on top of the bones?"

The young man pushed back his Tyvek hood and lowered his mask. "Yes, sir. It was sitting between the third and fourth ribs. It could have been attached to a piece of clothing, but there's no material left on the body. Or it could have been dumped in the hole before the body was covered." The young man covered back up and went back to work.

Buck took a picture of the item in the bag and took the bag with him as he headed for the fifth grave. He found Dr. Kellerman talking with the two students working on this site. He walked up to the group. Dr. Kellerman stopped her conversation and handed him a small evidence bag. He looked at the contents of the bag and held up the bag he had taken from the young man at the fourth site. Dr. Kellerman stared at the small ribbon.

Buck held up the bag she had just handed him. "This one I recognize. This is a Purple Heart ribbon."

"So, unless these bones belong to someone in the military, there's no reason that ribbon should be in the hole," she said.

Buck looked at the other items that had been placed on a white plastic pad. "Any fabric in there that might indicate a military uniform?"

"No, sir," said a young woman as she pulled down her hood and mask and wiped the sweat with the back of her sleeve. "We found several small pieces of fabric, but none of them look military."

"Doc, I know it's early, but any thoughts on how long this body has been in the ground?" asked Buck.

"We'll know more once we get these to the lab and clean them up, but I think we're looking at at least one year but no more than three or four."

She told Buck she was heading towards the sixth body and asked if he'd like to walk with her. Buck took the second bag, and they continued down the road.

The team working on the sixth body was farther ahead of the other two and had removed several bones from the hole, which were now sitting on a piece of white plastic. Dr. Kellerman kneeled, picked up one of the bones and wiped it off with her hand.

"These have been in the ground longer than the other two. I'd say three or four years."

Buck kneeled next to her and looked at the dirt in a small sieve that was next to the hole. He picked up a stick off the ground and pushed some of the dirt aside. "Doctor, take a look at this."

Dr. Kellerman walked over and looked at what Buck was pointing to. "That looks like the pin you identified at the last site, except all the material had disappeared."

She stood and looked at him. "Three sites with three military awards buried with the bodies. That can't be a coincidence."

"I don't think so," said Buck. "These were buried with the bodies on purpose."

"But I thought serial killers took items from their victims to keep as souvenirs. Why would the killer leave a memento?"

"That's a great question, Doctor," said Buck. He pulled out his phone and dialed a number.

"Hey, Buck. What's up?" asked Bax.

"How many autopsies have they completed?"

"We were walking into the third one as you called. Why?" asked Bax.

"Did you guys find anything unusual during the first two?" asked Buck.

"Yeah. The hyoid bones on the first two victims were crushed," said Bax.

Buck cut her off. "Anything not a part of the body, something that might have been buried with the victims?"

"Yeah," said Bax. "We found a military ribbon,

actually, a Silver Star ribbon in the bag with one body and a military button with the other. Why?"

"We found military ribbons with the third, fourth and fifth bodies," said Buck.

"Holy shit. We thought the items were odd, but now with five of them—wow! Could it be the killer's signature?" she asked.

Buck laughed. "How many serial killers have we investigated that left something with the victim? We know they take souvenirs, but to leave some? That's strange."

"You're right, but what do you make of it?" asked Bax.

"Not sure yet. Let me know if you find anything with the third victim."

Buck disconnected the call and looked at Dr. Kellerman. "Looks like we have another mystery, Doctor. I'll let you get back to your students."

He picked up an empty evidence bag and, using a pair of tweezers, placed the ribbon in the bag, sealed and signed it. He turned back towards the incident command center and pulled out his phone.

"Hi, Buck," said Mel. "What can I do for you?"

Buck explained about finding the military

ribbons and buttons at each site. "Do me a favor and get with the FBI and see if they have any information on any killings where they found something military-related with the body."

"You know, once I do that, the cat will be out of the bag, and you'll get a call from Hank Clancy," said Mel.

"That's okay. It was inevitable that the FBI would get involved at some point; it might as well be sooner rather than later," said Buck.

"Okay, Buck. I'll get right on it. Stay tuned."

Buck disconnected the call and walked into the trailer. He placed the three bags on the table in front of Paul and Detective Apodaca.

Paul and the detective picked up each bag and looked at the ribbons, and Paul put the last bag on the table. "Military ribbons. Someone trying to tell us something about our victims?"

Detective Apodaca looked at them both. "Or is someone trying to tell us something about the killer?"

"Both good questions," said Buck. "Bax has another ribbon, a Silver Star and an army uniform button that they found with the first two victims. I'm not sure what to think at this point. I've asked

Mel to get with the FBI and see if they have any unsolved cases with the same MO."

"Why would the killer want to draw attention to himself by leaving us clues with the bodies?" asked Detective Apodaca.

"Maybe to see how smart we are," said Paul. "Most serial killers never believe they are going to get caught. A lot of them think they are the smartest people in the room. It could also be some weird ritual our killer has. It could also be he's just nuts."

"Well, whatever he is," said Buck, "he's got some strength, because the hyoid bones in the first two victims were crushed, not just broken. That takes a lot of strength or a lot of anger."

"Or a lot of passion," said Paul. "I don't mean passion in a sexual way, but a passion for what he does."

Detective Apodaca looked serious. "You mean, you think our killer likes to kill. Damn, that's a scary thought."

Chapter Twenty-One

Bax and Detectives Ridgeway and Maldonado entered the autopsy suite and put on Tyvek suits and booties. They donned masks and stepped up to the table. Dr. Kalishe was examining what was left of the plastic that had contained the body. She looked up as they entered and noted into the microphone over the table that they had entered the autopsy suite. She asked the two assistants to roll the plastic back, and she examined the underside. Finding nothing of note, she asked the male assistant to wash off the plastic, carefully catching the runoff in a sterile bucket under the table drain. She stepped away from the table and lowered her mask.

"The plastic bag," she said, "is in bad shape. I think the body has been in the ground for a couple of years. It also looks like most of the fluid from the decomp was absorbed into the ground, as there is little left in the original wrap. I had Franklin take some samples of the dirt under the body to send to the crime lab. Based on what I read about the earlier autopsies, I don't think we will find anything earth-shattering, but who knows."

The assistant indicated he was done, and the doctor pulled up her mask and stepped over to the table along with Bax and the detectives. Using tweezers, she pulled away pieces of the original plastic bag and placed them in an evidence bag. The pieces crumbled as she pulled them, so it was slow going, but she cleared enough to see the bones. Her assistant took still pictures as she removed each bone from the wrap and placed them on the table behind her. She stopped when she got to the hyoid bone, or at least what was left of it. She looked at her visitors and spoke into the microphone over the table.

"The hyoid bone is crushed, similar to the last two victims." She pointed to the bones so that Bax could photograph them with her cell phone camera. She turned and placed them on the table. She continued removing bones and taking samples to send to the crime lab. She stopped at the dirt in the bottom of the bag and ran her fingers through it. She picked up a small brass button and looked at it under the magnifying glass.

"U.S. Army," she said. She handed it to Bax, and the group looked at it.

"A souvenir," said Bax. "Just like the last two and the ones they found on bodies four, five and six."

Dr. Kalishe stepped away from the table, pulled off her mask and removed the Tyvek hood, as did her visitors. Bax placed the button in an evidence bag and sealed it.

"Any thoughts?" asked Bax.

"The body is of a young man, mid to late twenties. He has no discernible abnormalities, broken bones or anything we can use to identify him. We will send a couple of his teeth to the crime lab to see if they can get a DNA profile. There is no way to tell ethnicity or whether he was injected like the other two. His hyoid bone is crushed, just like the last two bodies, so it looks like we have a serial killer on our hands."

"Great," said Detective Ridgeway.

Bax laughed. "Okay, thanks, Doc. I'll call for the secure courier to pick up the samples. What have you heard on the next set of bones?"

"I spoke with Buck just before we came in here. They have two of the remains out of the ground and by now, they should have the third as well. Franklin has exposed all the rest of the bodies, so the anthropologists can keep moving. Should have everything out of the ground by this time tomorrow."

"Thanks, Doc," said Bax. "Let me know when you and Dr. Kellerman are ready to look at the next set of bones, and I'll make sure I have time to get here."

Bax and the detectives walked out of the autopsy suite and dropped off their coveralls, booties and masks in the trash can by the door. She grabbed her backpack and put the bag containing the button inside. They left the suite and headed towards the parking lot.

"What's next?" asked Detective Maldonado when they reached her car.

Bax thought for a minute. "Let's swing by your office. I'd like to look at the missing person files on the two women, and then we start investigating."

Bax left the detectives and headed for her Jeep. She pulled out her phone and dialed Buck.

"Hey, Bax."

"Hey, Buck. There was nothing unusual on the third autopsy, but we found another military button."

"Okay," said Buck. "What's your next step?"

"We're gonna meet back at the detective bureau, grab the missing person files, and I think we'll head over and talk to Angie Wilde's roommates and see what they have to say."

"Good. Let me know what you find, and we'll keep working from here until we can get the last of the bones out of the ground."

She disconnected the call and sat in her Jeep for a few minutes, thinking about the autopsies. Since nothing brought about any clarity, she started her Jeep, pulled out of the parking lot and headed for Grand Junction Police Headquarters. They had a lot to do and little information to go on.

Chapter Twenty-Two

Sheriff Hal Buckman pulled to a stop next to Buck and Dr. Kellerman. They stood next to the tenth hole, watching two anthropology grad students clearing away the dirt from the now-exposed bones. The sheriff slid out of his SUV, tapped Buck on the sleeve and indicated for Buck to follow him. They stepped to the back of the sheriff's SUV; the sheriff pulled out his phone, opened his app with a few clicks and handed the screen to Buck. He read what was on the screen. He was not happy.

"How the fuck did they get this information?" asked Buck.

"I have no idea, but if I find out it was one of my people, someone's head is going to roll."

Buck read some more of the internet posts. He looked up at the sheriff. "They gave our killer a name," he said.

"Yeah," said Sheriff Buckman. "The Roadside Cross Killer. Sounds like one of those true crime shows on one of those streaming services. My wife loves those shows."

"What's worse," said Buck, "is they know how many bodies we discovered."

Buck read the rest of the article. "Do the major news agencies have it?"

"Yep. This is just one of the articles. I heard the Denver media picked it up and it was on all the morning shows," said the sheriff.

"Well, at least they don't have the info on the buttons and ribbons. We need to keep that to ourselves."

The sheriff looked confused. "What buttons and ribbons?"

"Let's go to the trailer," said Buck. He looked over at Dr. Kellerman. "Doc, I'll be back in a bit. Let me know if you find anything interesting."

Dr. Kellerman waved to him, and he and the sheriff slid into the SUV and headed for the command center. They parked in front of the door, and Buck led the way into the trailer. Paul looked up from his computer.

"We have a problem," he said, turning his laptop so Buck could see the news article.

"Yeah," said Buck. "How did you hear about it?"

"My wife called me," said Paul. "She heard it

on the morning news on one of the Denver TV stations. She said it's all over the internet."

Sheriff Buckman had stepped over to the counter and was looking at the evidence bags containing the ribbons and buttons. He pushed them around and looked at Buck.

"Serial killers usually take souvenirs, not leave them. What do you think this is all about?" he asked.

"Not sure what to make of this," said Buck. "Could be some military angle to the murders, could be someone trying to point us in a direction away from themselves and towards someone else. I don't know what to think at this point."

Paul looked up from his laptop. "I scanned several news sites and no one mentions the buttons and ribbons."

"Okay," said Sheriff Buckman. "I best go up and talk to the media folks. I'll make sure not to mention the buttons. You want to come along?"

Buck smiled. "No, sir. I'm not a big fan of the media. Let me know if you need anything. We should move the command center back to your office later this afternoon. We should have all the remains finished in a couple of hours, and then we can clear the site."

The sheriff acknowledged, pulled out his phone and asked the dispatcher to have one of the public works guys come up and pick up the trailer. He disconnected the call, looked again at the evidence bags and walked out of the trailer.

Buck, Paul and Detective Apodaca sat and looked at the whiteboard. Other than the pictures of the first two victims and some background information, there was very little to show for the last thirty-six hours of work.

"What's our next step?" asked Detective Apodaca.

Buck sat in silence and looked at the pictures. He took a sip from his Coke and gathered his thoughts.

"We have two options on the ribbons and the buttons. Our killer is a soldier, or our killer bought them online or at an army-navy store. The latter would be impossible to trace since they could have been purchased anywhere. The former isn't much easier because other than the Silver Star and the Purple Heart, the military issues hundreds of those and thousands depending on how far back we go. If we had the Silver Star medal, it's possible it could have a serial number on it that could be traced, but we don't, and the military didn't number ribbons. The buttons are common to military uniforms since World War One."

"Doesn't leave us much to work with," said Detective Apodaca.

"Until we get an ID on the third body, we're stuck," said Buck. He turned to Paul. "Did you send Mel and George the employees from the lodge? Anything back on them?"

Paul opened the investigation file and clicked on the background check tab. "Looks like they ran about half the employees so far." He read for a few minutes. "Nothing jumps out. A lot of seasonal workers. It looks like most are college students. It doesn't look like anyone from this group has been here more than a couple of years."

Buck was frustrated. He had eleven crime scenes, and other than the ribbons and buttons, he had nothing to work with. He took a long drink from his Coke bottle. "Any of those have military service?"

Paul reread the backgrounds. "No, no military, but that doesn't mean that someone in their family wasn't in the military. Do you want to go that deep on these folks?"

"Not yet," said Buck. "We'll keep that in our back pocket for now."

Buck looked at his watch. "Let's head over to the lodge and grab some lunch. Hopefully, we'll get more background checks while we're gone."

They left their backpacks and laptops and headed for Buck's Jeep. They needed one thread to pull on, but so far, they didn't have it.

Chapter Twenty-Three

Bax stopped behind Detective Maldonado's SUV, turned off her Jeep and looked at the small house on Bunting Avenue. She thought back to some of the houses she had lived in while she was in college and smiled. Three cars were in the driveway, and she hoped someone was home.

They had picked up the missing person files from Detective Blackthorn and had reviewed them during a lunch stop at a small Mexican restaurant. The reports were well written, and it was clear that Detective Blackthorn had professionally investigated each case, leaving no stone unturned.

Bax slid out of her Jeep, grabbed her backpack and joined Detectives Maldonado and Ridgeway on the front porch. Ridgeway knocked, and they heard the music volume on the other side of the door lower. The door opened, and a tall, thin blonde wearing shorts and a Mesa University T-shirt opened the door. Bax and the detectives held up their badges.

"You would be Lizzy?" asked Bax.

Lizzy smiled and pushed open the screen door. "Yeah. Is this about Angie?"

"May we come in?" asked Bax.

Not looking at all concerned to have three cops standing on her front porch, Lizzy Clayton nodded and stepped aside. They entered a small living room containing the typical college rental house furniture: a mismatched couch, two wingback chairs, and a couple of stained wooden tables. The carpet on the floor was threadbare, but overall, the room was clean and neat.

Lizzy pointed to the chairs and sat on the arm of the couch facing Bax. Bax opened the missing person file.

"Lizzy, how well did you know Angie?" she asked.

"Not well at all," said Lizzy. "We had just met that morning. That was our first trip to the bar after getting settled."

"How did you come to be roommates?" asked Bax.

"My friend Toni had taken some classes with Gabby last semester, and they got close. When Gabby found this place, she asked Toni if she wanted to join her and Angie and if she knew of anyone else who needed a room, and she suggested me. I wanted out of the place I was living in, so I jumped at the chance." She hesitated for a minute.

"Has something happened with Angie? Did you find her?"

Bax looked at Detective Maldonado. "We found a body up on Grand Mesa that we believe might be Angie Wilde," said Detective Maldonado. "So, this is no longer a missing person case."

Lizzy Clayton put her hand up to her mouth. She hesitated. "Was she murdered?"

Detective Maldonado nodded. "We believe so; that's why we need to revisit the information you gave to Detective Blackthorn."

Lizzy Clayton turned pale, and her hands shook. Detective Ridgeway stepped around the corner into the kitchen and returned with a glass of water, which he handed to Lizzy. She drank it in one gulp and looked embarrassed. She wrapped both hands around the glass.

Bax picked up the conversation. "Lizzy, did anything happen that day you all moved in that seemed out of the ordinary? Strangers near the house, odd phone calls, anything like that?"

Lizzy Clayton thought for a minute. She took a deep breath to calm herself down and looked at Bax. "No, nothing that I can think of. We all spent most of the day getting our rooms in order. Toni and I finished earlier than Angie and Gabby and we headed for Tiny's to make sure we got a table."

"What about at the bar?" asked Detective Maldonado. "Anything strange happen, any problems with anyone in the bar?"

"No, we had some beers and ordered dinner, listened to the band and danced with some of the guys, but no one caused a scene."

The front door opened, and a short, dark-haired woman with a mocha complexion stepped into the room, dropped her backpack and looked around. "Sorry, didn't know you had company." She reached for her backpack.

"Gabby," said Lizzy. "These are detectives. They found Angie."

Gabby Cruz let go of her backpack strap and stood up. Tears ran down her face, and her legs shook. Detective Ridgeway stood up, grabbed her arm and led her over to the couch. She sat next to Lizzy, reached over and took her hand. She looked at Bax and then at Detective Maldonado. She opened her mouth, but nothing came out.

"Gabby," said Bax. "You were Angie's best friend?"

Gabby nodded. "We grew up together on the rez. Where did you find her?"

Bax explained about the body they'd found on the Grand Mesa and asked her if there were any reasons Angie would be up on the mesa. Gabby shook her head.

"So, she didn't know anyone with a house or a cabin up there, who she might have gone to visit? Could she have met someone at the bar that maybe lived up there?" asked Bax.

Gabby used the sleeve of her sweatshirt to wipe her eyes. "I would have known if she was going someplace. She wouldn't have left without telling me. Angie was excited about school. She was getting her degree in sociology and had already secured a job on the rez at the medical center; her brother works there as a doctor. She was also waiting to hear about an internship with a small stipend at the VA Health Center. She was planning on a great year." Her body shook, and she held Lizzy's hand tighter. "Do her folks know?"

Bax nodded. "We've been in touch with the sheriff, and he was going over this morning to let them know. Gabby, was Angie afraid of anything or anybody? Did anything happen at the bar that night that might have caused her concern?"

Gabby shook her head but stopped and looked at Lizzy. "The creepy guy in the bar," she said.

Lizzy nodded. "Yeah, you told me about that. I didn't see him."

"Tell us about this guy?" asked Detective Maldonado.

"I've seen him in there a couple of times, even after Angie disappeared. He's kind of grubby with long hair, and he looks dirty. He never seems to bother anyone, just sits in the corner and drinks, but that night, I'm not sure what happened, but Angie got freaked out. She said he was watching her. After a while, she told me she was going outside to get some air. I wanted to go with her, but she said she would be right back. That was the last time I saw her." Tears flowed down her face.

"Did you go out to look for her when she didn't come back?" asked Detective Ridgeway.

More tears flowed down her face, and she leaned into Lizzy. "I guess I lost track of time and when we were ready to leave, I figured she had gone back to the house. When she wasn't here, I thought maybe she found someone to spend the night with."

"Did that happen often?" asked Bax. "Did she often go home with guys she just met?"

"No," said Gabby, and she jumped up and ran down the hall. They heard a door slam and what sounded like vomiting.

Lizzy looked at them. "That wasn't fair. You just told her that her best friend was dead, and then you insinuate that she did nothing to find her. You people are cruel." She stood and glared at them. "Please leave," she said.

Bax stood and walked towards the door, and the detectives walked past her onto the porch. Bax turned.

"Who called the cops when Angie didn't come home?"

"Fuck you," said Lizzy. "Get the hell out of my house."

Bax stepped onto the porch, and Lizzy slammed the door so hard the porch shook.

"So much for caring about their roommate," said Detective Ridgeway.

Bax blew on a piece of hair that had slipped from her ponytail and was hanging across her right eye. "Let's go see if the bar has any video."

Chapter Twenty-Four

Professor Brian Davidson finished his late morning American history class, looked at his watch and decided to grab something to eat before his afternoon lecture started. He walked across the campus, crossed North Twelfth Street and entered Tiny's Bar and Grill. The smell of greasy burgers, beer and vomit hit him as he opened the door. He pushed his sunglasses up onto his head and found a seat at the bar. He swung around on the barstool and faced the seating area. Several of the tables were occupied by faculty members he recognized, and he gave them a slight wave. He turned to face the bartender and ordered a draft beer, a cheeseburger and fries. Once the bartender left, he spun around and watched the waitress taking orders in the back of the room.

She must be new, since he hadn't seen her before. She was medium height and looked fit, with a nice pair of legs sticking out of her shorts, and she was amply endowed, filling out the T-shirt she wore. Her dark hair hung down her back in a long ponytail. She wasn't supermodel pretty, but if he were younger, he wouldn't kick her out of bed. He laughed to himself, turned and sipped the beer that sat in front of him.

The bartender set his burger and fries in front of him and asked if he needed anything else, and he shook his head and picked up the burger. He was about to take his first bite when three people, two wearing suit jackets and one wearing a dark windbreaker with cbi in big white letters emblazoned on the front, stepped up to the bar and asked to speak to the manager. The bartender picked up the phone behind the bar, pushed one button and spoke for a minute. "He'll be right out. Can I get you something?"

Bax looked at her watch, and since they hadn't eaten anything since breakfast, which seemed like hours ago, she thought food sounded like a great idea. She looked at the detectives, who thought the same thing, and they grabbed a couple of menus off the bar, walked over to a four-top table and sat. The waitress came by, took their drink orders—three coffees—and told them she would be right back.

The waitress was setting down their coffees when a huge bear of a man walked up to the table and introduced himself. Vic Kowalski was six foot five and weighed nearly three hundred pounds. He wore black tactical pants and a light blue button-down shirt with the sleeves rolled up. He was anything but tiny. He had bright blue eyes, and his gray hair was combed back. He had gray stubble on his face. He sat and looked at Bax and then at Detective Maldonado.

"Jessie, good to see you," he said. "Keeping busy?"

"You know me, Vic," she said. "Gotta keep moving."

She turned to Bax and Detective Ridgeway. "Vic and I went to school together about a thousand years ago, or so it seems." Vic nodded and laughed. She continued. "Later on, we were in some of the same regional weight-lifting competitions. Those were good times." She saluted him with her coffee cup.

"So," said Vic. "What brings the cops to my doorstep, complaints from the neighbors? Although I doubt they would send some detectives if it was that simple."

"Neighbors bustin' your ass again?" asked Detective Maldonado.

Vic Kowalski smiled. "You know how it is. Noise complaints from the band, parking complaints, kids hanging outside. Same shit, different day."

"Not this time," said Detective Maldonado. "We were hoping you might help us out with something."

Vic leaned into the table just as the waitress brought their food. Detective Maldonado continued. "You remember a month or so back, that young Native girl that disappeared? She was here having drinks, stepped outside and was never seen again."

Vic got a serious look on his face. "Yeah, that was sad. No one could figure out what happened to her. I put up a reward for any information. Got a lot of crap information, but I passed it all on to that female detective, uh." He hesitated, looking for a name.

"Detective Blackthorn," said Bax.

Vic nodded. "Yeah, Blackthorn. I'm not sure if anything ever came of it. What's your interest, Jess?"

Detective Maldonado leaned into the table and looked around. "We found a body up on the mesa that might be her. That took it from a missing person case to a homicide, and it landed on our desks."

Vic sat back and blew out a low-pitched whistle. He leaned into the table. "Murdered, huh? Poor kid. So how can I help?"

Bax picked up the conversation. "Her roommates told us that the victim got freaked out by some grungy guy sitting at one of the tables, and that's why she left. We were wondering, and we know it's been a while, but we were wondering if you had any CCTV for that night. We know it's a long shot."

"Shit," said Vic. "I try to get these kids to understand that if they have a problem to come get me or one of the bartenders. We're here to help. I wish she had come to me instead of leaving. Might have turned out different." He sat back.

"You guys are in luck. With all the complaints we get from the neighbors, I've got cameras all over the place, including outside, and since we've been threatened with lawsuits, I have the cameras backed up to the cloud. My lawyer told me not to erase anything, so I've got years of video in storage."

"Any chance you'd be willing to share the video with us from that night?" asked Bax.

"Yeah. Why don't you guys eat before it gets cold, and I'll go see what I have for you." He stood up and walked away, and they dug into their food. The spicy wings Bax ordered were some of the best she'd ever eaten, and by the time she was done, Vic returned to the table with a laptop, sat and turned it so they could see.

The screen showed the camera at the bar, from the night Angie Wilde had disappeared. The time stamp in the corner showed 7:00 p.m. Bax pushed the play button, and they squeezed closer together to watch the video. She flipped through several of the cameras and then stopped. She stared at the blurry picture of the long-haired guy by the window.

"That could be the guy that Gabby mentioned." She turned the laptop so Vic could see and pointed. "You know this guy?" she asked.

Vic pulled a pair of glasses out of his pocket, put them on and looked at the picture. "Yeah, he's been in here a couple of times. I think someone said his name was Ultra or something like that." He waved over the bartender, who looked at the picture.

"Yeah," said the bartender. "He's kind of a semi-regular. Folks around here call him Ultra; it seems he's always talking about aliens. I think his name is Mike something. Not sure."

"Any idea what the Ultra is about?" asked Detective Ridgeway.

The bartender laughed. "A long time ago, the CIA or somebody ran a psychological program where they fed people LSD, and a lot of them had bad experiences. Some saw aliens or some such crap. Well, anyway, I guess his initials are M. K., and that was the name of the program, MK-Ultra. Since he always seems a little out there, if you know what I mean, people just started calling him Ultra."

The bartender left to fill an order, and Bax looked at the detectives and advanced the video. After an hour of looking at different angles from different cameras, they came to one conclusion. Ultra may have freaked out Angie Wilde, but he never moved off the barstool until last call, and he didn't appear to show any interest in her other than to look her way once or twice. The outside camera showed him getting into an old pickup truck and heading north on Twelfth Street, but by the time he left, Angie Wilde had been gone from the bar for more than two hours.

The front outside camera caught her walking across the street and heading into the campus, but then they lost her, and she never came back. They would need to find CCTV footage from the campus to see where she went.

Bax asked if she could send the videos to one of her colleagues, and Vic agreed. She pulled up his email account, attached the cloud file and sent it to George and Melanie to see if they could enhance the picture enough so she could identify the grungy guy.

They paid the bill, left a nice tip for taking up so much table time, thanked Vic and headed towards their SUVs. They never noticed Brian Davidson pay his bill and rush out the door. He had been so interested in hearing what they were saying that he had to run to get to his lecture. What he heard, he didn't like. He would have to put the new waitress on hold until he figured out how much the cops knew.

Chapter Twenty-Five

Buck, Paul and Detective Apodaca were sitting in the restaurant at the Island Lake Lodge when a black U.S. government SUV pulled into the parking lot. The doors opened, and two men in suits headed towards the building. Paul was the first to notice, and he tapped Buck on the arm.

"Looks like the FBI has arrived," he said.

Buck looked over his shoulder and frowned. He knew the FBI would get involved as soon as Mel put an inquiry into their system requesting information on similar crimes, but he'd hoped he would have a little more time. The last thing he needed was the FBI breathing down his neck.

Special Agent in Charge Hank Clancy and Special Agent James Carpenter pulled open the front door, stepped into the lobby and looked around. They spotted Buck sitting in the dining room and headed his way. Hank and James wore the standard-issue FBI uniform, as Buck liked to kid him: gray slacks, black shoes, white shirt, navy-blue jacket and red-white-and-blue-striped tie.

Hank Clancy was the special agent in charge of the Denver Field Office of the FBI and one of

Buck's closest friends. Hank had been a deputy director until earlier in the year when he fell on his sword and took the blame for a rogue FBI agent. The agent, while working out of the Denver Field Office and fighting Buck at every turn during the investigation of the Christmas Day bombings, caused the deaths of several FBI agents and serious injuries to many others.

Buck had asked the Colorado governor to intervene on Hank's behalf, and as a result, they were able to save his job, but they couldn't prevent the demotion. Hank had had a long career with the FBI, and he was involved in many high-profile cases, and even though his wife wanted him to retire, Hank refused to end his career with a black eye.

Special Agent Carpenter was running a serial killer task force looking into the perpetrator of the mass shooting at the drag club located outside of Grand Junction. Mitchell Evans, also known as Bryce Tanner and Roger Shipman, was a serial killer turned mass murderer. As Roger Shipman, he had murdered his preacher, the director of the juvenile hall he was confined to and his father. As Bryce Tanner, he killed seventy-some people at the drag club and injured almost 250 others. He was also suspected of killing his mother in a nursing home. As Mitchell Evans, he killed a psychologist at Duke University. He had been arrested for lying to the police during a murder investigation, and the police found plans for another active shooting situation it appeared he was planning. He was now in a locked psych ward at St. Mary's in Grand Junction, where he was being evaluated by Carpenter and a team of experts to see if he was fit to stand trial.

They shook hands, and Buck grabbed a chair from another table and set it at their table.

"Hank, Agent Carpenter, good to see you guys," said Buck.

Hank didn't smile. "You're holding out on me again, Buck."

Buck smiled. "We didn't want to waste your time until we were certain what we have, which we still aren't a hundred percent certain of."

"Don't give me that shit. You guys sent in a VICAP request for information about similar crimes. You knew that request would hit my desk as soon as you sent it. So, let's cut the crap, and you tell me what's going on."

The waiter approached the table, and Buck asked his visitors if they had eaten. Hank and Agent Carpenter ordered coffee and lunch, and Buck filled them in on what they knew so far. Hank and Agent Carpenter listened without interrupting until Buck stopped to take a drink from his glass of Coke. The waiter brought their lunches, and Hank continued the conversation.

"So right now, you've got eleven burial sites, the most recent being a couple of weeks old and the oldest several years old. You've got military ribbons and buttons found at each site, which is weird since serial killers take souvenirs, they don't leave them, and you've identified two of the victims from local missing person reports. Does that about cover it?"

"Pretty much," said Buck.

Hank didn't respond for a minute then looked at Paul and back to Buck. "How the fuck do you keep getting yourself into these kinds of situations, and aren't you supposed to be on vacation?"

Buck laughed and told him about the call Bax had received from Vicky Talmadge and about Jasper, the cadaver dog, alerting at all the roadside crosses while they were taking a walk.

Hank sat back and rubbed his temples. "You've got to be kidding. A cadaver dog in the right place at the right time found eleven burial sites. That's an incredible story."

Agent Carpenter laughed. "That has to be a one in a million thing. Is there any way this woman is connected to the bodies?"

"None whatsoever," said Buck. "If she had decided to stay at home in Durango to recover from her most recent trip, we would have never found the bodies. Besides, when I got here and watched the dog myself, I had Bax confirm her whereabouts for the two bodies we'd identified. She was overseas working several earthquakes during the time frame of those abductions."

Buck gave them a debrief on where they were with the recovery of the remains and what was discovered during the autopsies. He also explained about looking at all local missing person cases.

"Okay, Buck. I was going to pull James and his team in the next couple of days since we are pretty much wrapped up in Grand Junction, but I am going to leave them on-site for a while and have them follow up on your VICAP request. If anything comes of it, we can dispatch agents to check out the particulars. Keep me posted as you identify the bodies, and we'll give you whatever help you will need."

He looked at Agent Carpenter. "James, you and your team will be available to help Buck and his team with whatever they need. I want to make myself clear. As of right now, this is not our investigation. That may change, but until it does, you will work with Buck's team. Keep me posted on whatever you guys find."

Agent Carpenter nodded that he understood. Hank picked up the bill off the table and handed the waiter his credit card. Once he signed the receipt, they all shook hands and headed for their SUVs.

Buck stepped away for a minute to use the restroom and when he came out, he spotted Vicky Talmadge and Jasper coming in the front door. Vicky stopped and waited as he approached. Buck looked down and saw the suitcase she was pulling behind her.

"Hey, Vicky. Change of plans?"

Vicky smiled, and Buck leaned down to pet Jasper. "I was a little nervous being in the campground all by myself with a serial killer running around, so I decided we should spend our last night in the lodge. We're heading out in the morning. First back to Durango to resupply, and then to Peru. An entire town was buried under a landslide caused by a massive earthquake. We're being told the death toll could be in the thousands."

"Wow," said Buck. "You sure live an interesting life."

"Listen," said Vicky. "If it's not too forward of me, would you like to join me tonight for dinner? I'd like to hear about your investigation so far, speaking of interesting lives."

"I'd love to," said Buck. "How about we meet here at six?"

She told Buck that would work fine and to be careful, and she and Jasper headed for their room. Buck headed to his Jeep. There was work to be done, and now that the FBI was involved, he needed to keep things tight.

Chapter Twenty-Six

Buck stepped into the mobile command center just as his phone rang. He looked at the number and pushed the green button.

"Hey, Max," he said.

"Buck Taylor, how's my favorite cop?" she asked.

"Good, Max. What's up?"

"We have a DNA match on your third victim. I sent it to Mel and George so they can run a background check, but I wanted to get it to you right away."

Buck put his phone on speaker and set it on the table. "Okay, Max. I've got you on speaker. Paul and Delta County Detective Apodaca are with me. What have you got?"

"Your victim is James Michael Chamberlain," said Max.

Buck looked at Paul. "Why does that name sound familiar?"

Paul opened his laptop and clicked some keys. "Son of a bitch. James Chamberlain is the son of the billionaire industrialist Warren Chamberlain. He disappeared from the family home in Palm Beach, Florida, twenty-three years ago. He was six years old. The police at the time thought it was a kidnapping for ransom, but they never received a ransom note. At the time, his father, Warren, was under indictment for tax evasion and fraud, and the FBI thought that Warren had sent the kid to Europe to keep him out of the limelight. That never proved out either. The boy was never found, and no one was ever charged in connection with the disappearance. Over the years, according to several newspaper articles, there were sightings of the kid all over the country. His old man put up a ten-million-dollar reward for his safe return. No one ever collected. The kid just vanished. Looks like the interest in the story waned about ten years ago."

"That's why I wanted to get you his name right away," said Max. "Once this gets out, it will cause a media frenzy."

"Thanks, Max. You just made my whole day."

Buck heard Max laughing on the other end of the line. "Always glad to help," she said. "What do you need us to do?"

"We'll take it from here, Max. Have you gotten

to the samples from the rest of the bodies?" asked Buck.

"Yeah. We're pushing everything to the DNA lab as soon as we get it." She hesitated for a minute. "How do you get yourself into these messes, Buck?"

"Just lucky, I guess," said Buck. "Keep me posted on the rest of the remains as they come in."

Max ended the call as always. "You're a good man, Buck Taylor. God will watch over you." The call disconnected, and Buck picked up his phone and hit the speed dial one button. Director Jackson answered right away.

"Hey, Buck. How'd your meeting go with the FBI?"

"Not too bad, sir. For now, they will assist as we need, but that's not why I'm calling, sir."

Buck filled him in on the discovery of James Chamberlain's remains. The director was quiet as Buck gave him the rundown.

"Shit, Buck," said the director. "That's a wrinkle no one could have seen coming. You said the anthropologist estimated the body has been in the ground for around a year, give or take. Where the hell has he been all these years? Did your serial killer have him all this time?"

"Good question, sir," said Buck. "But with no good answer yet."

"Okay, Buck. What do you need from me?"

"The one thing I can think of right now, sir, is to give the governor a heads-up. We're not sure how the media found out about the bodies, so it could just be a matter of time till they get this too."

"I'll let him know, but let's keep this pretty close to the vest until you find out who's leaking information to the press."

Director Jackson hung up and Buck clipped his phone to his belt. "Fuck," he said. "This is all we need."

Paul and Detective Apodaca nodded in agreement. "You realize that word will get out as soon as George and Mel reach out for the original investigation files. What do you want to do?" asked Paul.

Buck sat in the chair and rubbed his temples. "Yeah" was all he said, and he just sat there. Paul printed off the original missing person flyer, and Detective Apodaca taped it to the whiteboard. As Paul repeated the information, he filled in what they knew under the flyer. When they were finished, they had a long list of information, but nothing that would lead them to any understanding of where this young man had been for twenty-three years and how he'd ended up buried in a hole in Colorado.

Buck stared at the information written on the whiteboard. The little bug in his brain was moving around, but not as actively as usual when they got a lead. In this case, they had a lot of information but no good leads.

Buck leaned back in his chair and sipped from his bottle of Coke. He set the bottle on the table.

"There's no way we can solve this without the original files and everything since then." He hesitated. "We need to get this out there. For twenty-three years, this kid was out there until he ran into our killer."

He looked at Paul. "Tell George and Mel to talk to the original investigators on the case, and let's get the file. The media be damned. We have a case to solve."

Paul dialed his phone.

"Vince, call the sheriff and tell him what we know so far. There's going to be a firestorm from the media, and I don't want him to get blindsided."

Buck pulled out his phone, dialed a number and waited. Hank Clancy answered.

"What's up, Buck?"

Buck filled him in on the latest development. Hank was quiet for a minute.

"Fuck," he said. "What do you need?"

"This was a big case back then; I'm sure you guys were involved. I need everything the FBI has from back then right up until now. Since this is still an open investigation, I bet you have someone still working on it."

"Let me make some calls," said Hank. The call disconnected, and Buck sat back. The little bug in his brain was moving faster.

Chapter Twenty-Seven

Buck had checked in with Dr. Kellerman and her team, and she reported that the last of the remains were on their way to Grand Junction and that she was sending her team to a hotel near the hospital to get some sleep. She would meet up with Sima Kalishe in the morning to analyze the skeletal remains. Buck thanked her for her help and headed back to the mobile command center. He stepped inside and told Paul and Detective Apodaca to shut down and head home to spend some time with their families. They wouldn't be able to do anything until they got back some more information on the victims.

He took the evidence bags containing the ribbons and buttons and put them in his backpack. He looked around the command center to make sure he hadn't missed anything and then walked over, pulled down the three missing person flyers from the whiteboard and erased the board after taking a picture of the information they had written down about their third victim.

He grabbed his backpack, locked the door and stepped out into the fading light. The air was crisp, and he figured it wouldn't be long before the Grand

Mesa received its first snow of the season. He nodded to the Delta County public works driver and stood by as the driver hooked up the command center to the county flatbed truck and headed for Delta.

Buck slid into his Jeep and called the Delta County dispatcher while driving towards the lodge. He asked the dispatcher to release the deputies blocking the road at both ends. He didn't want to be around when the hordes of media people realized that they could now enter what was left of the crime scene. Earlier, he'd had a team from public works fill in all the holes and cover them with leaves and broken branches. He didn't want to give the media too much to look at.

He drove past the west blockade, waved to the deputy placing the barricades in the back of his SUV and continued up the road to the lodge. He parked in the lot, grabbed his backpack and headed for the front doors. He was early for dinner with Vicky Talmadge and figured he could finish some work before they ate. He planned to head for Grand Junction after dinner and sack out in his hotel room for a couple of hours. He wanted to get to the Delta County Sheriff's Office early so he could get the conference room set up to use as their new command center. He knew if he didn't get there early, Bax and Paul would beat him there.

The hostess showed him to a window seat

overlooking the lake and he set his backpack on the floor and pulled out his laptop.

"I see you're wrapping up on the other side of the lake."

Buck looked up and nodded to Ray Rasmussen, who'd appeared out of nowhere.

"Can't say I won't be happy to see you go," he said. "All those media folks are good for business, but I'm getting tired of telling them I don't know anything about anything. Would like to get back to normal."

Buck nodded. "Can't say I blame you. They can be relentless. Listen, thanks for your employee list. We're still checking some of the names, but other than some minor violations, your folks look good to go."

"That makes me feel good. Would hate to think I have a serial killer working here."

He spotted some folks stepping up to the front desk and excused himself, and Buck opened his laptop and opened the investigation file. Around the CBI office, Buck was known as a technological dinosaur. He was happiest when he had paper files and his little notebook, but the times were changing, and Buck tried to change with them.

CBI had gone digital a couple of years back,

so instead of having a blue binder for each case, Buck just had to open a program on his laptop. The new case was automatically assigned a case number, and Buck would list everyone who needed access to the file and send them email invites. All evidence, lab reports, photos, etc., that were part of the case would be uploaded to the file, and anyone needing access just had to open the file. That was much better than the old system, where everything had been placed in the binder by hand, and Buck would spend half his time tracking down who had the binder.

Even for a tech dinosaur like Buck, this made his life so much easier, and he had ready access to anything he needed. Buck just had to click on a file and open the chronology page, which was the first page in the file. Nothing was ever entered into the file without a note entered in the chronology first. The chronology kept track of everything that happened in the investigation.

Buck was reading through the autopsy reports on the first two victims. There was nothing out of the ordinary in either autopsy. The young women had been drugged and strangled and had died not long after being abducted, but how did that fit with the third victim? James Chamberlain had been missing for twenty-three years only to end up as a pile of bones at the bottom of a hole under a white cross. Two thoughts came to Buck at the same time. Did the person who abducted him twenty-three years ago kill him, and why, or had James Chamberlain run into the serial killer and was just another victim?

Buck had doubts about his first supposition. What made more sense was that James Chamberlain had been living someplace from the time he was six years old until a year or two ago and somehow encountered the serial killer. Buck, like most cops, didn't believe in coincidence, but he also was a realist and understood that sometimes things happened, coincidence or not.

He'd just made a note in the file to follow up on that thought when a shadow crossed his table. He looked up from his laptop and almost didn't recognize Vicky Talmadge. Each time he'd seen her, she was in baggy sweatshirts and khaki pants. The woman standing in front of him was stunning, and he couldn't help but stare. Vicky wore a skirt that stopped three inches above her knee and showed off her shapely legs. She wore high heels and a button-down blouse that accented a very nice figure. Buck stood, walked around and pulled out her chair. He glanced at himself in the fading light of the window and realized he was wearing a three-day-old T-shirt and dirty jeans. He felt self-conscious. He sat, closed his laptop and looked at Vicky.

"Wow," he said.

Vicky laughed. "In my line of work, men don't notice me. It's nice to dress up once in a while and be appreciated for being a woman and not just a dog handler."

She noticed Buck look at himself in the mirror and she laughed. He laughed along with her, and that seemed to break the ice. The waitress came by the table, and Buck ordered a Coke and Vicky ordered a glass of the house red wine. They spent a few minutes looking at the menus, ordered dinner and sat back for a casual conversation.

Buck found Vicky to be interesting and easy to talk to. He hadn't sat down in this kind of setting with a woman since Lucy had passed away and had been uncomfortable in the past. Vicky made the discomfort go away. They spent most of their dinner talking about their lives before today and how Vicky had gotten into working with cadaver dogs. He discovered it was a family business and that her father and brother had been involved with search and rescue dogs. Her father had passed on a couple of years back, and her brother and his dog were killed in an avalanche in California while searching for victims from a previous avalanche.

She was fascinated by some of Buck's past cases and asked a lot of questions. He also gave her a brief rundown on where he was today with this current case.

"What do you do when you run into a brick wall like you're describing?" she asked.

Buck smiled. "I go fly-fishing. I use that to help clear my mind. Once you settle on a nice stretch of river and cast your fly into the water, you have to clear your mind of everything except you, the fly and the fish. If you lose focus, you lose the fish."

Buck hadn't realized how late it had gotten, and he still had the hour drive back to Grand Junction ahead of him. He asked the waiter for the bill, which he paid with a credit card. He stepped around and pulled out Vicky's chair, and they walked into the lobby.

"If I'm out of line, please let me know, but would you like to spend the night here? With me?" she asked. Buck smiled, and she took his hand and led him towards the elevator.

* * *

Buck slid out of Vicky's bed and checked his watch. He grabbed a quick shower, dressed, walked around the bed and kissed her on the cheek. She started to stir, and he told her to go back to sleep and to be careful in Peru. He pet Jasper, who was sleeping near the door, and told him the same thing. He left the room and headed for his Jeep. He had a lot he wanted to get done today, and his mind was clearer than it had been in the past couple of days. He smiled and pulled out of the parking lot.

Chapter Twenty-Eight

Bax couldn't sleep, so she slid out of bed, grabbed a beer from the refrigerator and grabbed her laptop. She sat on the couch, curled her legs under her, pulled the blanket off the back and wrapped up in it. She propped the laptop on the arm of the couch and opened the investigation file.

Something was nagging at her, but she wasn't sure what it was. Buck always talked about the little bug that ran around in his brain during an investigation, and although she had never experienced a little bug, she understood what it felt like to have a thought running around she couldn't quite put her finger on.

She opened the chronology page, logged into the file and noticed that Buck had been in the file earlier in the evening. He left a note that he was reviewing the autopsy files. She checked the time and figured he was sleeping, so she didn't want to call him to see if he'd found anything they might have missed.

She skipped the autopsy files and opened the video file that Mel had uploaded about an hour ago. She wondered if Mel and George ever slept, or if they took turns, because one of them always seemed to be in the office. She clicked on the file and the note from Mel.

Mel: The file was shaking from the loud music vibrating the camera. I ran it through a stabilizer program, and this is the best I could get. I hope it helps. P.S. You should be sleeping instead of looking at videos.

Bax laughed and took a sip of her beer. It was funny how well Mel knew her. She clicked on the video and let it play. The image was better; she could make out more detail in the bar, but the grungy guy was still a bit blurry. She watched the video several more times and was about to turn it off when the guy stood up and walked towards the back of the bar. She wasn't sure how she had missed that before.

She checked the time stamp and noted it was still several hours after Angie Wilde had left the bar. She pulled up additional video files that she had gotten from Vic, and she found one that captured the hall leading to the restrooms. She let the video play and then slowed it as she approached the same time stamp. She advanced it frame by frame, and there, clear as day, was the grungy guy heading towards the men's restroom.

The guy in the video looked like Mike Kirby, the maintenance man from the lodge. He stepped into the well-lit hall and walked past the camera. She let the video run, and five minutes later, she spotted the back of his head as he headed back towards the bar.

She sat back and took another sip of beer. "The bar was a long way from Grand Mesa," she said out loud. "What was Mike Kirby doing there?"

She remembered what Vic, the owner of the bar, had said. The staff and customers called him Ultra. It made sense. Mike Kirby, M. K., MK-Ultra. She could understand why people would think he was on some drugs with the way he acted.

She ran the first video for another half hour when another man walked into the bar and sat opposite Mike Kirby. She paused the video. She wondered who this guy was. He was short and bald. He was thin, but he had a good build under his T-shirt. He signaled the bartender, and a beer was delivered to the table. He and Mike Kirby talked like old friends.

Bax looked at her watch. If she hurried, she could get to the bar just before closing time. She threw on a pair of jeans and a sweatshirt, clipped her gun and badge to her belt and raced out the door, laptop in hand. Since the streets were empty at this time of the morning, she ran as many stoplights as she could, then pulled up to the curb in front of Tiny's Bar and Grill. She grabbed her laptop and raced to the door, which was locked. She banged on the door, and when the bartender, who was stacking the chairs on the tables, shook his head no, she pulled out her badge and held it to the window in the door.

Not looking happy, the bartender glanced at the badge and unlocked the door. "Kind of late, Officer," he said. "Can't whatever this is wait until morning? I have a bunch of cleaning up to do."

Bax was out of breath. "I just need a minute of your time."

She pushed past him and set her laptop on the bar. She opened it and clicked on the video that was still on the screen. She turned it so the bartender could see it.

"Do you know who this guy is?" she asked, pointing to the guy sitting opposite Mike Kirby.

The bartender stepped around the bar and turned up the bar lights. He looked at the still frame from the video.

"Yeah," he said. "That's Ultra."

"What about the guy sitting opposite him?"

He looked at the frame again. "That's Joker."

Bax looked at him. "Are they friends?"

"I think so. I heard they were in the army

together and go to some thing at the VA Center a couple of nights a week. They come in here afterwards."

"What kind of thing?" she asked.

He pulled up the sleeve on his left arm, and she spotted the Semper Fi tattoo. "It's like a group session. Lots of guys go. It's a good chance to discuss any issues you might have adapting to civilian life." He pointed to the picture. "Don't know the specifics, but those two seem to have a lot of issues."

"Any idea where I can find this Joker, and do you happen to know his real name?" she asked.

"Don't know his real name," he said as he pulled the mop from the bucket of soapy water and started mopping the floor. "Might live around here somewhere since the VA Center is just down the street. A lot of guys who go to the VA Center live in the area. What'd he do, anyway?"

"Just need to talk to him about something. Have you seen him around?"

The bartender stopped mopping and thought for a beat. "Now that I think about it, I don't think I've seen him in here in a week or more, which is odd. I know the last time Ultra was in here, he was upset because he couldn't get ahold of him."

Bax closed her laptop, thanked him for his help and ran out the door. She slid into her Jeep and headed for the morgue at the hospital. She knew it was early, but someone was always on duty. She understood how Buck felt when his little bug started dancing around.

Chapter Twenty-Nine

Buck pulled into the parking lot for the Delta County Sheriff's Office and parked his Jeep. He grabbed his backpack and was sliding out of the seat when his phone chimed. He looked at the number and smiled.

"Hey, kiddo. What's got you up so early?"

"Dad," said Cassie. "The last time I talked to David and Jason, they told me you were on vacation. Why am I reading about you and another serial killer online?"

Buck laughed. Cassie was Buck's middle child and was every bit a middle child. In high school, she'd played soccer, ran track and played volleyball. She lettered in all three sports. She was also the one who got in trouble for violating curfew, drinking and whatever other mischief she could find to get into. Buck was surprised when she was accepted to the University of Arizona with a full volleyball scholarship. He was even more surprised when she was accepted into law school. Cassie was never much for regimented education.

Several years ago, she'd dropped out of law school, and her career path took a different track.

She joined the Forest Service and was now working as a wildland firefighter with the Helena Hotshots. The Helena Hotshots were one of the elite firefighting teams based out of Helena, Montana. Buck was not surprised. He never saw her sitting behind a desk as a lawyer. She loved the outdoors, and she was as tough as they came. Lucy wasn't pleased that she'd quit school without any discussion, and she worried whenever Cassie was called out on a fire, but she also knew her daughter, and if this was where she was happy, then so was her mom.

David was the oldest of Buck's three children and the only one to follow in his footsteps and enter the law enforcement field. He was a patrol sergeant with the Gunnison Police Department and worked as the night shift supervisor.

Jason, his youngest son, was an architect, and he lived in Boulder with his wife, Kate, and their three children. Of all of Buck's kids, Jason was the most sensitive, always worried about Buck's job. He was also the one who had continued to follow Catholicism, just like his mom, and seemed to get more involved in his church after Lucy died.

"I was on vacation," he said. "This case kind of fell into my lap."

He told her as much about the case as he felt comfortable sharing, and she listened without saying anything, like she always did, until he was finished. Since Lucy had passed away, Cassie acted as his sounding board when he needed a different perspective on a case.

"So let me get this straight," she said. "A cadaver dog out for a walk just happened to stumble on eleven old graves, and you have now determined that this is the work of a serial killer." She paused for a second. "I'll bet Hank Clancy is just thrilled with you again." She laughed, and Buck joined her. "That is the weirdest thing I've ever heard," she said.

They both laughed again, and she told him she was up this early because they were shipping out to California for another huge wildfire. He told her to be careful; she told him to do the same, and he disconnected the call.

He entered the lobby, checked in with the deputy on duty and was buzzed into the back area. He found the empty conference room, dragged in a whiteboard and fired up his laptop. He attached the pictures of the three identified victims to the whiteboard, opened his camera and rewrote the notes they had written earlier. He stepped back from the board and stared at it. He was lost in thought when his laptop chimed with an incoming message. He opened his laptop.

The file Hank sent on the James Chamberlain

kidnapping was thinner than Buck had hoped it would be. They'd interviewed twenty people who worked at the Chamberlain home, and no one stood out. Buck read the interview transcripts for each person. He had to agree with the FBI agent who did the interviews. Nothing jumped out at him either. There was some contact made with several known pedophiles in the area, but nothing came of that either. He looked at the forensic report, and other than one set of fingerprints that they never identified, there was no physical evidence that pointed to an intruder. It was as if James Chamberlain had disappeared into space.

Buck opened the investigation file that Mel had been able to get from the original Palm Beach detective, and it contained less than the FBI file. He set the file aside after reading what amounted to nothing. He looked back at the FBI file and opened a tab marked Sightings. Now, this file was a little more interesting. Over the past twenty years, there had been more than a hundred sightings of James Chamberlain, in almost every state. Buck read through them, and one report caught his attention. The FBI had interviewed a woman in Carbondale, Colorado, who swore that the picture looked like a kid who used to play with her kids. She said his father was a pastor, and the family had moved to Carbondale from someplace in Florida when the kid was seven or eight.

The FBI agent interviewing the woman noted

that she was a day drinker and seemed to be fixated on this case. Over the years, up until three years ago, she had made a dozen reports, which did not appear to have been taken seriously. The agent had spoken with the father, who looked at the picture and said it didn't look anything like his son and that the lady was nuts. The child was at school, and nothing in the notes indicated that the agent had followed up any further. Buck pulled up the rest of the reports the woman had filed, and she seemed coherent to him. He wondered why no one had followed up on any of the other reports. He sat back in his chair and rubbed his temples.

"Looks like some deep thinkin' goin' on," said Sheriff Buckman as he stepped into the room and chuckled.

"What's so funny, Sheriff?" asked Paul.

"I just read through the overnight reports. My deputies caught three high school kids at one a.m. with a pickup truck loaded with crosses that they were driving around and hammering into the ground. They thought it was funny until we called their parents at three a.m. to come get them. Then it wasn't so funny anymore."

He looked at the whiteboard. "The media is going nuts for more information. The switchboard has recorded over two hundred calls from the media and people looking for a reward. We're also inundated with calls from citizens reporting roadside crosses, and we're not alone. The news last night reported the same thing happening all over the country. People who have missing loved ones are calling the FBI and the local police to dig up crosses in their area to look for their missing. It's tragic. The cops in a town in Virginia found a guy digging holes along a rural highway. He was desperately searching for his missing daughter and believed she was buried under the cross. This isn't helping us any."

"You want to hear something even weirder?" said Detective Apodaca, who had entered the room behind the sheriff. "I was talking to Special Agent Carpenter last night, and there's a guy on the internet selling serial killer cross kits. He'll customize the quantity and even customize the design and color of the crosses if you want to create a signature. He's had forty-seven sales, and the FBI is tracking those people down."

Buck slid his laptop so the sheriff could see the screen. "Read this," he said. He sat there sipping his Coke while the sheriff read the sighting report. When he was finished, he slid the laptop back to Buck.

"You think there's something hinky about these reports?"

"I'm not sure," said Buck. "All the other reports

over the years were discounted for one reason or another, yet no one seemed to follow up with this woman after the original report was investigated. I'm wondering if there's more to this than the rantings of a drunk woman."

"Paul Weaver's the sheriff over there. Let me give him a call and see if he can have someone run over there and interview the lady. Email me those reports." Buck pulled up the sheriff's email and hit send.

Sheriff Buckman turned to leave. "Oh, I meant to tell you. We found out who leaked the story to the press. One of my overnight nine-one-one operators has a true crime podcast. He got wind of the story and thought he had an exclusive. He jumped from five hundred followers to over fifty thousand overnight. He also went from employed to unemployed."

There was a buzz in the room, and Buck let it go for a bit. Once everyone settled down, Buck walked them through the FBI report on James Chamberlain and the sightings report from Carbondale.

"You want me to go check it out?" asked Paul.

"Hal's going to call the Garfield County sheriff and see if he can spare a deputy to run by first. Let's see if he comes back with anything. Follow up with

Max and see if she has any new identities for us. Have you heard from Bax?"

"She left me a cryptic message that she was going to check out a couple of things and she'd see us later," said Paul.

Buck reached for his phone when it rang. He looked at the number and put it on speaker.

"Hey, George. What's going on?" said Buck.

"Hi, Buck. We finished up the background checks on the lodge employees and I wanted to run one of them by you. One of the employees, a guy who's been there about ten years, has a military file, but it's sealed. Wanted to see if you wanted me to go really deep or if you want to try some other sources first."

Buck didn't have to read between the lines to know what George was asking. A couple of months back, the team had been involved in an investigation into a dead state brand inspector and a bunch of dead cows. The investigation had also uncovered murder, human trafficking and baby farming. It was determined that the cows were killed by airborne botulinum toxin, and the general in charge of a secret lab that had been built in the Colorado mountains to replace Plum Island in New York was concerned that this lab might have been the cause of the deadly toxin. When the investigation stalled, the general gave Buck a sophisticated encryption breaking software to get into some government files. He let Buck keep the software with the promise to use it wisely.

"Let's hold off on that for a bit. Let me make a call and get back to you." Buck disconnected the call and dialed a number. Harriet answered right away.

"Good morning, Deputy Taylor. How can I help you?" said Harriet.

He had no idea how she did it, but the few times he had contacted Harriet, he always got what he needed. Harriet was a voice with a touch of a Southern accent who was at the other end of a number the U.S. Marshals Service had given him.

A year or so back, Buck had been testifying in federal court in Denver during the murder trial of a survivalist drug dealer who had killed a DEA agent. One day, after court was dismissed, Buck and Jess Gonzales, the special agent in charge of the DEA's Grand Junction Field Office and one of Buck's closest friends, were talking outside the courthouse when all hell broke loose, and people ran for cover. The marshals who were escorting the prisoner were ambushed in the parking garage, and Buck and Jess raced to their rescue.

Once the dust settled, the prisoner, one of the

marshals and the ambushers were dead, but a lot of people in the garage that afternoon survived, thanks to Buck and Jess. To honor Buck, the U.S. Marshals Service made him a full-fledged deputy marshal, and as part of that designation, he was given a special number that he could call anytime, day or night, and Harriet would get him whatever he needed. He had used the number several times and often wondered if Harriet was one woman or an entire team of women, but whatever she was, he appreciated the help.

Buck explained what he was looking for, and Harriet told him she would see what she could find out. She told him she would get back to him as soon as she had something to report. Buck disconnected the call and sat back. For some reason, he always felt like he was making progress when he spoke with Harriet. He hoped it would be the same this time.

Chapter Thirty

Bax parked outside the emergency room entrance at St. Mary's Medical Center, grabbed her backpack and slid out of her Jeep. She flashed her badge to the night attendant, grabbed the elevator and exited one floor down. She walked down the hall to the morgue.

Darcy Kingman was the overnight intake attendant, and she was sitting behind her desk reading a trashy romance novel when Bax walked in. Darcy looked up and smiled. Darcy was a middle-aged divorcée who was raising a teenage daughter on her own. She loved romance novels and enjoyed talking with Bax whenever she had the chance.

"Hey, Darc," said Bax. "Anything good?" she asked, pointing towards the book.

Darcy smiled. "Just daydreaming about the long-haired, muscular hunk of a man who someday will sweep me off my feet and carry me away from here."

Darcy and Bax laughed. She looked at the clock on the wall. "So, what brings you to my crypt at such an ungodly hour?" asked Darcy.

Bax pulled out her phone, found the picture she was looking for and handed the phone to Darcy. "You got any John Does on ice who look like this guy?"

Darcy looked at the picture on Bax's phone, turned on her computer, clicked on the morgue inventory page and worked her way down the page. "How far back are you thinking?" she asked Bax.

"Two, maybe three weeks. I know you release the unclaimed bodies after thirty days, so I'm hoping he might have come in after the last release."

Darcy worked her way down the screen for a few minutes, then returned to one picture and clicked on the file.

Bax walked around the desk, stood behind her chair and read the file. John Doe was found in an alley with a fentanyl overdose; the needle was still in his arm. EMTs noted the body was cold when they arrived on the scene.

Bax noticed something in the EMT's notes and pointed to it. The left pant leg was drenched with urine, and the syringe still contained enough fentanyl to kill a horse. There were also no track marks on either arm.

Bax was about to ask, but Darcy was way ahead of her and was pulling on a pair of nitrile gloves while pushing the button under the desk to unlock the door to the morgue. She consulted the sticky note in her hand and walked along the row of refrigerated drawers until she found the one she was looking for. She signed the small card stuck to the drawer, opened the door and pulled out the drawer.

Bax stepped next to her as she pulled down the sheet, exposing the face, and Bax compared the face with the picture on her phone.

"Sure looks like him," she said.

Bax pulled the sheet down, exposing both arms, and grabbed a small magnifying glass off the counter; she looked at his arms, legs, toes and groin area. Anyplace where a junkie would shoot up so no one would know. After twenty minutes, she looked up.

"There's just the one needle mark. Do you have the tox screen?"

Darcy walked over to the computer on the counter, logged in, entered the victim ID number and opened the file. She waved Bax over. While Bax read the report, Darcy entered a side room and came out with a clear plastic bag containing the John Doe's belongings. She signed the evidence log, opened the bag and laid the items on one of the autopsy tables.

Bax was reading the tox report when Dr. Eric

Faraday walked into the autopsy suite and looked around. "Good morning, Darcy, Agent Baxter. What's going on?"

Bax called him over to the computer. "Glad you're here, Doc." She pointed to the screen. "If I'm reading this right, his alcohol level was three times the legal limit." He nodded. "Tell me about the fentanyl number."

Dr. Faraday looked at the numbers on the screen. "Looks like this poor fella had enough fentanyl in him to kill him. There are no signs of any other drugs, which in itself is kind of unusual. Most victims of a fentanyl overdose die because they didn't know the drug they were injecting was mixed with fentanyl. Even street junkies know that shooting straight fentanyl is a death sentence. There's no way to control the dosage." He walked over to the table, picked up the syringe and looked at it.

"The EMT's note is correct. There's enough fentanyl left in this syringe to kill a horse and then some. Unless this guy was determined to kill himself, he would have never used up that much fentanyl. What's left in the syringe is worth two or three hundred dollars. Mixed right, that amount could last him three or four weeks."

Bax showed him the one needle mark, and he stood and thought for a minute. He took the magnifying glass Bax still held, started at the head and worked his way down the body. He called Bax over and pointed to the neck area.

"See the purple tint here on the neck and arm? Those are bruises. Someone grabbed this guy and then, probably using a forearm, pinned him to the wall where he was found."

"Why didn't that get caught on the autopsy?" asked Bax.

"It's not unusual for bruising to not show up for a day or two after the body has been refrigerated. This is light-colored, so it happened close to his death."

Darcy looked at Bax and then the doctor. "It sounds like this guy was murdered."

Dr. Faraday nodded. Bax pulled her phone off her belt and dialed a number. The phone rang several times, and a sleepy voice said, "Hello."

"Jess, it's Bax. I need you to grab some coffee and head over to the morgue. We just found another murder victim."

Bax pulled the fingerprint card from the victim's file and noted that the analyst did not get any hits on Joker's prints. She opened the investigation file, forwarded the prints to Mel and George and asked them to check the military database. She leaned against the counter. She knew she had learned a lot tonight, but did what she learned get them any closer to finding the killer?

She thanked Darcy and Dr. Faraday for their help, pulled out her phone and dialed Buck.

Chapter Thirty-One

Buck spent fifteen minutes talking to Bax while he was across the street from the sheriff's office, picking up breakfast burritos for the team. He walked back to the office and was buzzed in to the back. He put the burritos on the table and opened the bottle of Coke he'd bought.

"Just got off the phone with Bax. She played a hunch, and it paid off. Angie Wilde complained about a grungy-looking guy in the bar the night she disappeared. She felt he was watching her, and that's why she left the bar. Bax found him on the CCTV cameras from the bar. She also spotted him sitting at the table with another guy."

Buck continued explaining about Mike Kirby, the maintenance man at the lodge, and his connection to a guy named Joker, whom he was concerned about because he couldn't find him.

"Bax stopped by the morgue this morning and found this guy, Joker, listed as a John Doe. The cause of death was listed as a fentanyl overdose. They took another look this morning, and Bax and the pathologist now believe Joker was murdered. When Bax first interviewed him, Mike Kirby mentioned that Joker wanted to tell him something important."

"So," said Sheriff Buckman. "Bax identified the grungy man as this Mike Kirby from the lodge, and she believes the guy he met on the CCTV was this guy Joker, but who killed this Joker fella, and why? And what does this have to do with the eleven bodies we found?"

Paul set his burrito on the table. "It's about six degrees of separation. Angie Wilde was freaked out by this guy in the bar, which leads to Kirby. That's one degree. Kirby was in the military and knew this guy, Joker. That's two degrees. Joker is killed by someone unknown. That's three degrees. Angie was murdered along with ten other people, that's four degrees, and Kirby works at the lodge near where the bodies were found, that's five degrees."

"So, what's the sixth degree?" asked Sheriff Buckman. "Is this Mike Kirby our serial killer and the sixth degree?"

"It's possible. That's what we need to find out," said Buck. "I asked Bax to head over to the VA Health Center. The bartender told her that he thinks both Kirby and Joker go to the VA Center for group therapy."

Buck's phone chimed, and he checked the number and answered. "Hey, Mel."

"Buck, we got a match on the prints from that unknown body at the morgue. His name is Guy Martindale. He's not in our databases, so he hasn't had any run-ins with the law as a civilian, but his military record is a different story. Martindale left the army after ten years with a dishonorable discharge. He did two tours in Afghanistan, and then he punched out an officer. He spent five of his ten years in Leavenworth military prison and was released ten years ago."

"That's great, Mel. Did you give the info to Bax?"

"Yeah. She and Detective Maldonado were going into the VA Center."

"Hey, Mel. Just a thought. You had access to some of Mike Kirby's military records. Is there any chance their paths crossed? Maybe in Afghanistan."

George came on the line. "Hey, Buck. I went through the records as far as I could, and there's no crossover between those two. There are two possibilities: they met up sometime during the last ten years at some VA outpatient group thing, or Mike Kirby was also in Leavenworth, but we have no way of knowing which unless we can get that portion of his records. There has to be a reason his records are sealed, so my money is on the latter, that they met in prison."

Buck's phone chimed with another incoming call.

"George," said Buck. "Max is calling. Let me call you back."

"Hi, Max. What's going on?"

"Hi, Buck. How's my favorite cop?" asked Max.

"Good, Max."

"Great," said Max. "I wanted to let you know that we identified five more of your victims. I let Dr. Kalishe know so she can have the coroner notify the next of kin, and I loaded the details in the investigation file."

"That's awesome, Max. Any luck with the other three?"

"We got good samples from two sets of remains, but we can't find a match. We'll keep trying. The last set, the DNA was too degraded. We're gonna try the old-fashioned way. We took impressions of the teeth and are putting them out to the dental community. After all this time, it's a long shot, but we'll give it a try. Who knows? We might get lucky."

"Thanks, Max. Anything else?" asked Buck.

"We're going through what was left of the

clothes, but we're not getting much. I'll let you know if we find anything else."

"Thanks, Max."

"You're a good man, Buck Taylor. God will watch over you." Max disconnected the call.

Paul was busy clicking away on his laptop, and Detective Apodaca was hanging new missing person pictures and writing information on the whiteboard as Paul pulled it out of the file or off the internet. Buck was heading out the door when Sheriff Buckman waved him to his office.

Buck sat in one of the visitors' chairs, and the sheriff put his phone on speaker. "Go ahead, Paul. I've got Buck Taylor sitting here, and you're on speaker."

Paul Weaver, the Garfield County sheriff, came on the line. "Hey, Buck. It's been a while. I've got Sergeant Tallie McNeill sitting here. I sent Tallie to visit the woman who filed the report, Mrs. Elinore Hammersmith. Tallie, give them your thoughts."

"Yes, sir," said Tallie McNeill. She cleared her throat. "Mrs. Hammersmith still lives in the same house in Carbondale and has for over forty years. She remembers the child she reported to the FBI tip line. When I spoke with her this morning, I didn't get any impression that she was a drinker or had any memory issues. Seems pretty sharp for an older woman. Anyway. She said the kid the FBI was looking for was named Joshua Davenport, and when his family moved in, he was six or seven. She remembers that his parents were very protective of him. Would never allow him to come to parties or have sleepovers, nothing like that. They claimed he had a peanut allergy, so the kids only got to play together outside, and the mother was always around. She said that after the FBI came to talk to her and then went over to talk to the dad, from that point on, the parents were very cold to her. Each time the news would show an age progression picture of the kid, she would call the FBI, but she never received another response.

"She showed me a picture of the kid in question with her two kids when they were about nine. It's not a great picture, but it could be the kid they were looking for. We called her daughter, who lives in Kansas, and I emailed her the picture, and she confirmed what her mom said. Mrs. Hammersmith said Joshua disappeared from his parents' home three years ago. There was no missing person report filed since he was an adult. The neighbors all figured he just up and left. His dad had passed away several years before, and here's the odd thing. Several weeks after Joshua left home, his mother died from cardiac arrest. Mrs. Hammersmith said that Mrs. Davenport was in excellent health before she died."

Buck looked at Sheriff Buckman. He leaned into

the phone. "Excellent report, Sergeant. Paul, can you email us that picture of the three kids, and can you send us the autopsy report?"

"No problem, Buck. Sending them now. So, how does a kid go from a kidnap victim to the victim of a serial killer?"

"Great question, Paul. We'll let you know once we figure it out."

They disconnected the call, and Buck sat for a minute. The sheriff looked at him. "That's a good question." He looked at his watch and stood. "I promised the press a quick briefing this morning, so I'd better get to it."

They both walked out of the office, and Buck returned to the conference room, pulled up the picture and filled in Paul and Detective Apodaca on their call.

"Paul, let's run a background check on the parents of the kid in the picture and see what we can come up with, and let's see if Joshua might have crossed paths with Mike Kirby or Guy Martindale: military, work, social media, anything you can find."

Paul went back to work, and Buck sat looking at the whiteboard. They had a lot more information but not much evidence, and he was frustrated.

Chapter Thirty-Two

Bax and Detective Maldonado parked in the visitor's lot at the VA Health Center, grabbed their backpacks and slid out of their SUVs. They entered the lobby and asked to speak to someone in charge. The receptionist asked them to have a seat while she tracked someone down. They waited about ten minutes, and then a tall, thin, dark-haired man with glasses and wearing a dark suit stepped up to them and introduced himself as Dr. Timothy Abernathy, the hospital administrator. They shook hands, introduced themselves, and asked if there was someplace they could speak in private. He asked them to follow him and headed down a long corridor.

He held open the door to his office and asked them to have a seat, and he stepped behind the simple metal desk and sat.

"How can I help the police today?" he asked.

"Doctor," said Bax. "We appreciate you seeing us, and we'll try not to take up too much of your time. We're investigating several murders, and we are looking for some information on a couple of men who might be patients here. We know you are limited in what you can tell us under HIPAA rules, so we will try to keep this as generic as possible."

The doctor nodded in appreciation and smiled. Bax continued. "One of our victims is a man named Guy Martindale; you may also know him as Joker." Bax spotted the tell as soon as she mentioned the name. The doctor knew Joker. "We have reason to believe he was killed a week ago, and we were able to confirm his identity this morning. We spoke with several people who knew him, and they all told us that he was an outpatient here, in a group of some type."

The doctor regained his composure. "We have all been wondering what happened to Joker. He has missed his last several group sessions and it's not like him. He has been coming here for, I would guess, about ten years, and I can count on one hand the number of sessions he has missed. How was he killed?"

"He was found dead in an alley downtown with a needle full of fentanyl in his arm. He had no ID, so he was held at the morgue as a John Doe. We discovered his identity this morning, and we no longer believe his death was accidental."

"I would agree with that. Joker would never go near drugs of any kind."

"Why is that, Doctor?" asked Detective Maldonado.

"Don't get me wrong," said Dr. Abernathy. "Joker is no saint. He likes his alcohol, but we've been working hard to keep that under control. But he has never been into drugs of any kind, unlike many of our returning vets. Joker saw his share of death in Afghanistan, including many soldiers who died from drug overdoses, and he always said that was not for him."

"His blood alcohol level was three times the legal limit when he was found, Doctor. Would that surprise you?" asked Bax.

The doctor thought for a few seconds. "If he was troubled by something, I could see that happening. According to Dr. Davidson, the group leader, he seemed a little out of sorts during his last group session, but he wouldn't tell anyone what was bothering him. It makes me sad that he died alone and in that condition."

"Doctor, why was he sent here in the first place?" asked Bax.

The doctor looked serious. "I'm sure you've already seen his military record, so I guess there isn't much I could tell you. Joker has anger management issues. Once he was released from Leavenworth prison, he was assigned to us since he grew up in Grand Junction and wanted to return. He has kept those issues under control with a combination of medication, exercise and therapy. In Joker's case, he would have had to continue the therapy for the rest of his life. He was wound very tight."

"Doctor, we were told he was good friends with another patient, Mike Kirby. Have you seen him around?"

The doctor stared at Bax. "You don't think Mike killed him, do you? That's not possible. Those two were like two peas in a pod."

"His name came up during another investigation and we wanted to get some background. His file after his service in Afghanistan is sealed, and we were wondering why."

The doctor showed some agitation. "I'm afraid I can't get into that. Now, if you'll excuse me, I've got a meeting I need to get to."

They all stood, and Bax had just turned for the door when she stopped. "Doctor, one last thing. You mentioned a Dr. Davidson. We'd like to speak with him if he's around."

The doctor stammered a little and looked at his watch. "Dr. Davidson should be running a group for the next forty minutes. You'll find him in one of the meeting rooms down the corridor to the left of where you entered the building. Now, I must be going."

The doctor raced past Bax and Detective Maldonado and headed down the hallway. Bax looked at Detective Maldonado.

"What do you think that was all about?"

"I don't know," said Detective Maldonado, "but the good doctor sure didn't want to talk about Mike Kirby."

"Let's see if we have better luck with Dr. Davidson."

They returned to the reception area and stopped to talk to the receptionist, who pointed them towards a meeting room at the end of the corridor. When they reached the room, Bax looked through the small window in the door and saw twelve people, both men and women, sitting in a circle. One of those people was doing most of the talking, so she assumed he was the doctor, and they waited in the hall until the group broke up.

They pushed through the door and approached the doctor, who was placing some files in his backpack. He looked up, and Bax and Detective Maldonado flashed their badges.

"Dr. Davidson?" asked Bax.

The doctor nodded. He was of average height and weight, and his upper body was well-developed. He had short blond hair, was clean-shaven, and had a severely pockmarked face. He looked at their badges and stood up.

"How can I help you?" he asked. His mood was light, and he didn't show any of the agitation that Dr. Abernathy had displayed. He had an easygoing smile, and Bax figured he was planning to charm them. She was ready. She spent a few minutes giving him the same information they had given Dr. Abernathy, but he didn't display any anxiety. He sat in the chair next to him when Bax told him that Joker had been murdered, and he showed little to no emotion. To Bax, it seemed like he was keeping his emotions in check, which she found odd.

"I'm sorry to hear about Joker," he said. "We were all very concerned when he missed the last few sessions."

He told them the same thing when they mentioned the drug overdose. He didn't see that side of Joker, and he said he was having trouble wrapping his head around it, but it didn't look that way to Bax.

"Doctor," said Bax, looking around the room. "I didn't notice your name on the directory when we came in. If you don't mind me asking, what kind of doctor are you?" She smiled at him.

"I'm a psychiatrist, but I no longer practice. I volunteer here and monitor a dozen or so group sessions, but I no longer see patients."

"May I ask why?" she asked.

He focused his eyes on Bax, which made her feel uncomfortable, then he switched focus. "I spent a great deal of my life in the military, trying to put back together broken men and women, with little success. It got to be too much, and I decided to move on. I was always fascinated with history, so I am now a full professor on the faculty of Colorado Mesa University, in the history department. Teaching history does not require the same inner strength being a psychiatrist does."

"Doctor, what can you tell us about Mike Kirby? We were told he was in some of your group sessions."

"What would you like to know . . . Agent Baxter, is it?"

Bax nodded and watched him for tells. She had spent a lot of time working with Buck on understanding micro-expressions, those little tells that people don't even realize they have, and she had become very good at reading people.

"Anything you might be willing to share. We are having trouble accessing his file."

"Mike is a troubled man. He's also a gentle soul who has had some rough spots in his life. We have worked hard to keep him grounded."

"I got the impression from speaking with him that he might have suffered a brain injury during his time in the war. Do you know anything about that?" asked Bax.

"I'm sorry, Agent Baxter, HIPAA will not allow me to answer those kinds of specific questions. You will need to discuss those with the patient. Now, if you'll excuse me, I need to get back to the campus for an afternoon of enriching the minds of students on the truth about the Civil War."

"Doctor," said Bax. "This is a murder investigation, and anything you can tell us would be appreciated."

"I wish I could help, but I need to get going."

He picked up his backpack, shook their hands and walked out the door. Bax watched him go.

Detective Maldonado looked at Bax. "You get the feeling no one wants to talk about Mike Kirby? And what's the deal about giving up being a psychiatrist and becoming a history teacher? Guy gave me the creeps."

Bax nodded. "Yeah, I know what you mean."

She pulled out her phone and hit a button, and the phone rang on the other end.

"Hey, Bax," said Mel. "What's up?"

"Hiya, Mel. I need you to run a background check on Dr. Brian Davidson. He used to be a psychiatrist, and now he works part time as a volunteer at the VA Health Center and works the rest of the time as a history professor at Colorado Mesa. He also mentioned he spent a lot of years in the military."

"Seems odd someone would change professions that drastically," said Mel. "Let me dig into him and see what I can find."

Bax disconnected the call. "Why don't you start looking around on campus and see what you can find about the good doctor? I'm gonna head to Delta and talk to Buck."

They headed for their SUVs and left in different directions. Bax stopped on the way, grabbed a late fast-food lunch and ate in the parking lot.

She was troubled by Dr. Davidson, but she didn't know why. She couldn't find any tells when he spoke, like he was keeping his subconscious under control, and the way he looked at her made her feel creepy. She couldn't explain it, but there was something about him that was off-putting. She finished her lunch, scrunched up the wrapper from the burger, threw it into the back seat and pulled out of the parking lot. Maybe Buck could help her find the answers.

Chapter Thirty-Three

Brian Davidson drove the eight blocks back to the campus and parked in the staff parking lot. He turned off his truck and sat for a minute. He was trying to wrap his head around what had just happened, and it unnerved him. He was always in control of any situation he was involved in. That came from being smarter than everyone else, and that had always served him well, except for today.

He slid out of his truck, grabbed his backpack and headed to the lounge where he was holding class today. He hated the classroom environment, found it stuffy and overbearing. He tried to find different locations to hold his lectures. He liked the library and the cafeteria. Sometimes he would hold his classes off campus, under a tree in the parking lot or in the local coffee shop. He believed his students got more out of the lectures when they weren't confined to a square concrete room with no windows.

He raced up the stairs and entered the lounge. He was five minutes late, but from what he could tell, no one had left the lounge. He put his backpack down and started speaking. He knew he had their undivided attention because he taught real history, not the made-up, fake crap that someone had written into a history textbook.

Forty minutes later, the bell chimed, and the lounge emptied out. He slowed his breathing and allowed his mind to focus. He wasn't sure what it was about that Agent Baxter, but without knowing it she had pushed his buttons. The way she watched him like she was waiting for him to make a mistake so she could pounce on him. What had set her off? He had never met her before, but there was something about the way she looked at him like she was looking into his soul. He didn't like it much.

He took a sip from his water bottle and had to focus to get his hands to stop shaking. She reminded him of the CIA interrogators he worked with in Afghanistan. Those pompous pricks who thought they were better than everyone else. He wondered if deep down inside, she was laughing at him. No, that wasn't it. She was watching him, looking for something.

He set the water bottle down and stared at it. She had been looking for a tell, some tiny subconscious sign that he was not telling her the truth. She was going to have to work harder than she did to get him to crack. He was trained by the best the CIA and PSYOP had. He knew how to control his tells. He started to feel better, but then he started running the interrogation—that's what it felt like, an interrogation—through his head and he wondered if he had made any mistakes.

The more he thought, the more he was convinced that bitch, Agent Baxter, was trying to trick him. He knew she hadn't gotten to him, but then again, what if she had? He felt himself getting madder with each passing thought. He didn't like the way he felt.

The more he thought about it, the more he realized what had to be done. He was going to have to give them Mike Kirby. That would be the best way to get that bitch out from under his skin. He thought about what he needed to do. He would need to ingratiate himself into Agent Baxter's investigation.

He looked at his watch. He had another lecture starting in twenty minutes and he needed to get his head back in the game. He would figure out how to get involved in the investigation. He also might need to do something to take care of the anxiousness he was feeling. He thought for a minute. Maybe that fat cop who was with the bitch. She didn't look too tough. He smiled. He could see his plan coming together, and he liked what he saw.

Chapter Thirty-Four

Bax walked into the sheriff's office conference room and spotted Buck standing in the corner on the phone. She looked at the whiteboard.

"Looks like we got a few more names," she said. She pointed towards Buck.

"He's talking to Sima," said Paul. "You missed a lot. Our third victim was identified as a guy who disappeared as a kid. He was a rich kid, and it was a national story. He was never found until the other day. Our victim disappeared from Carbondale three years ago, where he had been living all this time. The woman posing as his mother died supposedly from a heart attack a couple of weeks later. Sima did the autopsy on the mom, and Buck is going over a couple of things."

Buck disconnected the call and walked back to the table. "Hey, Bax." He pulled out a chair and sat. "According to Sima, the mom was in excellent health. No sign of heart disease or anything that would explain the heart attack. She did find a tiny pinprick on her right arm and a small bruise on her neck, but her tox screen came back clear, and there were no signs of foul play. The body was cremated, and since she had no other relatives, her belongings were sold at auction, and the house has since been resold. So right now, that's a dead end."

Bax swiveled in her seat. "You think the mother, or whatever she was to our third victim, might have also been murdered after her son disappeared?"

"It's a string we needed to pull on," said Buck. "So, let's focus on the victims the lab identified. Paul."

Paul clicked a couple of keys on his laptop, and Detective Apodaca picked up the black marker and stood next to the whiteboard.

"Victim number four," said Paul. "Trudy Pembrook, Caucasian, thirty-seven, five foot nine, one twenty-five, blond over brown. Trudy was reported missing in July, four years ago, when she didn't show up for her cashier shift at the Rinse N Glow car wash in Buena Vista, Colorado. She was married and had two children, ages twelve and ten. According to the report, she liked to party but kept it to one night a week after her shift ended. Her husband works the night shift at the prison and didn't know she was missing until her boss called him when she was a no-show. He told the investigating officer that she was home all night with the kids, and the kids confirmed that she was there when they went to bed at ten p.m. No one saw her after that. Her car, phone and purse were still at home."

Paul looked at Apodaca to make sure he was ready to continue, and he nodded.

"Victim five. Elena DeRivera, Hispanic, twenty-two, five foot four, one-forty, dark brown over brown. Elena was reported missing by her parole officer after she missed four appointments. That was five years ago. She was a street person and was supposed to do a nickel for distribution but was paroled after two years. From the original missing person report, it doesn't look like anyone spent a lot of time looking for this young woman. They assumed she did a runner, so she fell through the cracks."

Apodaca finished writing and looked at Paul.

"Victim six," said Paul. "Jasmine Powell, Black, eighteen, five foot nine, one thirty-five, black over hazel. Disappeared six years ago. She was reported missing by her parents. She lived in South Carolina but was out here on vacation and looking at colleges. Since she checked in once a week, her parents were not sure where she disappeared. They last spoke to her when she was in Boulder, Colorado. She told her folks she was heading for Ouray, but the family she was going to stay with said she never arrived. The family checked out. Her car and backpack were found at Denver International Airport a week after she disappeared."

The door to the conference room opened, and

Special Agent Carpenter slipped into the room and sat next to Bax.

"Victim seven. Arlene Thurmond, Caucasian, sixty-seven, five foot seven, one-thirty, gray over hazel. Disappeared seven years ago. Arlene was a retired schoolteacher in Avon. According to her children, she was an avid bird-watcher, and on the day she disappeared, she was down on the Eagle River doing an Audubon bird count with some friends. Her friends last saw her when they headed home around six p.m., but Arlene told them she was going to stay for a bit. She was never seen after that. Her car was found in the parking lot where she met her friends.

"Victim eight. Gretchen Overton, Caucasian, thirty-one, five foot seven, one-forty, brown over brown. Gretchen left her home in Hamburg, Germany, nine years ago. According to her father, she took off to find herself. She was an artist, paint and sculpture, and she had a wild spirit. It was not usual for her family not to hear from her for months at a time, so they had no idea when she disappeared or where. The last postcard they received from her, a year after she left home, was from Pikes Peak.

"Max is still working on nine and ten, and the DNA for victim eleven is so degraded that we may never figure out who that person is."

Buck stood up and walked around the table. He hated sitting at a desk, and he needed to stretch.

"Okay," he said. "So, what do we have?"

Bax was the first to answer. "It looks like he was killing one victim a year, so why the change with victims one and two? They were killed three months apart."

"Good," said Buck. "What else?"

"Except for victim three," said Detective Apodaca, "they're all women, and they're all across the board, young, old, Black, White, Hispanic. There doesn't seem to be a pattern."

"Maybe that is the pattern," said Special Agent Carpenter. "Maybe the pattern is the randomness."

Buck looked at him and smiled. "Which will make our job even harder. This is the worst kind of killer, one who attacks for no obvious reason. We have no idea what sets this guy off. The one thing that is clear is that he enjoys killing."

They all thought about what Buck had said. They had a dilemma on their hands because they had no idea when this guy would strike again or where his next victim would come from. Bax broke the silence.

"Victim number one, Angie Wilde, was afraid of

a creepy guy in the bar she thought was watching her. Earlier today, we looked at video from the bar's CCTV cameras, and we think we have identified the creepy guy as Mike Kirby, the maintenance man from the lodge. We also identified his friend Joker. Joker was found dead a week ago in an alley with a fentanyl needle in his arm. He was listed as a John Doe, and the cause of death was an overdose. We reviewed those findings after we identified him, and the coroner has now changed the COD to homicide. Mike Kirby told me he was worried because he couldn't find Joker, who wanted to tell him something important."

Buck's phone chimed, and he looked at the number, excused himself and stepped out of the conference room.

"Buck Taylor."

"Deputy Taylor," said Harriet. "I secured the military file for Michael Kirby and uploaded it to your investigation file. A couple of things of note. I spoke with some of the people involved, and things don't add up."

She went on to explain to Buck what she had read in the file and the conversations she'd had with some people who were there. Buck listened without saying a word. When she finished, he thanked her and entered the conference room. Everyone stopped talking.

"Paul," said Buck. "Please go into the investigation file. The Marshals Service secured Mike Kirby's military record, including the part we were not allowed to see. Put it up on the screen, if you would."

Paul clicked some keys, and the file appeared on the large monitor hanging on the wall.

Buck filled them in on what Harriet had told him. "Kirby spent ten years in Leavenworth for killing five women while he was stationed in Afghanistan. Several months earlier, he had been injured in a raid on the camp and suffered a head trauma. After several months in the hospital, he returned to his unit, part of a military/CIA PSYOP program, but according to the call I just got off of, he had anger management issues and impulse control issues. His anger issues were well known, which is how he ended up in the army, after stabbing his abusive father. Over the course of a year, five Afghan women in the area were murdered. An Army CID investigation led them to Michael Kirby, who, when presented with the fact that his DNA had been recovered at the murder scenes after a lengthy interrogation, confessed to the murders. The five women were drugged and strangled. Their hyoid bones were crushed. There were no signs of sexual assault."

"Why such a light sentence?" asked Sheriff Buckman. "Seems like he should have gotten life."

"There were two reasons," said Buck. "First, we were in a bad way with the Afghan people, and the government wanted to push this under the rug as soon as possible. It was a political move to save face."

"What was the second thing?" asked Bax.

"The investigation was lacking at best. The DNA evidence linking Kirby to the crime was questionable and ended up missing, and other than the confession of a man who had anger issues and was almost incoherent by the time he confessed, according to one source, they had little else. While he was in the hospital, he assaulted several female nurses at the base hospital, so he had a history of violence towards women. They also found some personal items with the bodies that they linked to Kirby. Items like what we found, which, on the face of it, could have been linked to anyone in the military."

"This is interesting," said Paul. "Kirby was awarded a Silver Star and a Purple Heart. I wonder if he still has the ribbons for them?"

Buck's phone chimed; he checked the number and suggested they take a half-hour break. He walked out and answered the call.

Chapter Thirty-Five

Mike Kirby finished connecting the water line to the cabin and loaded the extra pipe onto the back of the ATV. He checked the time on his phone, climbed into the ATV and headed for the maintenance shed. Gus Kramer was putting away some paint cans from a project he had worked on earlier, and he nodded as Mike pulled to a stop outside the shed.

"Get that water line hooked up, Mike?" asked Gus.

Mike nodded but looked distracted. He slid out of the ATV, grabbed the roll of water line and hung it on the wall. Mike was typically more animated at the end of the day, and Gus wondered what was going on.

"You okay, Mike? You seem kind of out of sorts."

Mike shook his head but didn't say anything, so Gus backed off, finished stacking the paint cans and told Mike he'd see him in the morning. Mike liked working with Gus, but sometimes Gus asked too many questions, especially on days when Mike didn't feel like talking.

Mike sat at the desk and pulled out his phone. He opened the news app he had been streaming and reran the report from earlier. The sheriff was talking about one of the victims, a kid who had been kidnapped when he was young and ended up in one of the graves on the other side of the lake as an adult. Mike was having trouble wrapping his head around that. He listened as the sheriff described the condition of the bodies they found. He couldn't comprehend eleven bodies. That was a lot, and he worried. He paused the feed and looked at the picture of the guy who had been kidnapped. He wondered if he had known the guy as an adult. He thought back to the confession he had given when he was questioned by CID. Could he have killed this guy too? He stared at the picture until his eyes blurred.

He had walked along the road yesterday after work and stopped where he thought the graves were. He had no idea why he did it—curiosity, maybe, or something else. Someone did a good job covering up the holes. He spotted several newspeople taking pictures and talking into their cameras. It was like he was listening to a transcript from his trial. Several dead, all strangled. He'd read one article online that mentioned that the victims' hyoid bones were crushed. Could he have done that again? That was what they said he had done to those women in Afghanistan. But how could that be? He was on medication so he wouldn't do that anymore. He thought he should mention it to Dr.

Davidson during his next group. Maybe he needed stronger medicine. He never wanted to go back to being that person again.

The more articles he read and the more news programs he listened to, the more he became concerned that he was to blame. He looked down at his hands. "Could I have strangled eleven people with my bare hands?" he asked out loud. His whole body shook, and he reached into his pants pocket and pulled out his pill bottle. He popped the lid off, and several pills spilled onto the ground. He kneeled and picked them up one by one. He put a pill in his mouth, put the rest of them back in the bottle then dumped another pill into his palm. He put it in his mouth and swallowed water from the bottle next to him. Did he take one or two pills? He couldn't remember.

Mike locked up the maintenance shed and slid into his pickup truck. He pulled out of the parking lot and headed for his cabin. He felt funny, like his heart was racing. He ran off the road twice as the medicine kicked in, almost hitting a tree before making the correction. He parked next to the cabin, shut off the engine and fell out of the door. He stood and staggered to the door and pushed it open. He fell onto the small bed, his head spinning. He closed his eyes, but when he opened them, it wasn't any better.

He tried to stand, fell over and pulled out his

phone, focusing on the numbers that he couldn't get to stop spinning. He located the number and pushed send. The phone fell out of his hand and landed on the floor, and he passed out.

Chapter Thirty-Six

Detective Jessie Maldonado had parked on the outer edge of the grocery store parking lot and went in to pick up dinner and some assorted items for herself and her daughter. Tonight was her daughter's night to cook, and she had given her mom a list. After paying, Jessie walked through the crowded parking lot, got to her personal SUV and opened the back door. She had just placed the grocery bags on the seat when she sensed someone approach from behind her and felt a pressure on her left shoulder.

Her assailant wasn't expecting any resistance when he shoved the tip of the syringe into her shoulder. What he failed to know was that besides her stab-proof ballistic vest, Jessie Maldonado also wore a leather shoulder holster, and he had shoved the tip of the syringe straight into the thickest part of the leather. The tip of the syringe broke off just as he pushed the plunger, and the back of Jessie's jacket was now wet with fluid. He threw away the syringe, reached in and tried to wrap his hands around her throat. Jessie was a big woman, and he had trouble getting a grip on her neck.

Jessie reared back and pushed off the seat,

slamming into the side of the car next to her, and her assailant let go. He punched Jessie in the back of the head, and she saw stars but was able to turn around, grab him by his shirt and his belt and lift him over her head. She body-slammed him onto the hood of the car, and he fell off the hood. He jumped up and landed a hard roundhouse punch right into Jessie's temple and she went down on one knee. She shook her head. The assailant came in for another punch, and Jessie fell backwards. As she did, she sent a wicked snap kick; she connected with something solid and heard a crack. The assailant screamed and backed up.

Jessie reached for her pistol and, with blurry vision, tried to track the assailant, who was hobbling between cars. She dropped her pistol and pulled her ROVER radio off her belt.

She keyed the mic. "Detective four-one-five-seven. Officer down, grocery store, Twelfth and Patterson."

Jessie fell back against the car tire and closed her eyes. A crowd had gathered, and several people were talking to her, asking how they could help. One young man picked her pistol off the ground and placed it in her lap. Sirens could be heard as patrol cars swept into the parking lot from all directions, and people in the crowd waved them over.

The first responder on the scene kneeled next to her and secured her weapon. He keyed his mic and called for an ambulance and paramedics.

"Jessie," he said. "Who did this? Can you give me a description?"

By this point, several more officers had arrived and were working through the crowd, asking people if they saw what had happened and if anyone could describe the person. One man said he saw an average-sized guy wearing a ski mask hobbling across the parking lot. The witness thought he wore faded blue jeans and had some kind of leather jacket on, brown.

The officer put out the description over the radio, and then they kept Jessie comfortable until the ambulance arrived. Someone in the crowd pointed to a syringe lying under Jessie's SUV, and one of the officers took a couple of photos of it and then, with gloved hands, picked it up and placed it in an evidence bag.

Jessie, now conscious, was struggling to sit up when the paramedics arrived. They gave her a quick appraisal, saw the purple bruise on the side of her head and loaded her onto the gurney. The first responding officer locked her car and stayed to wait for the crime scene folks. Jessie, arguing that she was fine, was loaded into the ambulance and was taken to St. Mary's. The other patrol officers slid into their patrol vehicles and searched the area. Two officers remained behind and took witness statements from the folks in the crowd.

Detective Mark Ridgeway was the first detective to arrive at the scene, followed by several more detectives and the chief of detectives.

Detective Ridgeway approached the first responding officer, who handed him Jessie's keys. "So, what do we know so far?" he asked.

"According to several witnesses, none of whom saw how this all started, it appears Jessie was jumped from behind." The officer handed Detective Ridgeway the syringe as the chief of detectives walked up and listened to the conversation.

"We found this syringe under her car. It has a broken tip, and I noticed a large wet spot on the back of her jacket. She was wearing her vest, so it looks like the tip of the syringe broke off in the vest. Jessie must have been able to push her way out of the car, and that was when people heard the first thud. There's a dent in this door." He pointed to the door of the car next to where they were standing, and the chief of detectives examined the door.

"One witness in the next aisle over said the guy punched Jessie in the back of the head, and she started to go down, but she caught herself, grabbed the guy, lifted him over her head and slammed him onto the hood of the car. That's when the rest of the people in the parking lot heard the fight and came running. The guy hit Jessie on the side of the head, and as she went down, she did a snap kick and the guy screamed. He hobbled off towards Twelfth Street. That's when the crowd came to help her."

The chief of detectives took Mark Ridgeway aside. "Could this be related to what you guys have been working on?"

Mark Ridgeway thought for a few seconds. "It could. The syringe, as far as we know, is the weapon of choice for whoever killed those eleven people, but why would the killer risk it all to take on Jessie?"

"Maybe the guy got a surprise," said one of the other detectives. "If Jess was wearing her rumpled suit, she doesn't look like a weight lifter, she looks kind of fat. He might have underestimated her. We've all seen it happen with her before."

"But," said Ridgeway, "that would mean that Jessie and the killer crossed paths. She's seen him."

"Today was your day off," said the chief. "Do we know what Jessie was doing?"

"Yeah," said Ridgeway. "She was with Agent Baxter from CBI. They were doing autopsies and conducting interviews."

"Good. Get with Bax and fill her in, but first, get the groceries out of the back of the car and check on Jessie's daughter. She must be getting worried by now. I'll head over to the hospital to check on Jessie."

Detective Ridgeway unlocked Jessie's SUV and grabbed the bags of groceries off the seat. He walked to his SUV, placed the groceries on the back seat and slid into the driver's seat. He started the engine, pulled out his phone, dialed a number and pulled out of the parking lot.

Chapter Thirty-Seven

Buck clicked on the green button and answered the call. "Yes, sir."

"Buck," said Director Jackson. "The governor would like an update. What can you tell me?"

"Well, sir. We've identified eight victims so far, including the kid who went missing twenty years ago, James Chamberlain. The killer is all across the board, so we are looking at each victim to see if they have anything in common with each other or something or someone else. The FBI thinks the killer might be totally random, which is unusual but not unheard of. We asked the Garfield County sheriff to interview a woman who reported the kid to the FBI starting right after his family moved to Carbondale and reported him every couple of years after that. According to the sergeant who spoke with her, the woman seems credible. I've got George and Mel running background on the parents to see what we can come up with."

The director interrupted. "What a tragedy. To get kidnapped from your home only to end up years later as the victim of a serial killer."

Buck told him about the information they had

gotten from Bax's interviews and Mike Kirby's military file.

"So, this Kirby guy has had a hard time adapting to life after the military, but do we think he could be our serial killer? From what you're telling me, I don't see a lot of evidence in that direction."

"That's the problem, sir. We don't have anything conclusive. I'd like to ask him to come in for a voluntary interview and see if we can shake anything loose. The problem, though, is that, according to Bax, when she spoke with him the first time, he seemed a little unstable, and I don't want to push him over the edge."

"Okay, Buck. Let's see if the voluntary interview thing works. I'll give the governor some talking points for his next press conference. The news media is camped out on his doorstep. Let me know if you need anything from me."

The director disconnected the call, and Buck looked around and noticed it was later than he'd expected. He walked back into the office and filled everyone in on his call with the director.

"Bax, since you have already spoken with Mike Kirby once before, why don't you and Vince run up there tomorrow morning and see if you can get him to come in for a voluntary interview? Okay, everybody, good work today. Let's everyone get some downtime and we'll pick this up again in the morning."

Vince Apodaca and Bax agreed to meet at the lodge for breakfast and then approach Mike Kirby when he came on for his shift. Paul loaded his laptop into his backpack and wished everyone a good night. Buck took a seat next to Agent Carpenter and Sheriff Buckman.

"We made some progress today, Buck," said Sheriff Buckman. "I wish we had more to show for all this work, and now we have a twenty-three-year-old kidnapping case to deal with."

Agent Carpenter looked at them both. "Maybe this is where I can help. Since we had the original kidnap case and didn't do anything with it, how about if I assign two of my people to run with it and take some of the burden off you guys?"

Buck laughed. "FBI trying to cover its ass?"

Agent Carpenter smiled. "Yeah, but maybe we can keep that between the three of us. Let's call it governmental cooperation or goodwill between agencies."

They all laughed. Buck looked at the sheriff. "Hal, you good with that?"

"Yeah. Let's go with that governmental

cooperation thing. I like the sound of that for when I update the media tomorrow."

They grabbed their backpacks and headed out the door. Bax was waiting in the hall, talking to Deputy Sterling. She nodded and walked over to Buck.

"You want to grab some dinner?"

"Yeah, let's go Italian," he said.

They headed out the door into a cool evening. It wouldn't be long until the first snowfall, and Buck was glad the weather had held until they got all the remains out of the ground. They slid into their Jeeps and headed for downtown Grand Junction.

Buck found a parking space across the street from his favorite Italian restaurant and waited while Bax parked in the lot down the block. They met at the door and walked into the most incredible smells imaginable.

The owner greeted them and shook their hands. He made small talk as he led them to their table in the back corner. Buck sat with his back to the wall, and Bax sat across from him. The waiter, dressed in black pants, a white shirt and a black apron, walked up to the table and set a Coke in front of Buck and a glass of house red wine in front of Bax. He placed the basket of bread and the bowl of olive oil and herbs on the table and took their orders. Bax grabbed a piece of bread and dove into the olive oil mixture. Buck smiled.

As they waited for their food to arrive, Bax told Buck more about her conversations with the two doctors who worked with Mike Kirby.

"So, you got a creepy feeling from this psychiatrist turned history professor," he said.

"Yeah. Jessie said the same thing. It wasn't anything he did, just a feeling."

"Okay," said Buck. "What do we know about the doctor?"

"I've asked George and Mel to run background on him and see what else we can find. Seems odd that he would give up being a psychiatrist after all that schooling."

"Some people just burn out after a while," said Buck. "How do you think you want to approach Kirby?"

She started to answer, then sat back as the waiter placed their meals on the table. He stepped away from the table, and Bax leaned in.

"I thought we might interview him at the lodge, where he's a little more comfortable. He was on edge the last time we spoke, and I would like to keep it as light as possible."

Buck picked up a piece of ravioli with his fork. "That might be a good idea. Bringing him to the sheriff's office could agitate him, and we'll get nothing out of him. I like the lodge idea; keeping it informal might work."

"Do you think he could be our serial killer?" asked Bax. "I mean, yeah, he's odd, but I didn't get serial killer vibes from him. These deaths were cold and methodical. This guy has trouble focusing on one thing for more than ten minutes."

"Let's look at what we know about him," said Buck. "He's lived in the area for ten years, which is when the first murder took place. He has a history of violence towards women. He was in the military, and he was locked up for murdering five women overseas. If he's not our killer, he sure ticks a lot of boxes."

Bax was silent as she finished her dinner. "True, but I don't see it. He acts like he's afraid of everything, and when he talked about the alien in his cabin, he looked terrified. You could see it in his eyes. The head of the VA Health Center described him as a gentle soul. I just don't see it."

Buck was about to say something when Bax's phone rang. She looked at the number and answered it. "Hey, Mark. What's up?"

"Hey, Bax," said Detective Ridgeway. "Listen,

Jessie was attacked tonight. She's alive and seems okay, but they're taking her to the hospital to get her checked out. I'm on my way to her house to let her daughter know and to take her to the hospital. Thought you'd want to know."

"What happened?"

"We don't have the whole picture, but it looks like she was loading groceries into her SUV when she was attacked from behind. Here's the weird part. The assailant tried to stab her with a syringe. The tip broke off, so whatever was in the syringe ended up all over her jacket. We'll get that tested. The chief of detectives asked if it could be related to the eleven bodies."

"If it is," said Bax, "why would the assailant know to target Jess? You guys just got involved in the case yesterday." Bax stopped talking for a few seconds. "Unless we ran into the assailant today while we were doing interviews. Fuck. We might have been talking to the killer."

"Listen, I've got to go," said Mark Ridgeway, and he disconnected the call.

Buck had called for the bill while she was talking, and they each left money on the table. They grabbed their backpacks and headed for the door. It didn't look like they were going to get much sleep tonight.

Chapter Thirty-Eight

The gray mist had taken over the cabin, and Mike Kirby, once again, found himself frozen in place, unable to move or speak. The fuzzy shape of the alien stood at the end of the bed, but Mike couldn't tell if he was looking at him or something else in the cabin. Mike was afraid.

He hadn't heard the alien come in, but then he never did. He would show up out of the haze. The bright lights hurt Mike's eyes, but he knew he couldn't look away. He couldn't move his head at all. He could hear the alien talking, but he couldn't understand the words. The alien must be speaking Martian or something.

The alien moved around the cabin and was out of Mike's view for a few minutes. He could hear drawers being opened and closed, but he had no idea what the alien wanted or why he had come so often over the past couple of months. It wasn't like him to visit this often, or at least he hadn't visited as often since Mike had moved into the old cabin.

The alien stood beside him, but Mike couldn't make out his face. He shuddered and wanted to scream for help, but he knew even if he could, there was no one around for miles to hear him. He just had to lie there and wait for the alien to leave.

Mike thought about the first time the alien had come to visit. It was during his first tour in Afghanistan. His team and the guys from the CIA were surveilling a Taliban village, or maybe it was just him and the doctor. That part was never clear. He remembered talking to a young Afghan girl down by the spring. She was gathering water for her meager herd of goats. Mike was never clear on what happened next, but he remembered waking up and seeing the alien slip through the hazy mist. The alien was doing something to the little girl, but it was never clear. When he woke up, he was back in his bunk and was surprised to find a small hair ribbon in his hands. It looked like the one the little girl was wearing, or maybe not.

Now, the alien leaned over Mike and injected something into his arm. He felt all warm and gooey inside. Then, the alien did something he had never done before. He raised something long over his head and slammed it down onto Mike's right leg. Even paralyzed, Mike could feel that the pain was excruciating, and he passed out.

Mike woke the next morning, and the feeling of euphoria had been replaced by a horrible pain in his leg. He tried to get out of bed, but the pain from standing caused him to pass out, and he awoke a while later lying on the floor. Mike propped himself up against the bed and pulled up the leg of his sweatpants. The area just below his knee was purple and brown, and just touching it caused him to cry out in pain. He couldn't understand why the alien had hurt him.

He found a pill bottle on the small wooden table next to the bed and popped one pill in his mouth. He looked at the bottle and thought that it didn't look like the bottle his pills were usually in. He thought that was odd. The pills looked different. He tried to crawl into his bed, but the room started spinning. He fell to the floor and closed his eyes. He felt at peace for just a minute, and then something happened that hadn't happened before. Pain. Pain like he had never felt before. It felt like his chest was on fire, and he screamed in his head. Everything seemed to go into slow motion. The pain slowly subsided, but he couldn't open his eyes. He felt like he was floating.

His thoughts turned to the eleven graves on the other side of the lake, and he wondered again if maybe he was responsible for those deaths. He didn't remember hurting anyone, but then he didn't remember hurting those women in Afghanistan either. Yet everyone agreed he had. He didn't feel like a murderer, but then he had no idea what a murderer might feel like. He closed his eyes and let the medicine take him away, but the dreams followed, and he had nowhere to turn.

Chapter Thirty-Nine

Buck and Bax parked in the visitor's lot at the hospital, grabbed their backpacks and raced across the lot to the emergency room doors. They walked in, flashed their badges and were directed down the hall to the last door on the left.

They could hear Jessie Maldonado complaining before they reached the room.

"Jess, it's for your own good," said a voice through the partially open door. "Let them run the scan to make sure your brains haven't been scrambled."

"Just get me some aspirin and I'll be fine. I don't need an exam; I need to catch the son of a bitch who attacked me."

Buck pushed open the door and found Jessie lying on a hospital bed. She was still wearing her clothes except for her suit jacket. Detective Mark Ridgeway and the emergency room doctor stood next to the bed, looking dismayed. At the foot of the bed was Don Paladino, the Grand Junction Police chief of detectives. He stood by as Mark and the doctor tried to reason with Jessie. She was having none of it.

She looked at Bax and Buck. "Good. Will you please tell these guys I need to get back to work and find the asshole who did this?"

Bax walked over to the bed, leaned in and pushed Jessie's hair out of the way. She took a step back and looked at Jessie.

"That's a hell of a bruise you've got there, girl. Why don't you let these nice folks give you a quick scan, and then we can get out of here?"

"Not you too," said Jessie. "I thought you were my friend?"

Jessie looked pleadingly at Buck, who raised his hands in surrender. "Better to get you checked out now than to have you pass out when we need you," he said.

Jessie frowned and gave them both the middle finger. She looked at the doctor. "Okay, Doc. Let's get this done so I can get back to work."

The doctor left to call for transport and Bax sat on the edge of the bed. "What the hell happened?"

"I was loading the grocery bags into the back seat when I felt something pound down on my left shoulder. They told me it was a syringe that must have broken off when it hit my ballistic vest. The guy reached in and tried to get his hands around my throat. I'll tell you this. The guy had a hell of a grip.

I pushed back off the seat, and we slammed into the car next to me. That must have been when he hit me on the back of the head. I felt my legs get wobbly, so I knew I needed to end the fight right away. I turned around, grabbed him and slammed him down on the hood of the car. The fucker hit the hood, and I figured he'd be down for the count, but he bounced off the hood and threw a punch that caught me right on the temple." She raised her hand, touched the side of her head and winced. "I will admit, I saw stars, and as I was going down, I kicked out my right leg, connected with something hard and heard the guy scream. That's when I pulled my gun, and I must have passed out for a minute because the next thing I knew, there were a bunch of people standing around trying to help."

"Did you get a look at this guy?" asked Buck.

"He was average height and weighed one sixty-five. He was easy to pick up. I saw his arm under the rubber gloves, and he was white. He was also strong as hell. That's about all I got." She rubbed her head with her palms. "I know I hurt him when I kicked out."

The doctor came in, followed by an orderly with a wheelchair, and they helped Jessie into the chair and the orderly pushed her towards the door. When they were gone, Chief Paladino walked over to Buck and held up Jessie's shoulder holster. Buck looked where he was pointing and spotted the end of a tiny needle sticking in the leather.

"The hospital checked the syringe, and it contained sux," said the chief. "I'll bet this guy never expected her to be wearing a heavy leather shoulder holster and have on a stab-proof vest. Must have surprised the shit out of him when the needle broke off."

Buck nodded.

"Is this your serial killer?" asked the chief.

"The MO is similar," said Bax. "What I can't figure out is why he targeted Jess. She's the toughest woman I know."

"I think that's what saved her. Once again, people's first impression of Jess is a fat girl, no offense," said the chief. "She was damn lucky today. What I'd like to know is why she was targeted?"

Bax thought for a minute. "Jess wasn't with me when I went to speak to the bartender this morning. We didn't hook up until we got to the autopsies this morning, and after the autopsies, we interviewed the VA Health Center administrator and the doc who runs the group sessions."

She filled the chief in on the information they had about the latest victim being creeped out by a guy in the bar, and how they identified him and his friend Joker. She explained the reasons for reopening the John Doe case since they now believed that Joker was murdered.

"After that, Jess headed back to the office, and I headed to Delta."

"Any chance it was the VA administrator or this doctor that could be the connection to the eleven bodies?" asked the chief.

"Anything's possible," said Buck. "We just learned about those two today. We'll run their names and see if anything clicks."

Bax spoke up. "Come to think of it, Jessie and Mark were with me at the bar earlier yesterday watching their CCTV. That's how we found Kirby and Joker. Someone could have seen us there then."

"What about this Kirby guy?" asked the chief. "What's his story?"

Buck quickly debriefed him on the information they'd recovered from his military file. The chief turned his back and looked out the window, deep in thought. He turned back and faced Buck.

"What's your gut tell you, Buck?"

"We'll know more tomorrow, Chief. Bax and Detective Apodaca are going to take a run up to the lodge and see if they can interview Kirby. He ticks a lot of boxes, but Bax is concerned if he is stable enough to pull off these murders. They are almost flawless, and this guy's history seems like a jumbled mess."

"Okay, guys. Keep me posted if you will, and if Jess shows up ready to work, give her something easy to do. You know she's not going to sit still."

The chief pushed through the door and headed down the hallway. They turned and faced Detective Ridgeway, who was sitting in the chair next to the bed, staring at the heart monitor.

"Mark, what's up?" asked Bax.

Mark looked uneasy. He looked at Bax and then at Buck, then down at his hands. "I let her down," he said. "I didn't protect her."

Bax stepped over and put her hand on his shoulder. "I know it feels that way right now," she said. "But there was nothing you could have done. You were off today, yet from what I understand, you were the first detective on the scene when you got the word. That counts for something."

Mark looked at Bax and wiped a tear from his eye. "Yeah, I guess. When I heard the call, I couldn't get out the door fast enough. But I wish I could have done more."

"Look, Mark," said Buck. "Jess is one of the toughest people I know, and it sounds like she gave as good as she got. Nothing you could have done would have changed that. Our jobs are to find the person responsible and see that they are held accountable."

Mark stood up. "Okay, Buck. What do you need me to do?"

Buck smiled. "Right now, I want you to make sure your partner is comfortable, whether here or at home, and then I want you to finish your day off with the family. We'll talk tomorrow once we've had a chance to interview this Mike Kirby guy."

They shook hands, and Buck and Bax stepped through the door and headed for the elevator. As they reached the ground floor, Buck's phone rang. He looked at the number and pushed the green button.

"Hey, George."

"Buck, hope I didn't catch you at dinner," said George.

"No, you're good. Whatcha got?"

"We ran the background check on Dr. Brian Davidson, and there's something hinky there. We got shut out, just like we did with Mike Kirby, but the clearance required to get in is way more than with Kirby. We can go back as far as him being transferred to Leavenworth, but we can't get any further. What do you want to do?"

"George, did you say he was transferred to Leavenworth?" asked Bax. "When did the transfer take place?"

They heard George clicking keys. "Looks like he arrived there a month after Mike Kirby. He is listed as a resident psychiatrist."

Buck looked at Bax. "That's interesting. George, I think we need to go a lot deeper on the good doctor, if you know what I mean?"

"Gotcha. I'll let you know what I find."

Buck disconnected the call. "Did the doctor mention that he knew Mike Kirby while he was incarcerated in Leavenworth?"

"No, he didn't," said Bax. "I think we need to have another conversation with Dr. Davidson."

"I'll take the doctor. I would prefer you handle Mike Kirby. Send me his contact details, and I'll grab Paul, and we'll hit him first thing," said Buck.

Bax pulled out her phone and clicked a few buttons, and Buck's phone chimed.

"Let's get some sleep," said Buck. "We've got a lot to do tomorrow."

They slid into their Jeeps, Bax headed home, and Buck headed to his hotel. The little bug in his brain was moving. Not a lot, but enough to be noticed.

Chapter Forty

Buck's ringing phone woke him from a sound sleep, and he checked the number and answered. He noticed there was no light peeking through the gap in the curtains. He checked the time on his watch.

"Taylor."

"Buck. Jim Carpenter. Sorry to call so early, but I wanted to get you this before you started your day."

"No worries, Jim. Go ahead."

"I'm emailing you some information on similar crimes that your office requested. I don't have access to your investigation file, so I thought I'd send it to you and you can upload it. Our analysts have uncovered a dozen similar crimes. Now, these are crimes where the bodies were recovered. Since we have a general area for crimes, we can now look for missing person cases in the same general area. Take a look at these reports and let me know what you think. I'll let you know what the analysts find as far as the MISPERs."

"That's great news, Jim. Of course, you doubled

our workload, but the more information we have, the better."

"By the way, Buck. My agents visited the woman in Carbondale today, and they agreed with the deputy who interviewed her. They said she seemed sharp, and there was no sign of drinking or drug usage. She came across as a citizen who attempted to do her civic duty and was squashed at every turn. We have some directions to go on, and I'll let you know what we find. It would be nice to wrap up a twenty-year-old kidnapping that made national headlines. Maybe get rid of the agency's black eye. I have agents in Florida who will contact the family tomorrow, so prepare for more news media."

"Thanks, Jim. That's all we need. The sheriff will be so happy. I'll look over the reports and get back to you. Thanks again."

Buck clicked off and pulled out his laptop. He grabbed a bottle of Coke from the refrigerator under the counter and opened his email. The first rays of morning light shined through the crack between the curtains, and Buck opened the curtains to let in the light. The first thing he did was send a text to Sheriff Buckman, letting him know that the FBI were visiting the Chamberlain family so he could be prepared for the media onslaught.

He opened the email from Special Agent

Carpenter and worked his way through the murder files. Eight of the twelve murders had occurred in and around Kansas City, Kansas, and Kansas City, Missouri. The MOs were similar to the eleven murders in Colorado. Intact bodies, of which there were five, were found to have a small injection site in the area of the shoulder, and all the bodies had crushed hyoid bones. None of the bodies showed signs of sexual assault prior to death.

Four of the bodies were identified using DNA or other means because they were too decomposed to find any identifying marks. These four bodies were found in a rural area, in shallow graves along an isolated road, and there was evidence that at least two of the sites had a small roadside cross near the body.

Buck reread the other reports. Two mentioned a roadside cross. Several of the first eight bodies were found in alleys of construction sites and had been dumped out in the open.

Each body was found with a military ribbon, pin or button, and it was obvious to Buck that during these eight years, none of the agencies investigating the individual murders made a connection between the crimes. Buck leaned back in his chair.

The fact that Fort Leavenworth was in the area had most of the investigators looking into acting or former soldiers due to the military memorabilia.

Although several of the agencies came up with a list of potential suspects, it appeared that no one was held accountable for the murders. According to the file, one investigator interviewed several former Leavenworth inmates, but nothing ever came out of those. Several suspects were arrested during the investigations, but no one was ever charged.

Buck picked up his phone, checked the time and placed a call.

"Mornin', Buck," said George. "What's got you up so early?"

"I'm uploading some files from the FBI," said Buck. He told him about the crimes that had taken place in the Kansas City area. "Can you go through some old media stuff and see if the reporters found anything the investigator might have missed?"

"You looking for something specific?" asked George.

"I'm not sure. There were seven different agencies involved with these murders, yet no one put two and two together. I wonder if a local reporter might have, and it never took hold."

"No worries, Buck. I'll call you back. Listen, Mel wants to talk to you. Hold on a sec."

Mel came on the line. "Hi, Buck. I uploaded the military file for Dr. Brian Davidson. Interesting reading. I also had to go into the CIA archives. This guy's been in a lot of places and has worked under some odd government groups."

Buck interrupted. "Mel, are we protected? I'm not thrilled we had to go into the CIA's files."

Mel said, "The encryption software is designed to keep us anonymous, but I had concerns too, so I went through several servers. I'll save you the tech mumbo jumbo, but the short answer is, yeah, we're clean."

"Okay," said Buck, sounding unsure, but he had complete faith in George and Mel. "Give me the down and dirty."

"We already know he hasn't been a practicing psychiatrist since arriving in Colorado ten years ago, and we knew from the service file we accessed that he left the military as a colonel around the same time. He put in enough time in the army to get his monthly pension, but he was also in a position where if he had stayed for another twelve years, his pension would have almost doubled, and he would have left as a general.

"Now, here's where it gets strange. Before his time at Leavenworth, he did two tours in Afghanistan and Iraq. We know during that time he was part of a joint Army/CIA project. From what we can tell, it involved deep psychological warfare on Taliban leaders, but it also branched out to include other civilians. We know drugs and torture were involved. We also know that while focusing on those target villages, several Taliban leaders disappeared. Military targets are one thing, but there were also reports from an NGO working in the area that several women disappeared."

"How many is several, Mel?"

"This program operated for three years, and it's speculated that over thirty men, women and young girls disappeared during that time."

"How did you get this out of the doctor's file?"

"The doctor was investigated by Army CID. I found one small mention in the doctor's file, but it led me to another army file, which led me to a CIA file. Anyway, no charges were ever filed against the doctor or any of his team, but according to the CIA file, they did some horrible things to the Taliban men, women and young girls. It's all in the files I uploaded, but it's not pleasant reading."

"Anything else I need to know?" asked Buck.

"One more thing. Prior to his assignment with the PSYOP/CIA team, Dr. Brian Davidson was in six posts in seven years."

"That's a lot of moving for a young officer," said Buck. "Any indication what that was all about?"

"His fitness reports are vague, but if you read between the lines, I think the good doctor had some socialization issues. I don't think he worked and played well with others, but no one came out and specifically said it. They danced around the issues and kept moving him from unit to unit until he found the wackos at the CIA, where he seemed to fit right in."

"Thanks, Mel. We're going to see if we can catch up with him, ask him why he forgot to mention that he was at Leavenworth the same time Kirby was and see if we can get anything else out of him."

Mel disconnected the call, and Buck sat back in his chair. Dr. Davidson had led an interesting life before settling down to teach history. He wondered what that was all about. He grabbed a quick shower, put on his cleanest clothes and texted Paul to meet him for breakfast. Today could prove to be an interesting day.

Chapter Forty-One

Bax met up with Detective Apodaca and grabbed a quick bite to eat at a small restaurant in Delta. The breakfast burritos were excellent, and after a meal like that, Bax thought it would have been nice to go back home and grab a nap. But they had work to do, so they headed for Bax's Jeep, slid in and pulled out of the parking lot. They followed Highway 92 and then turned onto Highway 65 for the forty-minute drive to the lodge.

Bax turned into the parking lot and had no trouble finding a parking space. They grabbed their backpacks and walked towards the entrance. Once inside, they found Mr. Rasmussen standing behind the front desk counter, entering information into the computer. He looked up as they approached.

"Officers, what can I do for you this morning?"

The door behind him opened, and Mrs. Rasmussen stepped into the front desk area, spotted Bax and Apodaca, stared daggers at them and stepped back through the door, letting it slam.

Mr. Rasmussen looked embarrassed. "She'll be fine," he said. "It takes her a while to get over stuff. Now, what can I do for you?"

"We were hoping to talk with Mike Kirby this morning. Can you point us in the right direction?"

"Can I ask if Mike is in trouble? We talked about him having authority issues; I would hate to see you upset him."

"We just have some questions we didn't get to ask him the other day," said Bax. "Shouldn't take more than a few minutes."

"Do I need to call my lawyer?" asked Mr. Rasmussen. "I'm sure Mike doesn't have one and want to ensure he's protected."

"That's your right, and his as well," said Bax. "Like I said, we just need a few minutes, but if you would like to sit in with us, that would be okay. Since you are not his legal guardian, you will not be allowed to interfere, but if you are acting as his friend, then we are good."

Mr. Rasmussen stood looking at Bax, and she could see his mind working through the options. "I'm okay with that." He pushed through the door, said something to Mrs. Rasmussen and said he was ready.

"Mike should be working over at the new cabins with Gus. We can take the ATV over." He led them out the door to the four-passenger ATV parked next to the front doors. He slid into the driver's seat, started the engine and, when Bax and Apodaca were settled, pulled away and drove around the main building, following the path Bax had walked earlier.

Gus was unloading some paint cans from another ATV and taking them into the new cabin when they pulled up and parked. He walked over to the ATV.

"Mornin', folks. What's up?" he asked.

"Morning, Gus," said Mr. Rasmussen. "These folks would like to talk with Mike. Is he around?"

Gus looked confused. "No, sir. He didn't show up this morning." Gus looked at his watch. "He had a group session last night and I figured he was sleeping in. I know he stops for a couple of beers after group, and sometimes he's a little hungover. He should be here any minute."

"Is he typically this late?" asked Bax.

Gus hesitated. "No, ma'am."

Bax looked at Mr. Rasmussen. "You told us that he lives in a cabin not far from here?"

"That's right. It's about two miles west of the campground. Why?"

"If you wouldn't mind, can you take us there?"

Mr. Rasmussen nodded, and they climbed into the ATV. He thanked Gus, turned on the ATV, headed back to the lodge through the parking lot and headed west past the campground. Two miles later, they turned onto a dirt road, and after a half mile, they spotted a small lake and an old cabin sitting in front of it.

The cabin was rustic but had a great view over the small lake. Mike Kirby's pickup truck was parked haphazardly next to a small shed. It looked like the front bumper had pushed against the door, which was hanging off a bent top hinge.

They slid out of the ATV, and Mr. Rasmussen walked up to the door and banged on it with the side of his fist. "Mike. It's Ray. Are you in there?"

Detective Apodaca walked around the cabin and looked in all the windows. Through a crack in an old blind, he spotted what looked like a body lying on the floor. He raced back to the front door.

"We've got a body on the floor," he said.

Bax asked Mr. Rasmussen to return to the ATV, and she and Detective Apodaca pulled their pistols. Standing to the right of the door, Apodaca grabbed the lever handle and pushed down. The door wasn't latched. He looked at Bax, who nodded, and he pushed open the door, moving right while Bax moved left, leading with their pistols. The cabin was one room with a small attached bathroom, so they cleared it in a hurry, holstered their pistols and kneeled next to Mike Kirby.

Mike was breathing, but he was unconscious. Bax pulled off the old blanket that was wrapped around his waist and stared at the purple-and-black bruise on his right leg just below his knee.

Detective Apodaca grabbed his shoulders and shook him. "Mike. Mike. Can you hear me? Mike, open your eyes."

Mike Kirby mumbled something incoherent. Bax stepped away and moved towards the small table next to the bed.

"I think this is more than hungover," said Detective Apodaca.

Bax held out a pill bottle that was lying on the floor. She looked over as Mr. Rasmussen stepped into the cabin and kneeled next to Detective Apodaca. "Is he all right?" he asked. He looked at Bax.

Bax shook her head no and pulled out her phone. She called the Delta County dispatcher and requested an ambulance and paramedics.

Mr. Rasmussen stepped over to her and looked at the pill bottle. "Do you think he OD'd?" he asked.

"It's possible. These pills are pretty strong, but that doesn't explain the huge bruise on his leg," said Bax.

Mr. Rasmussen turned and looked down at the bruise. "Shit, it looks like someone beat him. You don't get that from banging into a chair leg."

Bax stepped away and spent a few minutes looking around the cabin. She spotted an old wooden footlocker and lifted the lid. Folded and sitting on top of some other clothes was an army dress uniform jacket. The first thing Bax noticed was that most of the buttons were missing, and several of the ribbons were missing from the ribbon bar. She called over Detective Apodaca.

"Shit," he said as Bax closed the lid and stepped over to a box sitting on the small kitchen counter. She looked in the box, which had no lid, and saw several small pieces of jewelry: a couple of rings and several gold and silver chains.

"Vince," she said as he stepped over to look at what she was looking at. "We're gonna need a search warrant."

She pulled her phone from her back pocket, dialed a number, explained what she needed to Franklin and disconnected the call. Apodaca was on the phone with the sheriff, who said he would get one of the clerks to write up the warrant application and get it over to the judge. He told the detective he was heading up that way.

Bax hung up with Franklin and dialed Buck. His phone went to voice mail, so she left him a detailed message about what they'd found in the cabin and Mike Kirby's condition. She disconnected the call and heard sirens in the distance; she asked Apodaca to take the ATV and run out to the road to lead the paramedics in.

Mr. Rasmussen looked at the box Bax was standing next to. "Do you think those are from all those victims? I can't believe Mike would be involved in something like that. In the ten years he's worked here, there's never been a hint of trouble."

Bax didn't respond. Instead, she led Mr. Rasmussen outside, and they stepped out of the way as the paramedics climbed out of the ambulance, grabbed their gear and headed inside. She asked Mr. Rasmussen to stay out of the way and went inside to speak with the paramedics.

Bax stood out of the way as the paramedics worked on Mike Kirby. The lead paramedic stood, pulled out his radio and asked the dispatcher to get Life Flight in the air. He gave the dispatcher the coordinates for the cabin and told her there was a large field south of the cabin, and they would be there. He stepped over to Bax.

"His leg might be fractured, I can't tell for sure, but that's not my worry. I think he overdosed on something. It could be the pills in the bottle. We'll take them with us, but we need to get him to St. Mary's."

With the help of Detective Apodaca and Mr. Rasmussen, the second paramedic carried the gurney across the dirt and into the cabin. They loaded Kirby onto the gurney, strapped him in, carried him outside and placed the gurney on the back of the ATV. With Mr. Rasmussen at the wheel, they walked alongside the ATV, keeping the gurney from falling off. They headed back down the small driveway to the field on the other side of the road.

Bax stepped outside the cabin and heard the Life Flight helicopter coming over the trees. A few minutes later, she heard the helicopter engine rev, and the helicopter headed for Grand Junction. The paramedics came back in the ATV, returned the equipment to the ambulance and headed back to Delta. Bax asked Mr. Rasmussen to take her back to the lodge so she could get her Jeep. Detective Apodaca stood guard over the cabin.

When Bax returned a few minutes later, she followed the sheriff down the dirt driveway and parked next to him. Once out of her Jeep, she explained what had gone on.

"Do you think he tried to OD out of remorse that we had found the bodies?" asked Sheriff Buckman.

"Could be," said Bax, "but I'm more concerned with how his leg got hurt."

She explained about the attack on Jessie Maldonado the night before and the fact that Jessie's kick had connected with the leg of her assailant and he had screamed in pain and hobbled away.

"Jessie's strong, but I don't know if one of her kicks could have caused that much damage. The bruise on Kirby's leg looked more uniform than I would expect to see from a kick, more like someone hit him with something. Once they get him stabilized, I'll arrest him for the assault on Jessie, and we'll see where that leads us."

She opened the footlocker, pointed out the missing buttons and ribbons and showed him the box with the jewelry pieces.

"Sure looks like our guy. What do you think?" asked the sheriff.

Bax didn't answer right away. She stepped outside to where Detective Apodaca was leaning against her Jeep. "Vince. I'd like you to take some pictures of the jewelry. Don't touch it; move it around with a pen or a stick. Then, head back to the office with the sheriff and call the relatives of the victims we've identified to see if they can tell us if their loved one owned any of those pieces.

"In answer to your question, Sheriff. I'm not sure," she said. "Let's see if Vince can get us some answers."

Sheriff Buckman nodded, and he and Detective Apodaca slid into the sheriff's SUV and left Bax standing on the cabin's front porch with just her thoughts. While she waited for Franklin and the forensic team to arrive, she called Detective Ridgeway and told him about the condition of Mike Kirby and his possible connection to the assault on Jessie Maldonado. She asked him to have a couple of officers assigned to guard him while he was in the hospital and to place him under arrest if he woke up before she got there.

She disconnected the call and leaned against the cabin. This was not how she expected her day to go. She redialed Buck, got his voice mail and left him a message to meet her at the hospital when he finished whatever he was doing. She disconnected the call and sat on the front step to wait.

Chapter Forty-Two

Buck entered the small Mexican restaurant down the street from his hotel and found Paul sitting by the window sipping his coffee. Buck pulled out the chair and sat. The waitress, an older Latina named Consuela, set a large glass of Coke on the table in front of him and took their orders. Buck asked her how her son was doing. He was in the final week of the police academy and would soon join the ranks of the Grand Junction Police Department. She told Buck he was excited to finish and couldn't wait to get on the job. She stepped away to put in their orders.

Paul laughed while sipping his coffee, and Buck gave him a "what?" look. Paul put down his cup. "Seriously, is there anyone in Colorado you don't know?" They both laughed.

Buck asked Paul to pull out his laptop and open the investigation file. He had him take a few minutes to review the crime reports from Kansas City. Paul read them, closing his laptop when Consuela brought their food and then continuing to read while he ate his breakfast burrito. He pushed the laptop aside and finished his coffee. Consuela was right there with a fresh pot and refilled his cup.

"The similarities are uncanny," said Paul. "But let's think about this for a second. During this period Mike Kirby was serving a ten-year sentence. His friend Joker was serving five years. How would either of them have been involved?"

Buck finished his huevos rancheros and slid the plate aside, sipping from his glass of Coke. He set the glass down. "That's the big question. Mike Kirby has a problem with women and was convicted of murdering five Afghan women. He has the background to be the killer, but Bax didn't feel it when she spoke with him the first time. Joker, on the other hand, was convicted of punching an officer. It's a big step from there to killing dozens of people."

"So, what's the answer?" asked Paul.

"Open the file Mel uploaded this morning for Dr. Brian Davidson and read his service record."

Paul clicked a few buttons and read the file. "Guy went to some good schools, had to be smart to get into these. The army sent him to medical school, a stint at Johns Hopkins, and onward to his psychiatric residency at Walter Reed. Impressive credentials. Top of his class everywhere he went."

Paul continued reading. After a few minutes, he sat back and looked at Buck. "With all his background, his early FITREPs are terrible. He kept getting bounced around like no one wanted him. Do we know why that is?"

"Mel is doing more digging," said Buck.

"Several tours in Afghanistan and then suddenly a major change in fitness."

Buck looked at him. "Yeah, right after he landed in the PSYOP program, he became the darling of the military. Top fitness reports, choice of jobs. Looks like he found his niche."

Paul opened the CIA file that Mel had included. He read for a few minutes and then stopped and looked at Buck. "This is some sick, twisted shit. No wonder the world is locked out of this file. Who does this kind of stuff to other human beings? It looks like they were developing newer and more diabolical ways to torture people."

Buck looked across the table. "Keep reading."

Paul read some more of the file. "Looks like things went a little overboard. People died horribly."

"What if all the good reports," asked Buck, "were a way to keep Dr. Davidson quiet about what they were doing?"

Paul stopped and stared at Buck. "Do we know if his path ever crossed with Mike Kirby?"

"We know Kirby was inside while Davidson was on the psychiatric staff, and we know they both landed in Colorado at about the same time. What we don't know is if they were connected pre-incarceration."

"Maybe we should find out," said Paul.

They each left a twenty on the table and headed for Buck's Jeep. Buck headed for the campus and parked in the main parking lot. They headed for the administration office, where a pleasant woman directed them to Dr. Davidson's office. They crossed the campus, climbed the stairs and entered a modern building. The offices were on the third floor, so they grabbed an elevator and pushed the button.

Buck and Paul stood outside the office with the sign that read professor brian davidson. Buck pushed open the door, and they walked into an office that would have driven Buck nuts. Buck was meticulous about his files and office, but this space went to the extreme. Everything was pure white, and the office almost glowed. The books on the shelves were organized not by the author but by the color of the cover. The office felt sterile.

A young blond woman sat behind a small desk and looked up as they entered. Buck held up his credentials. "Agents Taylor and Webber. We'd like a moment with Dr. Davidson?"

"May I ask what this is about?" she asked.

"Nothing you need to be concerned about. The doctor is helping us with a case, and we need a few minutes of his time," said Buck.

"I'm afraid the professor is not in today. He called and left a message that he would be working from home today."

"Is that unusual?" asked Buck.

"It happens occasionally, but he will miss the department staff meeting, which he has never missed in the two years I have worked for him."

"Do you have his home address?" Buck asked.

She hesitated, and Buck said, "We can get it from the admin office, but it would be easier if you could give it to us. Save us some time."

She pulled a piece of paper off a pad, wrote down the address and handed it to him. She didn't look happy.

Buck thanked her, and he and Paul left the office and headed for the parking lot. They slid into Buck's Jeep, and Buck entered the address into the navigation system. Once on the road, Paul said, "Some office. I couldn't work there. Felt like an operating room."

Buck smiled. "Yeah, I wonder how his assistant could have worked there for two years. Would have driven me crazy."

They followed Twenty-Six and a Half Road until the GPS told them to turn onto Roundhill Drive, and they pulled into the circular driveway. Buck slid out of the driver's seat and waited for Paul. They approached the front door and knocked.

The door was answered by a petite Afghan woman wearing a purple kaftan dress with gold embroidered trim. Her long dark hair was in a ponytail that hung to the middle of her back.

"May I help you?" she asked.

Buck held up his credentials. "We were hoping to have a word with Professor Davidson but were told by his assistant that he was working from home today. Is he here?"

"My husband isn't feeling well today, perhaps another day."

A voice from behind her said, "It's okay, Amina, show the gentlemen in."

She looked unhappy but stepped aside and waved them into the house. Buck and Paul entered a warm, comfortable house with bright-colored carpets and pillows. It was nothing like his office. Dr. Davidson was lying on a leather couch, and as they entered, he set his laptop down and closed the lid. "I apologize for not getting up to greet you, gentlemen. I had a little accident and am having trouble getting around. Please have a seat."

Buck reintroduced himself and Paul, and they sat in the two leather recliners that flanked the couch. Once they were seated, Dr. Davidson said, "Gentlemen, can I get you something to drink? My wife, Amina, makes the most incredible coffee. Amina, please get these officers some of your coffee."

Buck shook him off. "That's not necessary, sir. We shouldn't be here for more than a few minutes."

Dr. Davidson waved his hand, and his wife disappeared from the room. He relocated the pillow under his back and winced.

"Are you okay, Doctor?" asked Paul.

"Yes, yes, I'm fine, or at least I will be in a couple of days, according to the doctor. I had a run-in with a bicyclist on campus—totally my fault. I was running late for my next lecture, wasn't paying attention, and stepped right in front of this young lad on a bike. As my young students would say, the crash was epic, and I'm afraid I got the worst of it. I twisted my knee and have some bruising. The bike, I fear, is a total loss and I offered to purchase the young man a new one of his choosing. I feel like such an idiot. But enough about my misfortune. How can I help you, gentlemen?"

"Doctor, yesterday you spoke with one of my colleagues, Agent Baxter, about a member of one of your groups, Mike Kirby. We were wondering why you didn't mention to her that your paths had crossed while he was locked up in Leavenworth for the murder of five Afghan women."

The professor looked deep in thought. "Ah, yes. I do recall. It was right before my accident, and I'm afraid the painkillers have made me a bit forgetful. Yes, she and another detective visited me at the VA Center. I didn't mention it because she never asked, and I didn't see the point."

"So, you did know Mike Kirby before coming to Colorado?" asked Buck.

"Yes. Is Mike in some trouble?"

"We're investigating several old homicides, and his name has come up in connection to that case," said Buck.

"Oh, my," said the professor. "I was afraid something like this would happen sooner or later."

"Why do you say that, Doctor? Is it because of the five women in Afghanistan?"

The doctor looked surprised. "You are very well

informed, Agent Taylor. Yes, I have been worried that someday Mike might have a relapse. Mike suffered a traumatic brain injury while in Afghanistan, and he was never the same after that."

"How, so, Doctor?" asked Paul.

"I understand Mike was involved with a special PSYOP program with the CIA. His duties were security related, but I understand that he also helped out with certain programs the government has since outlawed."

"Enhanced interrogation programs, Doctor?" asked Buck.

"Correct, Agent Taylor, but I think they went beyond that. Mike had anger management issues before his brain injury, and I believe the CIA saw a chance to use him in their experiments. He was very easily manipulated, and I believe it was those experiments that led him to kill those Afghan women and others we may never know about."

"How did you get involved with him, Doctor?" asked Buck.

"In between his assignments, he came to see me complaining of headaches and nightmares. He believed he was being contacted by aliens, who made him do things against his will. He told me that he was given pills, and when he described the symptoms, I believed he was given LSD. Those side effects can last for years and manifest themselves in bad ways."

"So, you had contact with Mike, even before Leavenworth?" asked Paul.

"Yes, briefly. His team was constantly out in the field doing god knows what to god knows whom. We only met a couple of times, and I was never able to break through. After his arrest, I heard he was being transferred to Leavenworth and requested a transfer. I thought I could still help him, and up until yesterday, I thought we had made progress, but now you tell me he is being looked at for additional murders."

"Doctor, how come you didn't mention your contact with him at Leavenworth when you spoke with Agent Baxter?" asked Buck.

"I'm not sure, Agent Taylor. I was running late, and it must have slipped my mind. We only had a few meetings, so I guess maybe I didn't think it was important."

"Yet it was important enough for you to request a transfer to work with him at Leavenworth. Sounds kind of important to me, Doctor."

Buck watched the doctor as he ran his next comments around in his head. The question had caught the doctor off guard.

"I guess I found his case interesting, and since I had been in Afghanistan for several years and was looking for a change of scenery, I felt the timing was opportune."

"Doctor, after his incarceration and his treatment by you, do you think Mike Kirby is capable of committing murder?" asked Buck.

The doctor closed his eyes and rubbed his temples. He looked at Paul and then at Buck.

"Yes, gentlemen. I do believe Mike Kirby is capable of murder."

Buck and Paul stood, thanked the doctor and followed Amina, who'd appeared out of nowhere, to the front door. They thanked her and headed for the Jeep. Once seated, Buck pulled out his phone and dialed a number. Max Clinton answered the phone. "Buck Taylor, how's my favorite cop?"

"Hey, Max. I need a favor."

Chapter Forty-Three

Bax was sitting on the rickety porch when Franklin's black SUV came up the driveway, followed by the white forensic van. He parked and slid out of the Jeep.

"Hey, Bax. What have we got?"

Bax stood. "Hi, Franklin. We found Michael Kirby inside, incapacitated. His injuries suggest that he might have attacked Detective Maldonado. I did a quick look around and found an army uniform in a footlocker that was missing some of its buttons and ribbons. We also found some jewelry in a box."

"You think this guy, Kirby, is the serial killer?" asked Franklin.

"On the face, it looks like he could be. I'm just not sure right now. We need to go through the cabin with a fine-tooth comb. I'm waiting on a text from Sheriff Buckman that he has the warrant in hand."

"Okay, we'll suit up. Let me know when you're ready for us."

Franklin stepped away to talk with his team, and they started removing their equipment from the van. Bax looked at her phone, hoping that something would happen. She stretched and walked around the building to the small lake behind the cabin and stood at the shore. She spotted a pair of golden eagles perched on the other side of the lake, and she watched them until her phone rang.

She looked at the number and answered.

"Hey. I've been trying to get you for a while," she said.

"Yeah, sorry about that. Paul and I were talking with Dr. Davidson about Mike Kirby. I'll fill you in, but first, what's up? How did your interview with Kirby go?" asked Buck.

"It didn't happen," said Bax. "We found Kirby unconscious from an overdose in his cabin. He also has a big bruise on his leg. Life Flight took him to St. Mary's."

"You think he attacked Jessie?"

"It's possible. The paramedic said his symptoms might have been caused by an overdose of LSD. He might have been out of his head when he attacked Jess. As soon as I can release Franklin on the cabin, I was going to head to the hospital and arrest him."

Bax hesitated a few seconds. "There's more. When I did a quick look around the cabin while the paramedics were working on him, I found a uniform missing some of the buttons and ribbons and a box full of odd pieces of jewelry."

Buck was silent for a minute. "Funny you should mention LSD. Dr. Davidson said that he believed that Kirby was given LSD while working with the PSYOP unit in Afghanistan. Said the symptoms could manifest years later. He also told us that he believed Kirby was more than capable of murder."

"So, he did know Kirby before Leavenworth. I wonder why he never mentioned it?" asked Bax.

"He told me he was in a hurry and forgot. Said their contact was limited."

"Yet, he transferred to Leavenworth to be with him. That seems odd," said Bax.

Her phone chimed, and she looked at the text from the sheriff. She walked to the front of the cabin and waved to Franklin. His team grabbed their gear and headed for the cabin.

"Yeah," said Buck. "He said he needed a change of scenery. But here are two other odd things. The doctor mentioned that Kirby might have been exposed to LSD while working in Afghanistan, and he was laid up at home when we found him, recovering from a pedestrian/bicycle accident that left him bruised and with a twisted knee."

"He was fine when I spoke with him."

"He told us it happened after he left you when he was running to get to his next lecture and not paying attention."

Bax was deep in thought. Buck interrupted those thoughts. "By the way, something else we became aware of earlier this morning. The FBI discovered a dozen similar murders in the area around Kansas City while Kirby was incarcerated."

Bax's mind was running a thousand miles an hour. She sat on the front porch, deep in thought. She spoke up when she heard Buck calling her name.

"What the hell does it all mean?" she asked. "It sounds like the doctor was steering you towards Mike Kirby. What with the LSD and the dead Afghan women? But if it was Kirby who committed the murders here and in Kansas, how could he have done it while he was locked up? That makes no sense."

Bax's mind was working on the murders when she stopped and asked Buck to clarify what he had said about the doctor being in an accident.

"Interesting," she said after Buck retold her about the accident. "He gets in an accident right after Jessie is attacked and manages to injure her assailant. You don't think?"

"I don't know what to think, but it sounds

convenient. I'm waiting for some additional information."

Bax was dumbfounded. Could it be that they had two suspects in the attack on Jessie? She was sure her attacker had acted alone. She rubbed her forehead.

"I'm going to arrest Kirby for the attack on Jess. That will give us time to sit him down for a formal interview; then we can decide if the doctor fits into this mess."

Her phone chimed, and she told Buck she would meet him at the hospital, disconnected the call and answered the call from Detective Apodaca.

"Hi, Vince. What's up?"

"Hey, Bax. That jewelry you wanted me to ask the families about. I got a hit on the first call. One of the pieces was a small silver-and-turquoise pinky ring. The ring belonged to Angie Wilde. It was custom-made by her grandfather for her graduation from high school. Her mother told me she never went anywhere without it."

"That's awesome, Vince. That connects Mike Kirby to the murders. If you would, please call the DA and see if they will issue an arrest warrant based on the ring. I can arrest him for the murder at the same time I arrest him for the assault on Jessie. Great work."

"I am waiting on a couple of callbacks on some of the other pieces, but I feel good about this one."

Bax filled him in on the call from Buck. There was silence on the line, and Bax thought she might have dropped the call, then Vince came back on the line.

"Something doesn't make sense, Bax. Let's say this guy has been killing people for over twenty years, and he was so careful that even the FBI didn't know he was active. Why, all of a sudden, would he get sloppy and attack a cop? I don't see it. Think about it. We had some concerns with Kirby, but nothing concrete other than he had killed before, but that was twenty-some years ago. We had nothing that physically connected him to the murders, but now, what led us to think he might be the serial killer were the things we found in his cabin. And the reason we found those things was because we found him unconscious, with injuries that could have been caused by his attack on Jessie. It seems too, I don't know, too clean. And then how do we explain the doctor's injuries? I don't know, Bax. I can't see it."

Bax leaned her back against the cabin wall. That was more words than Vince Apodaca had spoken since they'd started this case, but what he said got in her head. He was right. They had nothing that connected Kirby to the murders except the six degrees of separation, and that was all circumstantial. Finding him with the leg injury led to a cursory search of the cabin, which led to the discovery of his mementos. Something else snuck into her head.

"I see what you're saying, Vince, but now think about this. In my first conversation with him, he mentioned this alien who visited him sometimes and left things in his cabin. Things he didn't recognize. Suppose someone was planting evidence in his cabin after the murders."

Vince laughed. "Looks like we may be stepping into the conspiracy theory zone, but you could be right. When Deputy Sterling told me about that conversation you guys had with him, she said he spoke about being immobilized when the alien came and that the alien was always fuzzy. Could be anyone."

"Keep thinking like that, Vince, and keep following up with the jewelry. I need to head to the hospital and talk to Mike Kirby. Call me when you hear back from the DA on the arrest warrant."

Bax disconnected the call, told Franklin she was leaving and slid into her Jeep. She knew if she had a little bug in her brain, like Buck, he would be dancing around. She drove away from the cabin and headed towards the hospital; she hoped Mike Kirby would be coherent when she got there.

Chapter Forty-Four

Dr. Brian Davidson hobbled to the front window and watched the two agents leave. He stared after them, wondering why he had a bad feeling in the pit of his stomach. He replayed the interview in his mind, and he'd given truthful answers to their questions: at least truthful enough that if they checked, they wouldn't find anything out of the ordinary. Or would they?

He thought back to his time in Afghanistan. He hated being there, but the army, in its infinite wisdom, chose to send him to units he shouldn't have been sent to. He hated it at first. He hated the heat, wind and dust, but more than anything, he hated the people. Not the soldiers he worked with, but the Afghan people. He had trouble adapting, and his fitness reports showed his dislike. His fellow officers, those who outranked him, didn't want to associate with him. He remembered one female officer telling him to his face that he made her skin crawl.

He never understood that. When he had to fight, he fought. When he talked to his patients, he tried to be the best doctor he could be, yet the other officers, particularly the female officers, felt uncomfortable around him. He never understood that, yet he knew it was true. Women avoided him like the plague.

When he was in grade school, he had few friends, and none of them were female. He was skinny and had a lot of acne, and he felt like he scared the girls in his class. The acne left his face pockmarked because his mother and father didn't believe in medicine, and the prayers they offered over him and his sister didn't do anything, but he couldn't tell them that. He hated them for it, and he hated them for what they had done to his little sister. He remembered her as being the sweetest little girl. How she ended up with those two as her parents baffled him. He could run away and hide from them, but his sister was too small to escape.

The pain in his sister's belly started after dinner one night. His mother blamed it on her eating too much and sent her to bed. A few hours later, she woke up the entire house with her screaming and crying. She was curled up in a ball on her bed and was running a high fever. Her face was contorted, and her hair stuck to the sweat running down her forehead.

His parents got on their knees and prayed, but after several hours, her discomfort continued. His father filled a large plastic pool with ice and water, and they stripped her clothes off and submerged her little body in the ice-cold water, and they prayed while his sister screamed. At one point he had run outside and hid under the juniper bush behind the house. It was his safe place, and he curled up and covered his ears, but it didn't help. Her screams penetrated his ears, and he wanted to scream for someone to do something.

By midafternoon the next day, his sister was exhausted, and her screams had turned to moans and sobs. The prayers weren't working, but instead of taking her to the hospital or a doctor, his parents called the rest of the congregation to help. At one point, ten or twelve people were standing around his sister, who was lying naked on the kitchen table, and they prayed some more.

At midnight, his little sister died. He remembered the silence as being worse than the screams. His father and several of the other men walked out to the back of the property and dug a hole. The next morning, his mother made him put on his Sunday suit, and the entire congregation gathered in the field behind the house and laid his little sister to rest. He stood watching those people praying to their god, and he hated every one of them.

During high school, he spent his time working out when others were dating and partying, and his strength improved. Girls still avoided him. His strength hadn't improved his pockmarked face, and the acne scars became more pronounced as he gained weight and muscle. There were three girls in high school who made fun of him and called him a monster. One of the girls lived two houses down the rural road, and her father was the minister of his parents' congregation. He had been one of the men who let his little sister die.

He found the girls at the home of the minister. His mother had asked him to drop off a roast for the dinner that always followed their service, and when he walked into the house, the girls screamed, laughed and called him horrible names. Something inside him snapped. He walked out of the kitchen, found a fireplace poker, walked back into the kitchen and started swinging.

When he was finished, there was blood everywhere, and he felt repulsed. It wasn't the death of the girls that bothered him; it was the blood. He hated the blood, but killing the girls gave him an incredible feeling of power. He felt great and wanted more, but he knew he needed to do away with the blood. He vowed to find a better way to kill someone—something more hands-on and with less blood.

He left the house, returned home, showered, went out to the shed, started a fire in the metal trash can and burned his clothes. DNA testing was not available yet, but he wasn't taking any chances someone would see the blood. The next few days were filled with services, burials and many meaningless prayers. He stood at the grave site and watched as the shattered bodies were laid to rest. Because it was a rural area, the local sheriff investigated to the best of his abilities and then declared that the murders were committed by a sexual pervert who had already left the area. Case closed.

He left for college the following year and never looked back. He joined the army; because of his test scores, the army sent him to medical school, and because he hated the blood, he went into psychiatry.

His career in the military sucked until he was assigned to work with the PSYOP/CIA group. He found a home, and the things they did to the people they experimented on made him feel free. That was where he met Mike Kirby.

Kirby was quiet and unassuming. He was assigned to a small security contingent and was responsible for securing the people they wanted for enhanced interrogation. Davidson found that he was easily manipulated and that with the addition of LSD, he could use him for special projects. Outside those special projects, he used him to cover his own tracks while he honed his skills. Kirby was the perfect patsy.

The five Afghan women helped him develop his skills, and he was surprised when the CID investigators showed up. He had left pieces of Mike

Kirby's life at each murder site, and when the investigation was concluded, Mike was hauled off to Leavenworth to get him out of the country.

Davidson knew that the truth would come out sooner or later, so he requested a transfer to Leavenworth to keep an eye on Mike. He knew one day, he would need to sacrifice him for his greater good. Mike was perfect. He hated female officers, and he assaulted several while in the hospital.

Davidson had continued his education in the Kansas City area and had found a young soldier in supply whom he could use to replace Mike until Mike was released. That young man proved unreliable and had to be dealt with. It was not his finest moment. Once in Colorado, he continued his education and made sure that if there were ever a problem with law enforcement, Mike would be in the frame.

He smiled as he watched the CBI agents drive away from his house, but he was worried about the accident story he had told them. He had been thinking on the fly, and that was the best he could come up with.

He called Amina and told her to go into the bedroom and get undressed and that she had better not disappoint him. He had killed her parents during a horrible enhanced interrogation session, and then he'd bought the thirteen-year-old from the local Taliban leader. She had been with him ever since, and he had taught her well. He walked away from the window and headed towards the bedroom. He needed to release some pressure.

Chapter Forty-Five

Buck's phone chimed as he pulled into the hospital parking lot. He pulled into a visitor's space, parked and told the entertainment system to answer the call.

"Buck Taylor, how's my favorite cop?" asked Max Clinton.

"Hi, Max. Were you able to find anything?" asked Buck.

"Maybe. I spoke with a friend, who spoke with a friend, and so on and so on. I have a name, but there is a good chance this person will not want to speak with you."

"Army or civilian issues?" asked Buck.

"Army," said Max. "He's getting a medical pension and may not want to risk the fallout."

"All we can do is try. Send me his details. And Max, thanks."

"Stay safe, Buck. God will watch over you." Max disconnected the call, and Buck's phone chimed with an incoming message.

Buck showed Paul the message. "Might as well see if his phone is on."

Buck dialed the number and waited through five rings. "Whatever you're selling, I'm not interested. Don't call back."

Buck redialed and waited through five more rings. "I told you not . . ."

"Joe, I'm with the police. Don't hang up," said Buck. There was silence on the other end of the line. Buck waited.

"How did you get this number?"

"We know people who know people," said Buck. "We need your help."

"How do I know you are who you say you are?"

"Access the internet and look up the Colorado Bureau of Investigation. Call the main switchboard number and ask for Agent Buck Taylor. They will connect you to my cell phone." Buck disconnected the call, and they sat and waited.

After five minutes, Paul looked up from his phone. "You think we scared him off?"

"Let's give him another five minutes," said Buck.

Three minutes later, Buck's phone rang with the main CBI number. He pushed the talk button.

"Buck Taylor."

"Colorado Bureau of Investigation, huh? Didn't know there was such a thing. What can I do for you, Agent Taylor?"

"We are investigating several murders, and someone you once worked with might be connected."

"Five women in Afghanistan," said Joe. "That was investigated, and the guy responsible went to jail. Now, if there's nothing else, I need to get back to my game show."

"Dr. Brian Davidson," said Buck. He waited.

"That's a name I hoped I would never hear again. What are you looking for, Agent Taylor?"

"We're trying to understand the relationship between Mike Kirby and Davidson, and I understand you worked with both men when you were on active duty. Looking for some background."

"Look, Agent. I'm not going to risk my pension. That was a long time ago, and I'd like to forget all about it."

"I can respect that," said Buck. "I served, but never in a war zone, but I had people I worked with that I respected and some I didn't. I need your help, sir."

There was a moment of silence. Buck waited. "Ask your questions."

"We have evidence similar to what was found in Afghanistan that puts Mike Kirby at the scene—"

Before Buck could finish, the voice on the other end of the phone said, "Mike Kirby didn't kill those women. I know that for a fact."

"How can you be so sure?" asked Buck. "According to the file, CID had evidence—"

"That's bullshit. Not sure how you got hold of the file, but nothing in that file is true. Mike was railroaded because the government needed someone, and Mike was the easiest person to blame shit on."

"Care to elaborate?" asked Buck.

"Davidson was treating Mike with a light dose of LSD. He was experimenting on Mike. The PSYOP folks were experimenting on locals with all kinds of drugs and chemicals. Davidson approved everything they used, and he told Mike he could help him with the nightmares he was having. Mike would have been fine, but by the time CID showed up, his brain was fried. He would have admitted to being the Pope if they had asked him to. He was in a fog most of the time."

"How long did this go on, and why didn't they send Kirby home?"

"Because Davidson ran the program and he needed Mike, so he faked his FITREPs and kept feeding him drugs."

"We interviewed Dr. Davidson, and he said his contact with Mike was limited to just a few occasions. Are you telling me that's not true?" asked Buck.

"Dr. Davidson, what a deranged son of a bitch. More like Dr. Mengele. The things they did to the locals under the guise of enhanced interrogations were disgusting. But to answer your question, Davidson and Mike were together every day. Mike was his pet project, and Mike would do whatever the doctor asked him to do."

"You said you know Mike Kirby didn't kill those women. How do you know that?" asked Buck.

"Because I watched Davidson do it."

Buck looked at Paul. "What do you mean you saw Davidson do it?"

"Just what I said. I knew he was setting Mike

up because I saw him enter the bunkhouse and rip a button off one of Mike's shirts. I was curious, so I followed him. The young girl was walking back from a well just outside our base. Davidson stabbed her in the back with a syringe and she went down. He dragged her into the bushes, wrapped his hands around her throat and squeezed. I could hear bones snap. I kept quiet until CID showed up. I tried to tell them that on at least that occasion, Mike was zoned out in his rack, but they weren't listening. The villagers were up in arms. Davidson fed CID a bunch of lies about Mike; the next we knew, he was on a plane stateside. A week later, I was coming back from a mail run to headquarters, and my Jeep was hit by an RPG. The guy with me died, and I lost my right leg below the knee."

"Is there any way to verify any of this? Is there someone else who knows what you know?" asked Buck.

"Find his journals. He wrote down everything he did. He was meticulous about keeping notes on all his experiments and victims."

The line went dead, and Buck hit the redial button, but the call went straight to voice mail. Buck sat for a minute.

"Is anything we know about this case true?" asked Paul. "Davidson just lied to our faces. He was a lot closer to Kirby than he let on."

Buck pulled out his laptop, opened the investigation file and pulled up the files from Kansas City. He read through each report until he found what he was looking for. He punched a phone number into the entertainment system and waited. "Detective Bureau, Detective Jordan."

"Hi," said Buck. "I'm looking for Detective Steven Blanchard?"

The detective asked him to hold, and the line went silent. A minute later, a female voice came on the line. "Captain Kohl, how can I help you?"

"Captain, my name is Buck Taylor. I'm with the Colorado Bureau of Investigation, and I was looking for a Detective Blanchard."

"Blanchard retired several years ago. Why were you looking for him?" she asked.

"We're investigating several murders out here that are similar to three murders Detective Blanchard investigated a dozen years or so back."

"Hold the line, Agent Taylor."

Buck sat patiently while Paul read through the files on his laptop.

"Thanks for holding, Agent Taylor," said Captain Kohl. "I needed to make sure you were who you said you were."

"No worries," said Buck.

"What's your interest in our murders, Agent Taylor?"

"As I said, we're investigating several cold case murders that were similar to yours, and I wanted to speak to Blanchard and get a feel for what he found."

"Are those the roadside cross killings I've been reading about on the internet?" she asked.

"Yeah. Gotta love the names the media can come up with," said Buck.

"Fascinating. I might be able to help you with that," she said. "I was one of the junior detectives working with the task force."

Buck could hear keys clicking in the background. "Let's see. There was a total of twelve women found; three of them ended up in our jurisdiction. No connection was ever made between the victims, and each victim was discovered with a military button or ribbon on or near the body." A few more buttons clicked. "Looks like the task force came up with a suspect. Private Sean McGill. He worked in the supply depot over at Leavenworth."

"What became of the suspect?" asked Buck. A few more key clicks.

"Ah, here it is. His body was discovered floating in the river. Got wedged in some spring debris. Cause of death was listed as suicide."

"That seems pretty convenient," said Buck.

"Yeah, Blanchard made a note to that effect in the file notes."

"Does it say how you guys identified the suspect?" asked Buck.

"Let me read through the notes; it's been a while. Let's see. No DNA to match to; the private had some medical issues. Here we go. Blanchard interviewed a doctor at Leavenworth who put him onto this private. He was being treated for depression and some antisocial disorder."

"Captain, what was the doctor's name?"

"Dr. Brian Davidson. According to the notes, he was a base psychiatrist." Buck looked at Paul.

"Is there anything else you can remember about the case, Captain?" asked Buck.

There was a pause. "Hold on a sec." She clicked more keys. "That's interesting. This file has been referred to our cold case unit for possible DNA profiling."

"You have DNA?" asked Buck.

"It seems there was dirt under one of the victim's fingernails. Back then, there was speculation that DNA could be recovered from dirt, but the technology didn't exist. She also had what the pathologist described as defensive wounds, scrapes on her heels and knees. It looks like she fought back. This case is on the list to be reevaluated in 2026."

"Captain, can you send us the samples? Our crime lab is cutting-edge, and they may be able to do something with the samples. We'd be happy to share the results if there are any."

"I don't see why not," said Captain Kohl. "Give me a few minutes to call downstairs and see if they can find the samples. I'll call you back."

Buck disconnected the call.

"Fuck," said Paul. "Could we get that lucky?"

"Let's not get our hopes up. She needs to find the samples first."

Twenty minutes later, Buck's phone chimed, and he answered the call. "Buck Taylor."

"Agent Taylor, Captain Kohl. You might want to buy a lottery ticket. The samples were in the evidence box, and the container appears to be sealed."

"That's awesome, Captain. My colleague is calling a secure courier service to swing by and pick them up." Buck relayed the contact details to Paul, and he gave them to the secure courier dispatcher.

"Agent Taylor, please let me know what you find out. It would be great to clear a few of these cases off our books. Good luck."

"Thanks for the help, Captain. If we get any results, you'll be our first call."

Buck disconnected the call and dialed Max Clinton. He explained what he had found out and told her the samples were on the way. She promised to push them ahead of everything else in the lab. Buck hung up and put his laptop back into his backpack.

"Let's go see if we can talk to Mike Kirby."

They slid out of his Jeep and headed for the hospital. The day was looking brighter, and he smiled.

Chapter Forty-Six

Bax was standing in the emergency room waiting area, talking on her phone, when Buck and Paul walked in. They stood next to Detective Ridgeway and waited until she finished the call. She disconnected and smiled.

"That was Vince Apodaca. He managed to get confirmation on three of the pieces of jewelry we found in Mike Kirby's cabin from three of the victims' families. We also have an arrest warrant. Now all we need is the all clear from the doctor."

Bax filled Buck and Paul in on what they'd found at the cabin.

"That's great news," said Buck. He told Bax and Detective Ridgeway about their conversation with Dr. Davidson and with Captain Kohl in Kansas City. They were excited about the possibility of DNA but were not optimistic it would help them.

They were interrupted by the emergency room doctor. He stepped up to Bax.

"The patient is awake. I can give you five minutes with him, but he's drifting in and out of consciousness, so you might not get much from him."

Bax thanked the doctor. "How do you want to handle this?" asked Bax.

"Why don't you and Mark go speak to him? We'll wait here," said Buck.

She nodded, and she and Mark Ridgeway headed deeper into the emergency room.

Buck pulled out his phone and dialed the director.

"Hey, Buck."

"Afternoon, sir. Wanted to give you a quick update."

Buck told him about his conversations related to Dr. Davidson and the Kansas City DNA.

"So, how do you think this doctor fits into all of this?" he asked Buck. "Is he the killer, or did he manipulate Mark Kirby to kill all these people, or does he have nothing to do with any of this? We're talking a lot of bodies."

"Yes, sir," said Buck. "We have no idea, but the problem is, even if we get a DNA match, we don't have any DNA from our crime scenes."

They spoke for a few more minutes and Buck disconnected the call. He was frustrated.

Bax and Detective Ridgeway pulled the curtain aside and stepped up to the bed. Mike Kirby looked terrible. He was pale, and his eyes fluttered, like he was trying to focus. He was hooked up to several monitors and had an oxygen cannula in his nose.

The doctor opened the curtain and stood next to them. Bax looked over.

"Was it an overdose, Doc?" she asked.

"I would say so," he said. "If those pills you sent along with him are any indication, he's been getting a low dose of LSD for a long time. It's also possible that the LSD is combined with something else. We found several injection sites on his right shoulder. We have no idea what those are all about. We did a quick tox screen when he came in. Nothing showed up, but he's been injected with something. I'd like to know who compounded the pills he was given. I'd have them reported to the pharmacy board and take their license."

Bax smiled at the doctor. "Well, Doc. If we find the guy, we will make sure that happens and worse. What about the leg injury?"

"The pattern is consistent. If I had to guess, it could have been made by a baseball bat or a piece of wood. It was something hard and round."

She stepped closer to the bed and leaned in. "Mike, it's Agent Baxter. Can you hear me?" She placed a hand on his shoulder, and he shuddered. "Mike. Who did this to you?"

His eyes opened wide, and he looked at her face. Fear filled his eyes. He shook, and the doctor checked the monitors. He opened his mouth, but nothing came out.

He closed his eyes, and the bed shook as bells went off. The doctor grabbed a small vial off the table next to the bed, picked up a syringe, filled it from the vial and stabbed it into the port on his hand. The bells stopped ringing, and Mike Kirby closed his eyes.

"The long-term effects of the LSD are playing havoc with his brain and his body. It's like something gave him a boost. I can't say if it was the overdose or that something else we spoke about, but his body is having trouble recovering. The truth is, he may never recover. I don't know at this point. I can't find anything in the literature to indicate what happens to the human body when it's exposed to LSD over a long period. We know the effects of even one dose of LSD can last for years, but prolonged use? No idea."

Bax thanked the doctor, and they walked back to the waiting area. Buck disconnected the call he was on as they walked up.

"Anything?" he asked Bax.

She shook her head. "Doc says besides the LSD overdose, he was injected with something."

"What the hell are we dealing with?" asked Paul. "None of this makes any sense."

Buck looked at his watch. "We're not gonna solve it standing here. Let's get some dinner and some rest. We can pick this up in the morning."

They headed for the exit, and Buck told the cop at the door to make sure no one bothered Mike Kirby. Detective Ridgeway told them he was going upstairs to visit Jessie Maldonado.

Bax offered to drive Paul home since his Jeep was at the sheriff's office in Delta, and he accepted. Buck slid into his Jeep.

Two hours later, Buck stood in the middle of the Colorado River with his fly rod. He was focusing his casts on a small area on the back side of a large boulder. The drought had left the river lower than he had seen in a long time, so the fish congregated in deeper pockets. Twice, he had gotten a strike but lost the fish. His focus was out of whack, and for some reason, fishing wasn't clearing his head. He stepped to the shore and sat for a minute on the bank. He closed his eyes and slowed his breathing.

Feeling calmer, he walked back to his spot and

dropped the fly right where he wanted it. The water around the dry fly exploded, and Buck set the hook. By the time he got the huge fish to shore, the sun had set behind the mountains to the west. He released the fish and walked back to his Jeep. His phone chimed with an incoming message, and he pulled it out of his pocket and read it.

Max had received the sample from Kansas City, and she had the lab working on it.

Buck drove to a small restaurant in Palisade, parked and slid out of his Jeep. He opened the door and stepped inside. A young woman in jeans and a T-shirt with the restaurant's name printed on it showed him to a table and took his drink order. She brought his glass of Coke, and he ordered the rib eye steak with a house salad. He leaned back in the chair and ran his fingers through his hair.

His phone chimed, and he checked the number and answered.

"Hey, Mel. What's up?"

"Hi, Buck. Did I catch you in the middle of a river?" she asked.

Buck laughed. His team knew him so well. "No, just grabbing some dinner."

"Listen, we scanned all the newspapers around Kansas City for any information on the murders. It was a big story for several months, then it fizzled out. The cops did have a suspect at one point, but it appears he committed suicide, which looks like it ended the investigation. Nothing after that. One interesting note. The suspect was a patient of Dr. Brian Davidson, and it looked like they consulted with him a lot during the investigation."

"Thanks, Mel. Anything on the family in Florida whose kid was snatched or on the family in Carbondale?"

"Yeah. We sent everything we could find over to Agent Carpenter at the FBI. The victim's family had serious money. His father owned a bunch of hotels and resorts. Nothing that we could find indicated anything shady with the family. The kidnapper ran a small church about three miles from the family's estate, but there was no indication of any connection. Oddly enough, when they moved to Carbondale after the kidnapping, the father opened another church. One of those nondenominational free spirit churches. He had a small congregation, and the family financials fit that kind of life. If they ever went after a ransom, it doesn't show up anywhere, and the victim's family swears they never got a ransom demand. Hold on a minute, Buck."

Buck waited, and George came on the line. "Hey, I just pulled this from a newspaper archive in West Virginia. We know from his military files that Brian Davidson was born and raised around Middlebourne, West Virginia. I checked the local papers in the area to see if anything noteworthy ever happened and found a couple of articles from when he was seventeen or eighteen. Three high school girls were viciously murdered in a house two doors down from where he lived. They were beaten to death with a fireplace poker. No one was ever charged with the crime, and it doesn't look like much of an investigation happened. I spoke with a local detective, who said that back in those days, the local police stayed away from that area of the county because it was inhabited by a religious sect. One of those laying on of hands, don't believe in science kind of things. The article said that one of the girls was the daughter of the local preacher.

"I did the same thing with Mike Kirby, and other than the incident with his alcoholic father, he lived a normal life."

Buck pushed his plate away. "That's interesting, George. Like everything else, we need to figure out what it means. Do me a favor and upload the articles. I'd like to read them."

George hung up, and Buck paid his bill, slid into his Jeep and headed for his hotel. He needed a good night's sleep.

Chapter Forty-Seven

Buck sat in the sheriff's conference room reading through the investigation file, looking for anything that made sense. "How can you have this many dead bodies and have no evidence?" he said out loud.

"You can't" came a voice from the door. Sheriff Buckman stepped into the room and grabbed the seat at the end of the table. "We've gathered a ton of information this week. The answer has to be in there somewhere."

"I agree, Hal. But I feel like we are missing a critical piece."

Sheriff Buckman turned his chair so he could look at the whiteboard. He was studying the faces of the eleven victims when Buck's phone rang. Buck looked at the number and answered, putting the call on speaker.

"Buck Taylor, how's my favorite cop?" asked Max.

Buck chuckled. He loved it when Max called because she didn't call unless she had something to offer.

"Hi, Max. Tell me you're calling to make my day?"

"Oh, now I'm hurt," said Max. "I thought I always made your day."

Buck and Sheriff Buckman laughed.

"Well," said Max. "This should make your day. The lab was at it all night, and we have a good DNA string from the dirt under the Kansas victim's nails."

Buck sat up in his chair. "Tell me you got a match."

"Not yet, but we are running it as we speak. If there's a match in the system, we'll find it."

"Max," said Buck. "Make sure you run it against Mike Kirby and Brian Davidson. They should both be in the military database."

Max said she would. Bax and Paul walked into the office as Max hung up, and they smiled. "Maybe some headway?" asked Bax.

"Maybe. If they're in the system," said Buck. "We know we have Kirby's DNA. Not sure about Davidson.

"Hal, can you contact the Grand Junction intelligence division and see if they can put a couple of people on Brian Davidson? He's smart, so tell them to stay back and stay loose. I don't want to spook him if the DNA comes back as a match."

Sheriff Buckman stepped out of the room and closed the door. Buck was staring at the board, and he started thinking out loud

"Okay, we have two viable suspects, and the evidence all points to Mike Kirby: the pins and buttons that are missing from his uniform and the jewelry that was in his cabin. His quirky behavior is odd but not evidentiary. Then we have Dr. Brian Davidson, who has lied to us several times about his relationship with Kirby, but we have no physical evidence to link him to any of the crimes. He could be the killer, he could be manipulating Kirby, or he could be completely innocent. Thoughts?"

Paul was about to answer when Buck's phone chimed. He checked the number and hit the speaker button.

"Max. Good news?"

Max Clinton got right to the point. "The DNA from the murder victim in Kansas City is a match to Brian Davidson. No doubt about it."

"Awesome, Max. Upload the test results to the file. I'll call the KC police and let them know. Thanks, Max."

Buck disconnected the call as Sheriff Buckman walked back into the room. He looked at the smiles. "What did I miss?"

Buck told him about the call and the DNA match.

"That's great, but it doesn't help our victims," he said.

Bax turned to face him. "You're right, Sheriff, but what it does do is allow us to arrest him, and then we can search his house and truck and see if anything jumps out at us."

Buck dialed a number and waited. "Agent Taylor, how can I help you?" asked Captain Kohl.

"Captain, we have a DNA match from your sample. The match is Brian Davidson."

"Son of a bitch," said Captain Kohl. "He made himself a part of the investigation and was in front of us the entire time. What's your next step?"

"Can you have someone send me the full file on the victim? What was her name?"

"Her name was Sarah Jane Calvin. What else?"

"I need a copy of the warrant. I'm going to email you the link to my investigation file. You'll have access to everything we have, and you can have someone upload the file and the warrant. We're going to put together an arrest team. I have one favor to ask. We have no links other than the MOs to our murders. I need you to sit on the extradition request and give us time to work on him."

"I'll talk to the DA and the cold case team. Since the cold case squad works for me, they won't be a problem, and I'll get this to one of the prosecutors who will work with us. Once you have Davidson in custody, I'm going to send a couple of my folks to connect with you. Any issues with that?"

"Thanks, Captain. I'll keep you posted."

Buck disconnected the call. "We're on the clock, guys. Kansas City will not let us keep him forever, so we need to work as fast as possible. Hal. Call intelligence back. Tell them that the situation has changed and is no longer just surveillance. If they see him, it's stop and arrest. Also, since he lives in the city, we'll need Grand Junction SWAT. Tell SWAT to prepare for a hard and fast entry. Bax. Call Franklin and have him gear up the team."

Buck asked Paul to pull up the satellite image of Davidson's house. He put it on the big screen, and Buck studied the image. He pointed to a church on the corner two blocks from the house. He checked his watch. "I don't want to wait. Let's meet at the church at two p.m. Paul call Mark Ridgeway and ask him to take a team to the doctor's office on campus. I also want another team to hit the VA Center simultaneously. We need this to go like clockwork. Let's move."

Buck called the director and filled him in. "Okay, Buck. What do you need from me?"

"We're good, sir. I'll let you know when it's over."

"Buck, stay safe." The director disconnected the call, and Buck grabbed his backpack and headed for his Jeep.

Chapter Forty-Eight

Buck was standing with the SWAT commander, looking at a map of the area. They had parked behind the church, out of view of the suspect's house, and were looking at points of access. The SWAT commander pointed to a small field of trees that bordered the house.

"I'm going to send one team through this field to cover the back of the house. The rest of the team will hit the front of the house in a blitz attack. Did you notice any weapons when you interviewed him?"

"No," said Buck. "Our killer uses his hands. None of the victims were shot or stabbed."

Bax, Vince Apodaca and Paul pulled into the parking lot. They slid out of their vehicles, pulled their ballistic vests out of the rear hatches and put them on. Paul pulled an AR-15 out of the secure gun locker and inserted a clip, placing several more in his vest. Bax strapped a second pistol to her thigh and added several magazines to her vest. Detective Apodaca stood next to them. They walked up to Buck and the SWAT commander and shook hands.

Both SWAT teams were geared up and standing

by their vehicles. Buck picked up the portable radio and pressed the mic button.

"Buck to Ridgeway, over."

"Ridgeway team on the campus, in position, over."

"Buck to Maldonado, over." Once Jessie Maldonado had heard about the arrest, Buck couldn't stop her from wanting to be a part. She had been released from the hospital and was resting at home when she got the call.

"Maldonado team in position at the VA, over."

Buck checked his watch. The SWAT commander twirled his finger in the air, and the teams loaded into their vehicles. The two vehicles, followed by Buck, Bax, Paul and Vince, pulled out of the parking lot. The first SWAT vehicle stopped next to the field, and the team raced out of the vehicle and took positions where they could watch the house. The rest of the group pulled to a stop.

Buck picked up the radio and keyed the mic. "Buck to all teams. Move!"

The SWAT vehicle took off, followed by the team. It rounded the corner, pulled into the circular drive, the back door flew open and the team raced towards the door. The front officer hit the front door with the forty-pound ram and stepped aside as the door blew off its hinges. The team ran into the house.

"Police, warrant!" could be heard throughout the house.

"On the ground. Hands where we can see them!"

"Clear, clear, clear!"

The SWAT commander stepped out of the door and waved to Buck. The rest of the team followed, and they stepped into the living room.

"Davidson was in the master bedroom. He surrendered without a fight. His wife was in the kitchen. Both are in custody."

One of the SWAT officers walked Davidson, limping, into the living room and sat him on the couch. He was wearing shorts, no shirt or shoes. The bruise on his leg was purple and brown, but the huge bruise on his back impressed Buck the most.

"I'll bet that hurt," said Buck with a smile.

"Agent Taylor, what the hell is the meaning of this? I'm going to sue your asses off. And look at my front door. What the fuck? You couldn't knock?"

Buck stepped up and dropped the warrant onto his lap. "Brian Davidson, you are under arrest for the murder of Sarah Jane Calvin." Davidson didn't react at all to the victim's name. Buck pulled the Miranda card out of his back pocket and read Davidson his rights.

"Do you understand these rights as I have read them to you?"

Davidson opened his mouth to protest, and Buck stared at him. He sat back and said he understood. Buck asked the SWAT officer to hand him over to the two patrol officers, who would transport him downtown. Bax was on her phone and gave Franklin the all clear. Buck gave the SWAT team the okay to pack up and clear out.

Five minutes later, Franklin pulled into the driveway, followed by his team. They had already geared up, so they grabbed their equipment from the back of the van and headed inside. Buck pulled Franklin aside.

"Top to bottom," he said. "We are also looking for journals. There could be a bunch of them. They're important if we can locate them." Franklin nodded.

Buck stepped into the kitchen, followed by Paul. The female SWAT officer stepped out of the room. Amina Davidson was sitting at the kitchen table with her hands cuffed behind her. Her face showed no emotion. Buck sat at the table opposite her, pulled the Miranda card out of his pocket and placed it on the table.

"Mrs. Davidson. I am going to read you your rights." He nodded towards Paul, who stepped behind Amina and removed the handcuffs. She rubbed her hands together, placed them in her lap and looked at Buck. "This is a formality and is to protect your rights." Buck read from the card and asked her if she understood her rights. She nodded.

"Yes," she said in a whisper.

"Are you willing to speak with us without an attorney present?"

"If you can get me my phone, I would like to call my attorney. She lives a few houses down the street."

Buck should have taken her downtown for a formal interview, but he sensed that she wanted to talk, so he had Paul get her phone from the bedroom and hand it to her. She dialed a number, spoke to someone and returned the phone to Paul.

"Thank you, Agent Taylor. She will be right here."

Buck sat back in the chair. "Mrs. Davidson, how long have you lived in this country? You speak English quite well."

She looked up, still twisting her hands together below the table. "Please call me Amina. I have lived here since I was thirteen. Before the Taliban took over my village, I was in school. The nuns taught us English and French."

Buck wanted to ask her more questions, but he didn't want to cross an important line. He asked her if she needed any water, and she said no and thanked him. They sat and waited.

Ten minutes later, Bax stepped into the kitchen and tapped Buck on the shoulder.

"Woman at the door says she is Mrs. Davidson's attorney."

"Bring her back," said Buck. He stood and turned towards the door. The woman who entered was not what he'd expected. She was a husky woman, wearing jeans, flip-flops and a T-shirt with a picture of a band he'd never heard of. Her hair was pulled back in a French braid. She stepped into the kitchen and shook Buck's hand.

"Hi, Gloria Danelli." She looked down at her clothes. "Please excuse my appearance; I was giving the dog a bath." She stepped past Buck, hugged Amina and kneeled next to her. "Are you okay, honey?"

Amina nodded and Gloria stood, pulled out the chair next to Amina and sat down. She pulled her phone out of her pocket, placed it on the table and clicked on a recording app. She looked at Buck. "You read her her rights?"

Buck said he had.

"Great, then let's get started."

Buck hit the record button on his phone and leaned into the table. He introduced everyone in the room.

"Amina, as of right now, you have not been arrested for any crimes. We would like to keep this interview informal, but your attorney will tell you that if we feel at any time you are attempting to be less than honest with us, we will arrest you and escort you to police headquarters for a more formal interview. Your attorney can stop this interview at any time. Are you okay with what I have said thus far?"

She looked at Gloria, nodded and said "Yes" in a soft voice.

"Great," said Buck. "Amina, we have arrested your husband on a warrant from Kansas City, Kansas, for the murder of a young woman. His DNA was a match for DNA taken from the victim. He is also a suspect in at least a dozen additional murders both here and in Kansas. Were you aware of his involvement in any crimes?"

Amina leaned towards Gloria and whispered in Gloria's ear. Gloria looked at her questioningly and then nodded.

"Agent Taylor, this may be out of the ordinary, but my client would like to tell you her story. Her one request is that you allow her to finish before you ask her any questions."

Buck sat back. "Please," he said.

Amina seemed to reach inside herself for some inner strength, and she began.

"My husband, Agent Taylor, is a monster, but you already know that. He has done all those things you mentioned and so much more that you are not aware of. Brian Davidson bought me when I was thirteen years old. As part of his job with the military, he tortured people from my and the surrounding villages for information on the Taliban. His methods were brutal, and the things he did to those people were horrendous. My father was one of those people. At some point during the torture, my father mercifully died, but not without suffering terrible indignation. Davidson had noticed me and took an interest. I watched one night as he strangled my mother and older sister, and then he paid a local Taliban leader one hundred U.S. dollars, and I became his. My mother and sisters were part of a group of five women who were used to arrest one of his soldiers for murder. Murders my husband committed."

Amina sat stone-faced, showing no emotion; she stopped for a few seconds to catch her breath. The room was silent.

"I was never married to Brian Davidson but was more of his sex slave. I knew when he committed his terrible acts because he would take me into his room, and the sex would be harsh and brutal. Over the years, he told me that I was in this country illegally and that if I tried to run, he would have me deported and sent back to Afghanistan. He also said he would wipe out my entire village, so I stayed and did as he asked. Waiting and hoping that someday I could escape from his control.

"My husband—and yes, I will call him that for now—kept meticulous records of everyone he tortured while in the army and everyone he killed once we moved to the United States. He found great pleasure in using various drugs to manipulate people into doing his will, and he enjoyed the killing. I have not read those journals, but he took great pleasure in writing down all his experiments. One of my jobs was to make sure his clothes were cleaned after he came home from doing whatever he was doing. I don't know if it will help, but in doing my job, I placed some of those clothes into plastic ziplock bags and hid them. I will be happy to give those to you after speaking with my attorney. I also know where his journals are. There are several boxes of them hidden away—those I will give you as well.

"All I ask is that you use those items to make sure my husband never hurts anyone again. As I mentioned, I am here illegally. I would like to remain in this country and try to have a life. Once I give you the items I mentioned, I would like my help in this matter considered in allowing me to remain here."

Relief flooded her face as she leaned back in the chair, and tears rolled down her face. Buck sat back and looked around the room. Everyone looked as stunned as he felt. He turned off the recording app and asked Gloria Danelli to follow him into the living room.

"Oh, my god," said Gloria. "She told me many times that she had a story to tell when the time was right, but I would have never guessed that this was it."

"I need to call the district attorney," said Buck. "Will you sit with her until I can get him here?"

Gloria nodded and walked back into the kitchen. Paul walked out and stood next to Buck. "Fuck. What are we going to do?"

Buck pulled out his phone, dialed a number and

talked to the person on the other end. He disconnected the call.

"The DA is on his way. We need to wait."

Buck dialed another number.

"Hey, Buck," said Hank Clancy. "What's up?"

Buck told Hank what he'd told the DA, and he listened without interrupting. When Buck finished speaking, he said, "Fuck, Buck. I need to make some calls. This is going to be a jurisdictional nightmare." Hank disconnected the call, and Buck called the director.

"So, you think she's for real?" asked the director.

"Yes, sir. If you had been able to watch her as we did, you would have no doubt," said Buck.

"Okay, Buck. When do you plan to interview Davidson?"

"I'm waiting on the DA, and once I've had a chance to talk to him, I'll let you know."

Buck hung up and looked at Bax, who had walked up and stood next to him. "Unbelievable," she said.

Forty minutes later, the Grand Junction district attorney, Harold Phelps, pulled to the curb and slid out of his SUV, along with three younger members of his staff. Buck met them on the porch and explained what was going on. He pulled out his phone and played the recording for the group. When the recording ended, Buck hooked his phone back onto his belt. The DA asked his staffers to wait in the living room, and he walked into the kitchen, followed by Buck and Bax.

The DA hugged Gloria Danelli. "Gloria, it's great to see you. Been a long time. I thought you retired?"

Gloria laughed. "Just helping out a friend."

The DA sat opposite Amina and placed his hands on top of hers on the table. He introduced himself and asked her if she could repeat her story for him. Amina sat up straight and went through the entire story a second time. When she was finished, the DA patted the top of her hand and asked Gloria and Buck to follow him. They stepped out of the kitchen.

"Gloria, what is she looking for?" asked the DA.

"Total immunity from everything related to Davidson's crimes and any knowledge she had of them, and she wants to stay in the United States and become a citizen."

"Buck, Bax, you guys good with that?" he asked.

Bax was the first to answer. "I think this woman has suffered enough living with that monster all those years. She deserves a medal."

The DA smiled. "Thought you'd feel that way. Buck, how about you?"

"I'm good, sir."

The DA looked at Gloria. "Okay, Gloria. Is my word good enough, or do we need to wait for the paperwork?"

"Your words have always been good enough for me, Harold. Let's get this done. Agent Taylor and his team still have a lot of work to do, and I need to get home and finish washing the dog."

They all laughed and headed back into the kitchen.

Chapter Forty-Nine

Buck stepped into the interrogation room and set the manila folder on the table. Brian Davidson looked up, his hands shackled to the bar on the table. They had held him overnight, and he was not happy. His attorney had a notebook sitting open and a pen resting on the lined page. Buck liked people who still used paper and pens to take notes. He would have done the same thing, but there were a lot of people waiting on the video and audio from this interview. There was also quite a crowd standing outside the interrogation room window.

Buck pulled his Miranda card out of his pocket. For the benefit of the tape, he introduced the people in the room. "I am going to read your client his rights, even though this was done at the time of his arrest."

Buck read from the card and asked Davidson if he understood his rights. He looked at his attorney, who nodded and said he did.

"Since your attorney is in the room, I assume you are not willing to talk with us without him present; is that correct?"

Davidson smiled. "Correct."

Buck opened the manila folder and, one by one, placed pictures of the eleven victims in Colorado on the table face up, facing Davidson. He watched Davidson for a reaction but got nothing but a smirk. He placed the morgue photo of Joker on the table and saw a tiny flinch in the smirk. Buck read off each name as he tapped the photos.

"Mr. Davidson, do you know why you have been arrested?"

Davidson whispered with his attorney and faced Buck. "On the advice of counsel, I plead the fifth."

Buck had figured out how this was going to go, so the answer did not surprise him. Davidson thought he was smarter than everyone else and figured if he refused to answer the questions, they would have nothing to convict him with. He knew he had not left anything on the victims that could be used against him, which meant he was surprised that they would arrest him without any evidence.

Buck picked up the next batch of papers from the folder and laid the twelve pictures out on the table. Buck could see a crack in Davidson's façade as he looked at the pictures. Buck read off the names of the victims who had been identified by the authorities in Kansas. He tapped the middle picture.

"Have you ever seen this woman before?"

"No, I have not," said Davidson.

Buck smiled. "You may not know her, but she has told us an awful lot about you."

Davidson broke a tiny bit. "I doubt that, since you said she was dead."

"Well, I never said she was dead, but we'll come back to that," said Buck.

He picked up another piece of paper. "Yep, a lot of information. For instance. She told us that you are Scottish on your father's side and Welsh on your mother's. She told us that you are one percent Neanderthal, which is below the average. Oh, and she told us that you are prone to heart disease and are at risk for obesity. She also told us you have twelve first cousins, fifteen second and third cousins and forty-seven fourth cousins. That's quite the family."

Davidson appeared agitated. "What the hell are you talking about? This is bullshit." His attorney grabbed his arm and pulled him close so he could whisper in his ear, and Davidson pulled away.

"Brian—can I call you Brian?" asked Buck. "Brian, would you like to look at the picture again and see if you recognize her?"

"I don't know her."

"Her name is Sarah Jane Calvin, and she died in an alley in Kansas City, Kansas. She was twenty-two years old and was going to be a teacher. She didn't die easily, and you must have been pretty dirty by the time you killed her, but you left her a gift under her fingernails so she could eventually nail you for what you did to her. You left her the gift of dirt. Dirt that contained your DNA."

Davidson jumped out of the seat and strained against the shackles. "That's ridiculous, you're making this shit up. You can't get DNA from dirt."

His lawyer pulled him back into the seat and whispered to him for a few minutes. His mouth dropped, and the smirk disappeared. Brian Davidson stared daggers at Buck.

"Did you know any of your victims by name, or did you pick them at random?" asked Buck.

"On the advice of counsel, I plead the fifth."

The questioning continued for two more hours, with Buck asking questions and Davidson pleading the fifth. Davidson looked at Buck.

"Since all you have is dirt, am I free to go?"

Buck sat back in the chair and laughed. Davidson stared at him.

"Oh, we're just getting started," said Buck.

He reached back and tapped on the glass. A

minute later, the door opened, and Bax laid a handful of plastic evidence bags on the desk next to Buck. She left the room, and Buck picked up the first bag. He placed it in front of Davidson, who appeared shocked until he caught himself and pulled back. "What's this?" he asked.

"What's it look like?" asked Buck.

"It looks like some old T-shirt for a band. So what?"

Buck placed the rest of the bags in front of Davidson, side by side, and sat back. Davidson stared at them. Buck noticed a slight tremor in his hand, and his lips trembled.

"Would it surprise you if I told you that we have a signed affidavit from your wife saying all these shirts are yours?"

"So what?" said Davidson.

"Would it also surprise you if I told you that your wife never washed these after you killed all these people, but saved them in freezer bags to use if she decided to escape from your clutches? These should help us learn a lot about the people you were close to when you were wearing them."

The lawyer reached for his arms, but it was too late. Davidson flew out of the chair.

"That stupid bitch. I gave her a great life, and this is the way she repays me. I should have killed her . . ."

Davidson caught himself and looked at his lawyer, who shook his head, and he sat back down. He looked at Buck.

"I apologize, Agent Taylor, for my outburst. Of course I would never hurt my wife." He took a few deep breaths to try to regain control.

Buck knew it was time. He tapped on the glass a second time and waited. When the door opened, a tall black man with a bald head stood ramrod straight in the doorway. His suit was cut sharp, and he held an old banker's box. He stepped into the room and set the box on the table next to Buck, and he sat in the empty seat next to Buck.

"For the benefit of the recording, we are being joined by John Winthrop. John is a major with the United States Army Criminal Investigation Division and is stationed in Washington, DC."

Sweat formed on Davidson's forehead. He looked at his lawyer, who shrugged.

Buck opened the box, pulled out the top journal and placed it on the table.

"Brian, have you ever seen this before?"

Davidson pled the fifth.

Buck pulled out a second and third journal and placed them on top of the first.

"Brian, would you believe we have seventeen boxes of these journals?" He wasn't expecting an answer; Brian Davidson looked deflated.

"That's okay," said Buck. "You don't need to respond. An FBI handwriting analyst has confirmed that these were written by you, as has your wife, who graciously gave us access to a small space under your house where these were hidden—nothing like a woman scorned. We've had a team of folks from the FBI, CID and CBI up all night reading through them. Gotta love the detail. I'll spare you sitting here and listening from my reading of some of what you've written. Let's just say it's very graphic and not to everyone's liking."

Buck picked up the last paper from the manila folder as Major Winthrop placed the journals back into the box and closed the lid.

"Brian Davidson, you are being charged with twenty-four counts of murder in the first degree in both Colorado and Kansas. You will be charged by the United States Army, along with other members of your team, for murder and war crimes for your activities while stationed in Afghanistan. You will also be charged with kidnapping, murder and human trafficking pertaining to the purchase of an underage minor while in Afghanistan. That minor being identified as Amina Davidson. CID is also going to reopen the investigation into the five women murdered in Afghanistan that resulted in Mike Kirby being incarcerated."

Buck put down the paper and looked at Davidson. "Once these investigations are concluded, I am certain there will be more charges to come. By the way, we've been in touch with the West Virginia State Police, and they will be reopening the investigation into the brutal slaying of three high school girls in a house two doors down from your family home. They will also be investigating the disappearance of your sister."

Buck stood up, leaned on the table and waved his hand. "All of this is because of Sarah Jane Calvin, a brave young woman who refused to stop fighting for the truth, even in death. Interview ended."

Major Winthrop picked up the banker's box, and Buck picked up all the pictures and evidence bags, and they walked out of the room, leaving Davidson with his face buried in his hands and his lawyer looking bewildered.

Epilogue

Buck pulled his Jeep to the curb and parked behind the black government SUV. He turned off the Jeep and sat for a moment. It had been a while since he had been to Carbondale and he was amazed at the growth. He slid out of the Jeep and walked up to the people gathered on the lawn.

Hank Clancy and Special Agent Carpenter shook his hand and introduced him to Elinore Hammersmith, her daughter Judith Castleton and Constance Chamberlain. Buck shook everyone's hands and offered his condolences to Constance Chamberlain. Sergeant Tallie McNeill, wearing her uniform, stepped up and extended her hand.

"Agent Taylor, it's a pleasure to meet you. The sheriff speaks very highly of you."

Buck shook her hand. "The pleasure is all mine, Sergeant, and thank you for your help with this case."

"I was just telling Mrs. Hammersmith that the FBI apologizes for how her concerns relating to James Michael Chamberlain were handled, and that we appreciate that she kept pushing," said Hank Clancy.

"Constance and I were just having a nice glass of iced tea. We spent a lovely morning talking about her son," said Elinore Hammersmith.

Constance Chamberlain smiled through tear-filled eyes. "I appreciate Sheriff Buckman bringing James's ashes to me this morning, personally. That meant a lot. I wish his father was alive. He passed away several years ago, hoping James would return to us someday."

Mrs. Hammersmith led everyone to the small patio table in front of the house, where she poured glasses of iced tea and passed them out. Judith Castleton looked at Buck.

"Agent Taylor. I was curious. During your investigation, did you find any information about what became of Joshua—I'm sorry, James Michael's sister?"

Buck looked sideways. "I'm sorry, Mrs. Castleton. I don't know anything about a sister. Can you enlighten me?"

"I remember we were playing in the street, and I happened to look up and there was a girl standing in front of the picture window. She had curly dark hair and was wearing what looked like a robe. I saw Mrs. Davenport take her by the arm, pull her away and then close the curtains. I asked Joshua about it, and all he said was she was younger than him and ill."

The bug in Buck's brain kicked him in the side of the head. Was it possible?

"I would like to show you a picture and see if you recognize her."

He walked back to his Jeep, opened his backpack and pulled out an old beat-up manila folder. He opened the folder and removed a picture. He walked back to the group and handed the picture to Judith Castleton.

Judith looked at the picture for several minutes and handed it back to him. "It was a long time ago, but it could be her. The hair looks the same, but I only got a quick glimpse of her face. Who is she?"

Buck looked at the picture. "An old case of mine. She was thirteen when she disappeared without a trace from her home in Aspen."

Elinore Hammersmith set down her glass. "I wonder if Maggie across the street would know anything. I don't think anyone cleaned out the house after Mrs. Davenport passed away. I know there was a lot of junk when they bought the place." She stood. "Follow me, Agent Taylor."

Buck followed Elinore and Judith across the street, and she knocked on the front door. Maggie, a young woman wearing a painter's Tyvek coverall, opened the door. Elinore introduced Buck and asked if they could come in. She told her about the young girl and asked her if they'd found anything when they were cleaning out the house that might help.

"We threw a lot of junk away when we moved in. The basement was a mess. We're still working on replacing all the drywall."

"Maggie, was there anything unusual in the basement that led to the mess?" asked Buck.

Maggie laughed. "Vandals had broken some windows, and the basement flooded. We had to remove the drywall and the odd insulation."

"What was odd about the insulation?" asked Buck.

Maggie pulled out her phone. "I think I have a couple of pictures of it. My brother-in-law is a contractor, and he said it was soundproofing." She paused at a picture and handed Buck her phone. "Tom couldn't figure out why they put soundproofing in the walls unless they used the basement as a studio or something like that."

Buck was intrigued. Peeking out from behind a broken piece of drywall was a black panel with cones on it. Buck handed her back her phone.

"Could we look in the basement?" asked Buck.

"Sure, follow me," said Maggie. "We still have a bunch of drywall to hang, but the framing is done."

They followed her into the construction zone in the basement, and Buck started looking around the space. He was looking in the framed bathroom when Judith called out to him. He walked over to an exposed wooden column, and Judith pointed to some faint letters scratched in the post. Buck pulled out his camera and took a picture of the letters using the flash. He looked at the picture and almost dropped his phone.

"That looks like it spells Becky," said Judith. "What is your missing girl's name?"

Buck composed himself. "Her name is Rebecca. She goes by Becky."

The three women stared at him. No one was sure what to say. Buck stood for a minute before he gathered himself. They all headed up the stairs, and Buck thanked Maggie. They walked back to the rest of the group, and Hank stepped up to Buck.

"Anything?" he asked.

Buck showed him the picture. "Son of a . . . gun," he said, correcting his words. "Do you think that could be her?"

"Don't know, but it could mean she was still alive a few years after she was kidnapped. There's still a chance."

They finished their iced tea, and Buck thanked Elinore for her hospitality. He said goodbye and walked to his Jeep. Today was a good day. He put the picture back in the folder and put the folder in its special place in his backpack. "There is still a reason to keep looking," he said to himself.

He had just pulled away from the curb when his phone rang. He pushed the button on the entertainment system.

"Hey, Bax. What's up?"

"Hi, Buck. The two investigators from Kansas City PD just left. They interviewed Davidson, but he was as close-lipped as he's been all week. I gave them access to the investigation file so they could go through the evidence."

"Thanks, Bax."

"One more thing, Mike Kirby died this morning. Jessie just called me."

"Okay, Bax. Thanks for letting me know. Ask the sheriff to have someone notify the Rasmussens, and call the VA Health Center and see if they can arrange a funeral. He'll never get the chance to live as an innocent man, but the least we can do is get him a veteran's funeral."

"Vince is on his way up to see the Rasmussens right now, and I'll call the VA. Get some rest."

Buck turned onto the highway. He was going to take a couple of days off, go home and hug his grandkids. He needed a vacation from his vacation.

His phone chimed, and he pulled to the side of the road to open the text. He smiled when he saw the picture. Vicky Talmadge and Jasper, wearing their yellow safety gear and hard hats, were standing next to a pile of debris with a group of smiling rescue workers behind them. Vicky held a sign that said we found a little girl alive. They looked tired but happy, and Buck laughed when he looked down and spotted Jasper wearing his work boots.

Acknowledgments

A special thank-you to my daughter Christina J. Morgan, my unofficial collaborator.

Thanks to my editor, Laura Dragonette, whose efforts helped turn my manuscript into a polished novel. Her help is greatly appreciated. Any mistakes the reader may find are solely the responsibility of the author.

Special thanks to my daughter Stephanie Morgan, my beta reader. Stephanie has read every novel in its rough stages and rarely gets to see the completed product. Her insight and critique have been critical to making sure the stories make sense.

Also, I would like to thank my family for their encouragement. I have been telling them stories since they were little, and I always told them that someone should be writing this stuff down. I decided to write it down myself.

I want to thank my closest friend, Trish Moakler-Herud. She has been encouraging me for years to write my stories down. I hope this will make her proud.

A special thanks to my late wife, Jane. She

pushed me for years to become a writer, and my biggest regret is that she didn't live long enough to see it happen. I love her with all my heart and miss her every day. I think she would be pleased.

Finally, thanks to the readers. Without you, none of this would be important.

About the Author

2019 Pacific Book Awards Best Mystery Finalist . . . *Crime Delayed*

2020 Pacific Book Awards Best Mystery Winner . . . *Crime Denied*

2020 Chanticleer International Book Awards: 1st Place Blue Ribbon, CLUE Book Awards for Suspense, Thriller Fiction . . . *Crime Denied*

2021 Chanticleer International Book Awards Finalist, CLUE Book Awards for Suspense, Thriller Fiction . . . *Crime Conspiracy*

2021 Chanticleer International Book Awards Finalist, Book Series, CLUE Book Awards for Suspense, Thriller Fiction . . . Crime Series, The Buck Taylor Novels

2022 Chanticleer International Book Awards Finalist, CLUE Book Awards for Suspense, Thriller Fiction . . . *Crime Exploded*

2022 Chanticleer International Book Awards Finalist, CLUE Book Awards for Suspense, Thriller Fiction . . . *Crime Spree*

2023 Chanticleer International Book Awards Finalist, CLUE Book Awards for Suspense, Thriller Fiction . . . *Crime Scene*

2023 Chanticleer International Book Awards Series Finalist, Mystery & Mayhem Book Awards . . . Crime Series, The Buck Taylor Novels

Chuck Morgan attended Seton Hall University and Regis College and spent thirty-five years as a construction project manager. He is an avid outdoorsman, an Eagle Scout and a licensed private pilot. He enjoys camping, hiking, mountain biking and fly-fishing.

He is the author of the Crime series, featuring Colorado Bureau of Investigation agent Buck Taylor. The series includes *Crime Interrupted, Crime Delayed, Crime Unsolved, Crime Exposed, Crime Denied, Crime Conspiracy, Crime Unknown, Crime Exploded, Crime Spree* and *Crime Scene*.

He is also the author of *Her Name Was Jane*, a memoir about his late wife's nine-year battle with breast cancer. He has three children, four grandchildren and a Siberian Husky. He resides in Lone Tree, Colorado.

Other Books by the Author

Dear Reader, thank you for reading this novel. Please enjoy the other books in this series and follow Colorado Bureau of Investigation Agent Buck Taylor and his team as they investigate new and sometimes unusual crimes in the Colorado mountains. Each novel is a separate story, and they can be read in any order, but you might find it more enjoyable to read them in order.

Happy Reading,

Chuck Morgan

"Crime Interrupted: A Buck Taylor Novel by Chuck Morgan is a gripping, edge-of-the-seat novel. Right from page one, the action kicks off and never stops, gaining pace as each chapter

passes." Reviewed by Anne-Marie Reynolds for Readers' Favorite.

Finalist . . . 2019 Pacific Book Awards Best Mystery

"This crime novel reads like a great thriller. *The writing is atmospheric, laced with vivid descriptions that capture the setting in great detail while allowing readers to follow the intensity of the action and the emotional and psychological depth of the story." Reviewed by Divine Zape for Readers' Favorite.*

"Professionally written in the style of a

**best-selling crime novelist, such as Tom Clancy,
Crime Unsolved: A Buck Taylor Novel by Chuck
Morgan is a spellbinding suspense novel with an
environmental flair.** *Intriguing subplots of fraud,
survivalist paranoia and murder weave their way
through the fabric of the plot, creating a dynamic
story. This is an action-filled, stimulating tale
which contains fascinating details that are relevant
in our present climate." Reviewed by Susan Sewell
for Readers' Favorite.*

**"Chuck Morgan has a unique gift for plot,
one that makes Crime Exposed: A Buck Taylor
Novel a hard-to-put-down book.** *From the start,
readers know what happens to Barb, but they
become curious as they follow the investigation,
wondering if the characters will find out what
happened to her. The descriptions are filled with
clarity, and they offer readers great images. The
prose is elegant, and it captures both the emotional
and psychological elements of the novel clearly
while offering vivid descriptions of scenes and
characters. This is a fast-paced thriller with*

memorable characters and a criminal investigation that is so real readers will believe it could happen." Reviewed by Romuald Dzemo for Readers' Favorite.

Winner . . . 2020 Pacific Book Awards Best Mystery

2020 Chanticleer International Book Awards: 1st Place Blue Ribbon, CLUE Book Awards for Suspense, Thriller Fiction

"It's really progressiveto see a female serial killer portrayed with such intelligent writing and depth of character, and the cat and mouse chase dynamic is thrown off nicely by the switching of genders. What results is a really enjoyable thriller and crime mystery novel, and overall Crime Denied is certain to please fans of both hard-boiled detective tales and action/adventure crime novels." Reviewed by K.C. Finn for Readers' Favorite.

2021 Chanticleer International Book Awards Finalist, CLUE Book Awards for Suspense, Thriller Fiction . . . *Crime Conspiracy*

"This makes for a truly dynamic story where anything is possible, and a hero you can root for even when it looks like all is lost." Reviewed by K.C. Finn for Readers' Favorite.

"This is a book you can't put down, which will entertain you on many levels, and at times make your skin crawl; the kind of book that remains in your thoughts long after you finish reading." Reviewed by Steven Robson for Readers' Favorite.

"I read Crime Unknown in one sitting. The plot is intense and the main character, Agent Buck Taylor,is a hero like no other. This book has everything a thriller needs to be and more. I thought I knew the story at the beginning. Buck will solve a tricky murder case, I thought. But Chuck Morgan adds a twist to this story that expands it and makes it one of the most enjoyable books I've read in this genre. I loved that the lead was such an awesome well-rounded fellow but that he also had a support team who were just as important to the story." Reviewed by Maureen Dangarembizi for Readers' Favorite.*

"Crime Unknown is a thoroughly enjoyable read and I would not hesitate to recommend this book to fans of the crime genre and those looking for a gateway in." Reviewed by K.C. Finn for Readers' Favorite.*

2022 Chanticleer International Book Awards Finalist, CLUE Book Awards for Suspense, Thriller Fiction . . . *Crime Exploded*

"Action-packed and fast-paced, I was sucked into the story the moment I opened the novel. The author built the story to perfection. Chuck Morgan gave just the right amount of suspense, mystery, and action to keep readers' attention on Buck and his team. There was never a dull moment in the story. The narrative ran smoothly until the end; it followed the development of the story and the pace set by the characters. I enjoyed the twists and turns. What I loved more than anything else in the plot was how calculating Buck was. He was smart; he didn't let the FBI discourage him and kept his head in the game. The action gave me an adrenaline rush. Absolutely brilliant!" Reviewed by Rabia Tanveer for Readers' Favorite.*

2022 Chanticleer International Book Awards Finalist, CLUE Book Awards for Suspense, Thriller Fiction . . . *Crime Spree*

"It is one of the best crime novels I have read in a long while, with real characters developed in a way to let you get to know them intimately,

understand them, and appreciate their strengths and weaknesses. The plot is tight, exciting, and tense, with plenty of action, and it will grip you from the start. The bizarre storyline is enthralling, written in descriptive prose that lands you right in the middle of the action. Forget sleep; once you pick this book up, you won't want to put it down until it's finished. Fantastic story, and highly recommended for fans of high-octane crime thrillers." Reviewed by Anne-Marie Reynolds for Readers' Favorite.

"*Crime Family* is the tenth book in the Buck Taylor series. Chuck Morgan had me hooked from the first page until the end. *There was never a dull moment with all the action; one chapter flowed into the next. The story was fast-paced and kept me on the edge of my seat. I kept turning the pages to find out what would happen next. I was intrigued, and with all the twists and turns, I could not predict what was looming. The characters were well-developed. Each had a background*

description, and it was fun getting to know some of them. The story was excellently written with a fitting ending." Reviewed by Alma Boucher for Readers' Favorite.

"Crime Scene is a must-read for lovers of mystery sleuth and murder tales with a touch of conspiracy." *Readers' Favorite review.*

"Crime Scene has a carefully designed intrigue that deepens with every unforeseeable turn of events,and a dynamic narrative." *Readers' Favorite review.*

"This is a great book. Holds your attention and you don't want to put it down. I would recommend this book to anyone who loves a good crime novel." *Amazon review.*

"Spellbinding, gripping, powerful, and relevant are just a few words that come to mind after turning the last page of Crime Scene: A

Buck Taylor Novel, book 11, by Chuck Morgan."
Amazon Review.